DARK KNIGHT

KNIGHT'S RIDGE EMPIRE #10

TRACY LORRAINE

CALLI

I sit on the floor of my new bedroom with my tablet on my lap and the products I've designed over the past few weeks surrounding me.

This hobby is new, something inspired by the custom lettering I put on our pink ladies jackets back in October for the Halloween party.

Something good had to come out of that night, I guess.

And with everything that's gone on recently with my new friends, it's helped take my mind off the fact that they've both dived headfirst into my world and immediately found themselves more exciting lives.

Things might have changed for me in the past few months—I've done things I never thought I would, experienced things I believed I was destined to miss out on—but still, here I am.

Alone.

I might have moved into Nico's den of sin and

turned it into my little piece of craft heaven, but still, I'm alone.

I blow out a breath, wondering what my friends are up to tonight.

They all made their excuses earlier, so they're probably having a night in with their fellas.

Everyone's been on high alert this week, stressed to the max with everything going on. But as usual, I'm not party to the details. Even now, I'm kept on the periphery. All I know is that it involves Jodie's father and the Italians. But what's new there? Both have been causing trouble for long enough that their drama is just part of normal life now.

Anger and frustration swirl in my stomach. The need to do something to make them all trust me, to let me in just as deep as they are burns within me.

I let out a sigh as I allow my thoughts to flicker between two guys—neither of whom should be taking up space in my head. But in spite of everything, both of them seem to have taken up residence over the past few months.

I shake my head, trying to force them out. Wanting to rebel and break out of my sheltered life was meant to be a bit of fun. I wasn't meant to find myself obsessing about two guys I shouldn't want.

As if he knows I'm thinking about him, my phone vibrates on the rug next to me.

Ant: You busy tonight?

I stare at the message, my fingers tapping on the side of my phone as I regret opening it.

He'll have seen I've read it and will be expecting a reply.

It's not that I don't want to talk to him. I do. I always want to. But as the weeks have gone on, the chance of us getting caught only grows. And now, with the war between our families only escalating, it makes the risk so much more real. I'm terrified. Not so much for me... But for him.

If—when—our time is up, he's the one who's going to suffer the pain from spending time with me. More than he already has.

I still vividly remember the day Nico and Seb laid into Ant and Enzo outside the cinema just for hanging out with Stella and me.

If they discovered even after all these months later that we were still in touch, that we still hang out...

No.

That can't happen.

Ever.

They might think Ant is the enemy because of his Italian blood, but it's not true.

Ant's a good guy.

I know he is.

I feel it when we're together, every time he looks at me. Every time he kisses me...

Calli: Nothing. Home alone. *sad face emoji*

I regret the sad face the second I hit send, but it's too late. It's out there now, and I already know how he's going to reply.

The bouncing dots start almost immediately.

Ant: Come hang with me. I miss you.

Excitement stirs in my belly. I shouldn't go. We're on borrowed time as it is, but I can't deny the thrill that rushes through me every single time I defy expectations and spend time with him at his place.

Butterflies erupt within me as I consider sneaking to the other side of town and spending the night with him.

I glance down at my tablet, the screen now dark and only showing my reflection.

My hair is pulled back, my face clear of today's makeup. I'm wearing leggings and a Christmas jumper that I should have packed away weeks ago, but it's comfy and warm and quite frankly, I don't really care.

Do I really want to get dressed up and go out?

I think about my friends, who are all probably enjoying themselves. Then, I think about my parents, who more than likely aren't home, which is nothing new. And my brother, who's probably out partying somewhere, treating some poor, unsuspecting woman to a night of less-than-mind-blowing sex.

"Ugh." A shudder rips down my spine. "Fuck it."

I could use some fun, some excitement.

Some attention.

Calli: Give me an hour. *smiley face emoji*

Another thrill shoots through me as I jump up. I'm not sure I'll ever get used to the rush I get from rebelling against all the rules and expectations that have been placed on me.

If only I knew this kind of fun existed before.

Leaving everything where it is, I strip out of my clothes and walk straight into the shower to freshen up.

I scrub every inch of my body and shave all the parts that need to be. Once I'm out and dry, I rub my favourite smelling moisturiser into my skin.

Feeling good, I pull out my sexiest underwear—which isn't all that sexy, but at least it's lace, not cotton—and I search through my wardrobe for something suitable.

Since Stella and Emmie entered my life, my wardrobe has seen a huge improvement. They haven't just had an influence on how I act, but also how I look. Stella was the one who convinced me to shed the blonde hair Mum had demanded I keep, when deep down I'd craved to try something darker and to cut off the length that Mum always told me was as pretty as a princess.

I didn't want to be a princess. The good girl who did as she was told and lived the dullest life in the world while locked up in her castle.

I wanted to experience life like Nico did. I wanted to paint the town red, be a teenager, or at least have the option to do so.

Happy with my reflection, I smooth my hair down once more and stuff my feet into my Uggs.

Grabbing my bag, I drop my phone into it and head out via my new back door.

Nico moving out was one of the best things to happen to me. I love having my own space, my own door, my freedom. Even if on most days I don't take advantage of it, considering I have nothing to do. Just the knowledge that I have it, that my parents finally trust me at least a little bit, is enough.

The journey to the Italian side of town takes longer than I'm expecting, and I get more than one message from Ant on the way asking if I'm still coming.

His impatience to see me makes me smile as I pull up on the street, one over from the converted warehouse he calls home.

Everyone else parks right out the front of the building. But by slipping through the trees at the back, it's allowed me to climb in and out unnoticed over the past few months.

The second I step out of the car, hidden in the shadows, I see him, standing under a streetlamp beside the gap in the trees.

"Hey, stranger," he breathes, stepping forward to meet me. "I've missed you."

His hand slips around the back of my neck and his lips brush against mine in the sweetest of kisses.

That's just Ant, though. Everything he does is sweet, thoughtful.

Nothing like *him*.

Ant would never touch me, kiss me, take me the way *he* did that night.

Is that the reason I still crave him?

The darkness he showed me. The pleasure.

He took what he wanted, what he knew I needed—although I'm not sure how he knew—and gave me something I'm never going to be able to forget.

"I'm sorry I've been so busy," he whispers, pulling back, cupping my jaw as he stares down into my eyes.

"It's okay, I get it." And I really do. He works for the Mariano Family, but he's also doing his first year at university and he's in the final stretch to exams. I understand why he needs to put that first. Why he has to put his Family first, because if he didn't and anyone found out that it was because of me, because of a Cirillo...

I shove reality away, trying to focus on him when he slides his hand into mine and twists our fingers together.

"Come on, I've already ordered food."

My stomach growls on cue.

"Sorry I took so long; the traffic was horrendous."

"You're here now," he says, lifting our joined hands to his lips.

Everything inside me relaxes in his presence. It's one of the many reasons I know my brother and cousin are wrong.

Ant's not playing me. He's not trying to get intel on us, our Family. He's never so much as asked me anything about my life outside of school or normal stuff. He's never given me any reason to believe that he wants anything more than just to spend time with me... well, maybe something. But he's been nothing but a gentleman and followed my lead.

I'd told him the first time we hung out after Halloween when he tried to make a move on me that I wanted to take it slow, and he accepted my request without argument, even though I knew he wanted to take it further. It showed me that he wanted to put my needs before his own.

I wanted it. To be physical with him like that. But after him, I just couldn't.

I'd have compared everything, then I'd get stuck in my own head with the way he did it.

I just needed time to push him and thoughts of that night from my mind like it seemed he did the second he walked out the door.

Discovering who he was and watching him forget it ever happened hurt. Seeing him later that evening while both Seb and Toby were lying in hospital beds was torture, but it had nothing on the way he looked at me like it was any other day, nodded in greeting and then walked away as if I hadn't come all over his face only hours before. Hell, he could probably still taste me, yet he dismissed me like I was nothing.

Like I was a regrettable mistake he'd happily never think of again.

"What's wrong?" Ant asks, sensing my mood shift.

"Nothing," I say, plastering on a smile. "It's just been a long week."

"Well then, you've come to the perfect place for you to relax."

We emerge through the trees at the back of the building and find the window to Ant's ground floor flat open and ready to climb through.

"Didn't you want to hang out with the guys tonight?" I ask as we come to a stop by the window.

"Over spending time with you? Not a chance," he breathes in my ear, stepping right up behind me and pressing the length of his body against mine.

I swoon hard as his hands brush up my sides, finally resting on the curve of my waist to help lift me through the window into his room.

It should be a glaring red flag that I can't just walk in through the front door to be with him. It should be enough to tell me what a stupid idea all of this is. But it doesn't stop me.

Spending time with Ant is just so easy. He makes me smile, laugh. He doesn't take life too seriously despite the ugliness of what we're entangled with because of our surnames, and he makes me feel important, worthy, sexy.

"I love this skirt on you, Cal," he tells me as I climb inside and wait for him to join me.

"Thanks," I say, my cheeks heating at the compliment. I knew he'd like it. It's short, and I made the possibly dangerous decision to forgo tights or leggings. It might be a little forward and could possibly be sending him the wrong message, seeing as I keep telling him that I want to wait. But I was feeling extra rebellious tonight and I crave the feeling of being wanted.

He makes my blood boil, and my stomach flutters wildly as he looks at me as if I'm the only girl in the world.

I barely notice the scent of Chinese food that fills the room as he locks the window and turns back toward me, closing the space between us.

"Hey," he says again, a lopsided smile tugging at one side of his lips.

My stomach clenches as he reaches for me once more.

His burning hand wraps around the side of my neck as his head dips.

My eyes flutter closed as his lips brush mine.

"Damn, I've missed you, Sunshine."

"Ant," I moan, my hand wrapping around his side and pulling him closer.

He peppers gentle kisses along my lips as he backs me up against the wall and rests his arm beside my head.

I gasp when the hardness of his body presses

against mine, the evidence of how much he's holding himself back more than obvious against my belly.

He makes the most of my parted lips and plunges his tongue inside, a move I eagerly mimic, quickly losing myself in his drugging kisses.

We don't part until we're both breathless and gasping for air.

"I guess we should eat, huh?"

I swallow down my need to tell him that I'm not all that hungry for food and regretfully release him when he rips himself from my body.

Lifting his hand, he pushes his dark hair back from his brow. His cheeks are flushed and his lips swollen from our kiss.

He looks hot. I mean, he's always hot, he's got that sexy Italian blood running through his veins. Tall, dark, and oh so very handsome.

The rapid movement of his chest drags my gaze from his hooded eyes before they drop lower to the more-than-obvious bulge in his jeans.

My fingers curl into fists.

It would be so easy right now to step up to him and tell him that I want it—him. That I'm fed up with waiting and finally give in to replace my memories of that dark room that night, of *his* touch with Ant's.

It's what any sane person would have done weeks ago.

Apparently, though, that's not what I am where these two are concerned.

"Shit," he hisses, reaching down to rearrange himself and turning toward the bags of takeout.

I fight to find something to say, to come up with an excuse for the reason I continually put a barrier up between us.

I stand awkwardly with my back still against the wall as he pulls the containers out and places them on a tray.

When he finally turns back around, his face is relaxed once more and he's got a soft smile playing on his lips.

"It's okay, Cal," he tells me honestly. "I get it."

I smile back at him, blown away by his understanding but also wishing he wouldn't be so considerate. A part of me wants him to throw caution to the wind, to sweep me up and just take what he wants. To force his way through the wall I keep putting up and rip it to shreds.

"Come eat. You wanna pick a film to watch?"

I look between him, the tray of food, then at the massive fifty-inch TV he's got strapped to the wall, and I shake my head. "Nah, you can choose."

I climb onto his bed, sitting back against the headboard as he lowers the tray and sits on the other side of it, passing me a fork.

Just as he picks up the remote, there's a huge roar from the other side of the door.

My entire body locks up at the realisation that the enemy—my Family's enemy—is only a room away. Hell, what am I thinking... Ant is the enemy.

But when it's just the two of us, our surnames, our connections, don't matter.

"It's okay," he says, reaching over and uncurling my fists. "They're all watching some fight. It's probably getting a little heated."

The reason I have to climb into his room via the window is because to get to it from the front door, we'd have to walk through a massive room that the younger members of the Mariano Family have converted to a massive den.

It's dangerous being here, but we figured that it was safer than being out in public where anyone from either Family could see us.

Here, we're locked in his room where no one should bother us.

Well, that's what we hope for.

"You don't want to watch?" I ask, once again feeling like I'm keeping him from his friends by being here.

Lowering the remote, he just stares at me.

"No, Calli. I wouldn't rather be out there with a bunch of sweaty, angry dickheads when I could be in here with you... in this skirt." He bites down on his bottom lip and wiggles his brows.

"You're an idiot."

He shrugs, not having a care in the world as he shamelessly checks out my legs.

"Eat up, Sunshine. I've got plans for you tonight."

A wave of heat races through my body, burning me from the inside out.

"Your parents aren't expecting you home, right?"

I scoff. "You think they've even noticed I'm out?"

He gives me a sad smile, but I know he understands. Having a big brother who's stolen the spotlight almost all his life, he gets what it's like, living in the shadows and expected to behave in a certain way. The only difference is that he's expected to step up now and become a soldier.

I, however, am expected to do what? Find a nice Greek guy and pop out some future soldiers?

I blow out a frustrated breath.

"It's a good job I called you over, then. We wouldn't want you home alone and lonely." His words drip with lust.

"I was just working," I say, throwing a little cold water on his train of thought.

"Sure you were." He wiggles his brows suggestively.

"You're a nightmare."

"You love it," he counters, finally picking the remote back up and hitting play on the number one film that comes up on Netflix. I don't even get a chance to see what it is other than it looks kinda romance-y. Not that I have an issue with that. I just can't imagine him being into it.

Grabbing one of the containers and a fork, Ant spears a piece of shredded chicken and holds it up for me.

"Your favourite," he murmurs as I part my lips, accepting it from him.

An appreciative moan rumbles in my chest as the

flavours explode in my mouth and he watches as my tongue sneaks out to lick up the sauce.

"Do you know how hard it's been to focus this week, knowing I couldn't see you?"

"Ant," I sigh, wishing he wouldn't say such swoony things to me.

I love it really, but it's just a massive reminder that no matter how we really feel about each other, it can never work. Our parents would never allow it.

He smiles at me, refusing to deal with our reality, and instead we just secretly spend time together enjoying ourselves.

The film plays out in the background, but neither of us pays it any attention as we eat and talk about anything other than our families.

He tells me about uni and the exams he's got coming up while I chat reluctantly about school and my classes. I hate talking about school, or even thinking about it really.

It was okay when it was just secondary school, but now we're in sixth form, everyone expects me to know what I'm doing with my life, and the truth is, I have no clue.

I don't fit in anywhere. I'm mediocre at best in all my subjects. I'm an okay gymnast and cheerleader, but it's not exactly a career option.

Nothing is.

And I don't want to be a stay-at-home mum. Yeah, I want kids one day, but it's not the only thing I want.

I want a life of my own. A purpose. A career. I just don't know what that might look like yet.

"Hey," Ant says, dragging me from my thoughts. "You finished?" he asks, nodding at the mostly empty tray between us.

"Y-yeah," I say, my eyes dropping to the last spring roll.

A wicked smile twitches at his lips as he climbs from the bed and moves the tray to the floor.

Walking over to the light switch, he dims it a little, then turns back to me, pausing to run his eyes up my legs where I've stretched them out in front of me.

He eats up the space between us quickly and he bends down, grabbing something before rejoining me on the bed and straddling my legs.

"Want it?" he asks, lifting the spring roll between us.

He runs it along my bottom lip, his eyes following its journey.

"Y-yeah, I do," I say, wondering if we're still talking about food right now.

"Open wide then," he says, waiting for my lips to part.

The second they do, he pushes it into my mouth and watches, his eyes darkening as I wrap my lips around it and bite.

"Fuck, Sunshine," he grunts. "You have no idea how hot you are, do you?"

I smile as I chew before watching him steal the other end of the spring roll and throw it into his mouth.

"Lie back," he breathes, gently pushing my shoulder until I'm exactly where he wants me, beneath him on his bed.

My heart thunders in my chest as I stare up at him.

"All you gotta do is say the word and I'll stop, you know that, right?" he asks.

"I trust you," I breathe.

A smile that makes my stomach flip and my thighs clench appears on his lips. Reaching behind him, he pulls his shirt from his body in one smooth move that does little for the desire that's already coursing through my veins.

It's not the first time I've seen him shirtless. He's given me the pleasure of witnessing, even touching his insanely cut torso before, and something tells me I've not done a very good job of hiding how much I love it.

Unable to stop myself, I reach out, running my fingertips from his chest all the way down to his waistband.

In a move I'd never even consider if I wasn't drunk on him already, I tuck my fingers under his waistband and tug him closer, needing more.

"Kiss me," I demand.

"Like you need to ask, Sunshine."

His lips descend on mine, his muscular body lowering and pressing my much smaller one into the mattress. My legs automatically wrap around his waist, pinning us together as he kisses me as if I'm the air he needs to survive.

My skin burns with need as his hand slips under my jumper, his fingers splaying across my ribs.

His hips roll, his hard length rubbing against my core, sending pleasure shooting through me.

"Fuck, Calli," he groans, ripping his lips from mine and kissing across my jaw and down my neck. "You get me so hot."

Goosebumps erupt across my skin as he sucks on my neck, grazing my sensitive skin with his teeth.

"Ant, God," I moan, my nails scratching across his back.

He kisses down my chest that's exposed by the deep V of my jumper before slipping his hand higher and cupping my breast.

My back arches with my need for more.

"Oh God," I moan when he pinches my nipple through the lace of my bra.

"I love watching you come apart. It's all I've been able to think about this week."

It's not the first time things have gotten this far with us, but it's never gone further than him losing his shirt and dry humping me until I shatter while he's probably about to come in his pants.

Every time he's made me come, I've been flooded with guilt that I haven't returned the favour, but he's always assured me that it's fine and he hasn't pushed for more.

Such a freaking sweetheart.

It should be everything I could want. But there's always someone else in my head. Someone who wasn't going to let me off easy. Someone who was going to take everything.

Sitting up a little, Ant pushes my jumper up, exposing my stomach and bra.

"Shit, this is sexy," he murmurs, running his finger around the lace edge.

A quiet, needy whimper escapes my lips.

"More?" he asks, a wicked glint in his eyes.

I hesitate for a second and he sees it, but thankfully, he doesn't question me this time. Instead, he drags my jumper up and off my body, throwing it to the floor with his. He lowers his head once more and presses his lips to the swell of my breast, tucking his fingers beneath the fabric and exposing me.

His eyes hold mine the whole time, telling me that I can stop whenever I want. But even if I wanted to, I'd be incapable of saying the word as I watch as his full lips wrap around my nipple.

All the air rushes from my lungs as his heat surrounds me.

"Oh shit," I gasp when he sucks hard.

He teases me until I can barely stand it as my body edges closer to release, his hips still slowly rocking into me.

With my fingers twisted in his hair, holding him against me, he begins kissing lower, over the soft skin of my stomach before dipping his tongue into my belly button.

My stomach clenches hard as I read his intentions in his eyes.

"I want to taste you, Calli. Tell me I can," he damn near begs.

Mindlessly, I nod, and the most breathtaking smile appears on his lips a beat before he drops to his stomach between my legs.

Oh God.

I squeeze my eyes closed when he reaches under my skirt and wraps his fingers around the sides of my knickers.

Sucking in a breath and dragging some confidence with it, I lift my hips right as a loud crash sounds out beyond the door.

Our eyes collide and my heart jumps into my throat.

"It's okay," Ant assures me, discarding my underwear over the side of the bed. "They're probably just wasted and the wrong guy won."

I nod, trusting him not to do anything that will end up with us being caught, or worse.

"Ignore them."

I nod again, my teeth sinking into my bottom lip as he presses his hands against the sensitive skin of my inner thighs and spreads me wide for him.

His eyes hold mine for a few seconds as the chaos seems to continue outside the door, but I do as he suggested and just focus on him, on us.

Happy that I'm still here with him in the moment, his eyes drop from mine, getting back to where he was before we were distracted.

"Fuck," he hisses. "You're perfect."

He licks his lips as if he's just been handed a giant bowl of his favourite dessert and surges forward, but he never gets a chance to make contact because his bedroom door flies open.

I sit up in a rush, reaching for something to cover up with as Ant barks, "Get the fuck—"

But everything comes crashing down around me when my eyes connect with the person standing in his doorway, his eyes locked on mine.

His face is the same hard, cold mask that I'm more than used to, but his eyes... they're not just deadly, they're blazing with contempt, with the need to burn this entire place to the ground and raise hell in its place.

"Daemon?"

2

———

DAEMON

Tonight has been... Fuck. I drag my hand down my face as I think of the events that have unfolded.

We knew Jonas was fucked in the head. But I don't think any of us truly appreciated just how fucking crazy he was.

Toby was adamant that Jonas would hurt Jodie and Joanne, and while I was hoping he wouldn't, the past that Toby and Maria have suffered sure points toward the fact that Jonas is more than happy hurting his own family.

We just hoped that Jodie would be different. But then, why would she be? He sent his own son to the fucking slaughter by pitting him against us.

Did he really have such little faith in the soldiers he helped to train?

I shake my head as I slouch in my seat and close my eyes for a beat.

The image of those houses exploding right in front of us fills my mind, along with the all-too-fresh panic I felt in those few moments of not knowing if we'd all made it out.

I might be the outsider in our little group, but hell if I want to see any of them hurt. Or for Jonas and the Italians to take something from us. Not when we've been working so hard to bring them down.

While Damien, the boss, and Evan, the underboss, had been dealing with the shit with the Reapers and the Wolves that Theo and Emmie found themselves tangled up in recently, my father had been focusing his efforts on the Italians.

After they confessed to working for Jonas the night of the last Circuit fight that went up in flames—quite literally—they'd gone quiet.

Too fucking quiet.

And we discovered there was a very good reason for it when Dad managed to plant a snake and uncover their plans for taking over our businesses that border their side of the city.

They tried with Marco's diner last year but failed. We'd hoped they might have given up, but it seems that was wishful thinking. They'd just gone back to the drawing board and had come up with a plan that included a lot of intentional blood loss on both sides.

It's just a shame they didn't grass on Jonas's most recent plans. That could have saved Toby yet another week of suffering at that twisted motherfucker's hands.

It's no surprise that the peace that's existed

between the two families for years has been shattered so soon after Ricardo took over as Boss, his father standing down because of bad health. He's always been unhinged, power hungry. It was inevitable that he'd drag us into a war sooner or later.

I glance over at the car parked beside mine and lock eyes with Theo's. Bloodlust for these motherfuckers who are trying to take things that belong to us shines just as bright in his eyes as I know it does in mine.

We're parked on the street over from the Italians' warehouse. The rest of our soldiers are planted at intervals around the building, waiting for the second signal from my dad.

This isn't their main headquarters, but from the intel we've managed to get, it's where the majority of them are tonight. Enough to send a message to Ricardo, at least.

Pulling out my weapons from my glovebox, I double check that each of my guns are loaded before tucking two into my waistband and another into my shoulder holster under my jacket. Spare rounds go into my pockets before I strap one knife to my ankle and secure another into the holster.

Then, I wait.

The second my phone buzzes and Dad's name pops up with the signal, I push my door open and climb out, while Theo, Seb, Nico, and my twin, Alex do the same, before Toby appears.

I do a double take, not expecting to see him here after the night he's had. But I don't let his presence distract me. If he wants a hand in delivering this hopefully bloody message to the Italians, he's more than welcome. I nod in their direction, but my focus is solely on the building before us.

As far as we're aware, this is going to be an ambush. But while we've had a mole in their ranks, it would be foolish to think this attack might not have got back to them. Recent events are proof enough that we might just have loyalties in the wrong places. The two almost dead bodies we have currently locked away are evidence of that enough.

We surround the building, hiding in the shadows before we get the final signal.

A smile curls at my lips as we storm inside with our guns raised and discover that the Italians couldn't be any less unprepared for this attack.

The stupid fucks scramble to defend themselves, but they're too slow as the boys and I take them down with little effort.

Alex, Nico, and Seb go for them using their fists, while Theo, Toby, and I use our guns, the silencers ensuring we don't get jumped by any of their members who might be hiding out in their rooms.

We don't shoot to kill. We're not here for that. We're here to deliver a message. To point out that we're always one step ahead of them, and that if we wanted to cut down their numbers, we could easily do so.

"Go check all the rooms," Dad booms at the six of us when it's clear we've got control of the little party they were having.

Turning away from his other soldiers who are tidying up the mess we've left behind, we split up, three upstairs and three down.

I aim for the first door while Alex and Nico overtake me to hit up the next two.

I push the handle down, but it doesn't budge.

Assuming that it's empty, I almost walk away, but something stops me.

I have no idea what it is, but the niggle of uncertainty in my gut means I ram my shoulder into the light wood, throwing all my weight into it.

The lock pretty much melts under the force and the door swings open, revealing a guy's legs hanging off the end of the bed, quite clearly in the middle of something important.

A slight smirk curls at my lips and I step into the room as the guy sits up and barks, "Get the fuck—" but the second our eyes lock and he realises who's just walked in, his words immediately cut off.

Smart guy.

But the joy at my gut feeling being right only lasts a split second, because I step farther into the room and my eyes land on the woman with that Italian cunt between her legs.

She freezes in shock as our eyes connect and something akin to lightning cracks between us.

"Daemon," she breathes, suddenly jumping into action, scrambling up the bed and trying to cover herself up.

But it's too late, I've already seen it.

I've already seen her with another fucking guy, a fucking Italian, about to...

"You're going to fucking die for this." My voice is cold, colder than even I recognise as the words fall from my lips and I lift my arm, aiming my gun right at his head.

"Daemon, no," Calli cries, scrambling from the bed, but she's too slow.

Before her feet even hit the floor, I squeeze the trigger, sending Antonio Santoro flying back into the wall.

"Nooo," she screams, but I don't give her a chance to look back and see where I hit him. I drop down in front of her and throw her body over my shoulder, marching her out of the room while she screams bloody murder behind me, her tiny fists slamming into my arse.

It's only my dad who looks up as I pass through all the bloody and broken bodies that he and his guys are rounding up. With Calli upside down behind me, I don't worry that he'll recognise her, and when he doesn't even spare the woman hanging over my shoulder a second glance, I keep moving, getting her the hell out of this shitshow.

She doesn't stop screaming and fighting even when I come to a stop beside my car and place her back on her feet.

"What the fuck are you doing?" she screams, her arms flying at me, hitting wherever she can make contact.

Tears cascade down her cheeks, coating them in black makeup as she stands there in just her bra and tiny skirt.

Fuck. She's never looked better.

My cock aches as images from that night flicker through my mind like a fucking movie.

I was so close. So fucking close to having the one thing I've allowed myself to crave all these fucking years.

Calli Cirillo.

My obsession.

My addiction.

My ultimate fucking weakness.

"Stop," I boom, my hand finding her throat as I force her back against the car.

Her screams stop as her chin drops in shock.

"Stop fucking screaming," I seethe, getting right in her face. "Unless you want all the others out here seeing you looking like a dirty little whore."

Her breath catches at my vicious words a second before her palm connects with my cheek.

Pain blooms across my skin. It does nothing but feed the fucking devil that lives inside me.

Her chest heaves as she glares at me.

"I hate you," she hisses through the sobs that are still wracking her body. "I fucking hate you, and I'll never forgive you for this. Ever."

A smile curls at my lips.

Those are the words I always thought I needed to hear. The words that might shatter the hold she's always had over me. But standing here before her, feeling her pulse thunder beneath my fingers, I realise they come nowhere near to severing this thing between us.

If anything, it only makes my obsession, my need to prove her wrong, to fucking own her, even more irrational.

I told myself for years that if I kept a distance between us, it would lessen. I'd find someone else to focus my efforts, my dark, twisted desires on.

But it's never happened.

Since we were six years old, it's always been Calli.

And until that night, it was my darkest secret.

One I was willing to take to the grave in order to give her the life she deserves, to allow her to find the kind of man she deserves.

Because that sure as fuck isn't a screwed-up, cold arsehole like me.

But something snapped in me that night.

Something that I can't explain even now.

And I still can't decide if it was the best or worst thing to ever happen in my life.

"Get in the fucking car, Callista."

"Fuck you," she spits, slapping me again and making a loud growl rumble deep in my throat.

"You're playing with fire," I warn her, two seconds from snapping. And that means I'm either about to strangle the fucking life out of her or take what I should have that night right here against my car for her brother and the rest of the guys to witness.

"Then watch me burn, arsehole."

Reaching out, I rip open the back door of my car, and, with my hand still around her throat, I grasp her waist with the other and throw her inside.

"You can't do this," she screams.

"I thought you knew, beautiful," I sneer. "I can do whatever the fuck I want."

"You're a fucking psycho."

"I know. It's fun, isn't it?"

The smile I give her is full of malice, but beneath it, there's nothing but desire.

Slamming the door shut, I engage the locks before she has a chance to escape. Then, I quickly unlock just the driver's door before getting in and flooring the accelerator before anyone sees me leaving with her.

I might be willing to reveal the level of my obsession with the little girl who helped me all those years ago to her, but like fuck will I let anyone else see that I care about anything.

3

———

CALLI

The almost-silent gunshot that pierces the room forces a scream from my throat.

The voice startles me, and my eyes fly open.

"What the—"

I try to sit up, but my arms are stuck behind my head.

My head is fuzzy, really fucking fuzzy.

I still, trying to focus, trying to drag up memories of how I went from being on Ant's bed with his head...

Everything slams into me with the force of an articulated lorry, and I kick my legs out as I try once more to get up.

Ant.

Daemon.

The gunshot.

"Noooo," I shriek, my heart racing so hard it makes my head even fuzzier. "Daemon," I cry.

Silence.

"DAEMON! DAEMON!" I scream his name until my throat is hoarse, but nothing happens. No one comes.

Looking up toward the headboard, I find my wrists have been bound with silk scarves, and when I remember that he dragged me from that warehouse in just my bra and skirt, I look down at what I have on.

"Jesus," I mutter, taking in the black men's shirt I'm now wearing.

Did he fucking change me?

"Daemon," I scream once more, but just like I expect, nothing happens.

He's either ignoring me, or he's left me here. Wherever here is.

I look around the room, trying to find something that might clue me in as to where I am.

The walls are white and the furniture is a dark walnut. It all looks expensive, but surely, it's not Daemon's place.

I'd expect that to be as black as Theo's, to match his soul.

A sob rips up my throat as I think about Ant.

Is that where Daemon's gone? To clean up his body?

Rolling onto my front, I bury my face into the pillow and let my tears spill free as I mourn something that never could have been mine anyway.

I never wanted this, yet I knew it was the risk we were both taking.

We were both naïve to think we weren't going to get caught.

I just never imagined that it would be by him.

Daemon.

My Batman.

My tears only come faster as I think back to that night and the way he's avoided and ignored me ever since.

He knew I'd seen him, yet he's never once tried talking to me about it.

It hurt to know that he regretted it so much when I truly believed every word he'd said to me that night.

I knew going anywhere near Ant after discovering that he was part of the Mariano Family was a bad idea. But he was so sweet. He saw me as just Calli—not the Cirillo princess—and he made me feel like no one else I'd ever met.

He was my secret. Something I chose for myself when every other part of my life is dictated by my parents, by the Family.

But it was selfish of me to drag him into my fucked-up life.

I have no idea how long I lie there sobbing, but eventually, I cry myself back to sleep.

When I wake up, I know that something is different before I've even opened my eyes.

I feel *him*.

His stare, his presence. His breath wafting softly over my face.

For a few seconds, I allow myself to remember how safe, how wanted he made me feel that night, but that contentment is soon washed away when I remember what happened tonight.

Was it even tonight?

How long have I been out of it?

Ant.

My eyes fly open and they collide with his dark pair.

He's lying on the bed beside me, staring at me with his hand tucked under his cheek.

The sight of him looking completely relaxed after everything he's done ignites a fire in my belly.

I tug at my arms, hoping that he's taken pity on me and released me now that he's here, but no such luck.

"What the fuck is your problem?" I seethe, my voice rough with emotion when all he does is lie there and stare at me as if he can't really believe that I'm here.

"Shh, it's okay, beautiful," he whispers softly, reaching out and tucking a lock of my hair behind my ear. "It's okay. Everything is okay."

"Are you actually fucking insane?" I snap, my eyes

bouncing between his, waiting for some kind of reaction, but all he does is smile.

It's not something he does all that often, and the sight of his dimples makes something odd happen inside me.

"Your assurances and your smile aren't helping the situation," I hiss, although I regret it the second his lips flatten once more.

"I'm not going to hurt you, beautiful. I'd never hurt you."

"Untie me then. My arms ache."

He looks up to where my wrists are bound and then back to my eyes.

"I can't," he confesses.

"Why?"

He studies me for so long that I don't think he's going to respond. But eventually, he reaches out once more, brushing his fingertips down my cheek and then along the edge of my jaw as if I'm something precious, something that might vanish at any moment.

"Because you'll leave."

"Damn fucking right I'll leave. You abducted me. You killed Ant." My expression hardens, grief washing through me as red-hot tears burn my eyes and my heart fractures.

Something flickers in his eyes, something dark that makes my stomach clench with fear.

I know Daemon is dangerous. I've known that for years. But I've never been scared of him quite like I have been tonight. I always thought his wrath was aimed only toward the enemy—I mean, I guess it was tonight too—but still, I can't help feeling like I'm suddenly one of them.

"He was touching you. He was..." His jaw clenches so hard, I can't help thinking it must hurt.

"I wanted him to," I shout when I realise that he's not going to finish that thought, making him rear back a little. "I wanted him to be touching me. I wanted to be his. And he wanted me too. He wasn't hiding from me. He wasn't walking away." With every word, my voice gets louder, angrier.

But despite the fire burning in his eyes, he doesn't bite back. And when he speaks again, it's soft.

"He doesn't deserve you, beautiful."

A bitter laugh falls from my lips. "And you do?"

"Never."

"This is insane. Let me go."

"No."

"Daemon, I swear to fucking God, if you don't let me go I'll..." I don't have any words to finish that threat, so instead, I start thrashing about, kicking my legs and shoving the sheets he's covered me with from my body in my need to hurt him.

The second my foot makes contact with his shin, pain shoots up from my toes, swiftly halting my movements.

"Callista," he warns, his hand wrapping around my thigh, drawing me closer to him.

My breath catches as his touch sends a bolt of electricity shooting through my body. It makes me achingly aware of how little I'm wearing. The fact that he's clearly already seen everything, considering I might not have exactly been dressed when he threw me over his shoulder and marched me out of Ant's room, I still felt significantly more covered than I am now.

"Do not chastise me like a child. Like I'm being an irrational brat, Nikolas."

His breath catches at my use of his real name. The one given to him at birth that I know he hates, one that everyone seems to have forgotten exists seeing as Daemon, his middle name, suits him so much better.

"Don't," he warns, his voice low and deadly.

"Or what? You'll shoot me too?"

He freezes, his grip on my thigh tightening on me for a beat, revealing that my words have some kind of impact on him.

"Never," he breathes, pushing up on his elbow so he can look down at me, but he doesn't release my leg, his fingertips digging into my soft flesh.

My breath catches when I find the deep scratches on the cheek he was lying on, but I drag my eyes away.

His eyes search my face. It's as if he's committing every inch of me to his memory before they drop lower, taking in his shirt that I'm wrapped in before moving down to my bare legs and the contrast of his darker skin against mine.

"You're the only person on this planet that I'd never harm. You're a fucking angel, Calli."

His eyes find mine again and my breath catches in my throat at the intensity of them.

He really means those words.

So why the hell are we here?

Swallowing down the lump that's crawled up my throat and blinking away the tears that are burning the backs of my eyes, I hold his stare, summoning up all the courage I possess.

"If that's true, then you need to release me."

"So you can go back to him." It's not a question. It's a statement, as if he knows he's already lost.

I mean, I can understand why. Anyone in their right mind would go running back to the nice guy right now, had he not just been taken out of the equation.

A sob erupts once more as I think about Ant.

It's my fault.

All of this is my fault, and he's just paid the ultimate price.

One of my tears slips free, and Daemon watches as it tracks down my temple before soaking into my hairline.

"Fuck, you're beautiful."

And you're fucking deranged, I think, but I keep it to myself. Something tells me that offending him isn't the way to get out of this.

Leaning forward, he presses his lips to my temple, his tongue licking at the remnants of my tear.

"W-what are you doing?" I ask, hating the way my voice sounds from one single kiss from him.

"He doesn't deserve you, Calli. You're too beautiful for the likes of him. Too pure." My breath catches as I remember telling him on Halloween night that I'd never been with anyone before. His response was that he knew.

Had he been keeping tabs on what I was—or wasn't—doing?

"So you killed him?"

His hand slips higher up my thigh, and it makes my entire body burn with need.

Stupid, traitorous body.

Swallowing down my emotions, my desire, I hold his eyes. "I need the bathroom," I tell him as softly as I can.

His gaze flicks across the room—I assume to the en suite—before coming back to me.

"Please. I need to pee and freshen up." I've no idea how long I've been asleep for, but the state of my mouth tells me it's been a while.

He hesitates, and for a few seconds, I actually expect him to refuse my request. But after another uncertain look in the direction of the bathroom, he reaches for the silk scarves and begins untying them.

My arms ache worse than I thought as I lower them and begin to twirl my wrists around, but my arm is soon captured in his grasp and he takes over my movements, helping me loosen my muscles before pressing a soft kiss to the inside of my wrist, his eyes locked on mine.

"Daemon," I breathe as he repeats the action on the other arm.

His tenderness confuses me after his brutality in Ant's room and the way he threw me into the back of his car and tied me up here when I was unconscious.

Tugging my hand free of his hold, I roll off the bed and stand on my feet.

My head spins and my knees almost give out, reminding me of something else he's done.

"You drugged me."

The last thing I remember was launching myself at him from the back of the car as he drove away from the Italians' warehouse. The next thing I knew, I woke up tied to his bed.

He pushes to stand before me, and I flinch away when he reaches out for me.

Pain shoots through his eyes, but he covers it up quickly, allowing his hand to drop to his side.

"It was for your own good."

"How? How was drugging me for my own good?"

"I'd have crashed the car if you continued freaking out," he says, calmly.

My eyes narrow on the scratches on his face as hazy memories of clawing at him around the driver's seat come back to me.

Pride swells in my chest that I managed that, that I actually managed to cause him even a little bit of pain for what he'd just done.

My lips turn down into a grimace as I stare at him, unable to keep up the act any longer.

"I hate you." My arm moves before I even register what I'm doing, and pain explodes on my palm as it connects with his cheek again.

His face turns feral, his eyes murderous as his

fingers wrap around my wrist, holding my hand where it landed against his face.

All the air rushes from my lungs when I collide with the wall, immediately crushed between it and Daemon's hard body as he stares down at me, his harsh breaths racing over my face.

"Say it again," he dares.

"I. Hate. You."

Before I know what's happening, his lips are on mine, his tongue is in my mouth and his hand is gripping the back of my neck, holding me in place.

For a good ten seconds, I return his kiss with as much fervour, my mind and body going straight back to Halloween when I lost myself in him so completely, but then everything comes crashing back to me and I slam my palms down on his chest.

"No," I cry. "You don't get to do this. You don't get to keep dropping in and out of my life pretending you care for a few minutes. No," I spit, slipping out from between his body and the wall. "You don't care about me. If you did, you wouldn't have ignored what happened between us like it was all a dream for months."

His chest heaves, his lips are swollen, and his fists are curled at his sides.

As always, he's dressed head to toe in black, only he's a little more casual with a black t-shirt. Just like on Halloween. Only, he's missing his cape and mask.

Superhero, my fucking arse.

A manic laugh falls from my lips.

"If you cared, you'd have found me. You'd have said something. Anything. But no, you've happily sat in the same room as me and pretended like nothing happened. That you didn't kiss me, that you didn't—"

"Make you come?" he finishes for me.

My cheeks burn red hot as the memories slam into me, and my thighs clench to ease the ache with the need to feel it again.

Things have been good with Ant. He's made me feel good. And I can lie to myself as much as I like, but it was never as good as that night.

I told myself over and over that it was just the mystery. The high of not knowing who I was with in that dark room. The wildness, the rebellion.

But I know none of it was true.

It was him.

My Batman.

"The things you said that night. The way you touched me, I thought..."

"You thought what?" he asks, taking a step toward me. "You thought it was the beginning of something? That I was going to claim you in front of everyone and make you mine?"

I shake my head, wishing that his words weren't true.

I knew the second he refused to reveal his identity that my hopes for any kind of future between us were a fantasy.

"I can't have you, Calli," he says, the sadness and

defeat in his tone enough to make a little of my anger ebb away.

"So why am I here? What the hell is all this about if you don't want me?"

"No," he barks. "I said I can't have you, not that I don't want you."

I stare at him, trying to process all of this while whatever he drugged me with still fogs the edges of my consciousness.

In the end, I turn my back on all of it, both figuratively and literally and I race toward the bathroom, slamming the door behind me and flicking to lock it before he has a chance to join me.

I manage to keep myself together while I pee, but the second I stand in front of the basin and look in the mirror, seeing the evidence left behind from Ant's drugging kisses to my neck and the pure fucking exhaustion in my eyes from everything else that's happened since, I shatter.

Loud, ugly sobs wrack my body, and my legs give out, leaving me in a heap on the floor.

4

CALLI

The next time I wake up, I'm once again back in his bed, only this time, I know I'm alone. I don't feel his presence, his stare, his heat.

Cracking my eyes open, the first thing I notice is the bathroom door hanging off its bottom hinges at a funny angle. The second is that I'm no longer tied to the bed.

Pushing my messy bed hair back from my face, I sit up and look around.

Every part of my body aches, but nowhere near the pain in my heart. Thoughts of Ant's infectious smile, his kind nature and supportive ways crack my chest wide open.

I knew he was going to end up paying the price for us sneaking around. But I never could have imagined this.

I still don't know where I am, but equally, I'm

having a hard job imagining that this is Daemon's home.

It's so... normal.

I sit there for long seconds just listening, trying to work out where he is.

A part of me wonders if he's left me, but after waking up tied to the bed the last time, I doubt he'd let me go that easily.

Something tells me that I'm going to have to work harder than just waltzing out the front door to discover the fallout of all this.

How long have I even been here?

Each time I've slept, it's been so deep that it could have been days, or could it be the effects of whatever drug he gave me making me lose my grip on reality.

Climbing out of the bed, I'm relieved when my legs are steadier than the last time I stood, and I make my way over to the window.

Pulling aside the blackout curtains, I discover that the sun is high in the sky. But the sight of it does little to lift my dark mood as grief continues to dig its claws into me.

Seeing that we're a long way from the ground only confirms my first assumption that we're in his flat.

"Jesus," I breathe, spinning back around to look for a clock.

There's one on the other side of the bed that shows eleven forty-five.

But what day?

It must still be the weekend. Someone will have

noticed if I just didn't turn up at school. Maybe not my parents, Jocelyn, our housekeeper, certainly would. Stella and Emmie also. Possibly even my brother.

A crash from somewhere beyond the bedroom makes my heart jump into my throat.

After another trip to the bathroom where I'm barely able to shut the busted door, I finger brush my teeth with the toothpaste left on the side of the basin and head out in search of the enigma that is Nikolas Daemon Deimos.

My eyes widen with every step I take through what can only be his home.

Because it looks exactly like that. A home.

The guys always joke about him living in a dark basement where he worships the devil and other shit along those lines, and I can't deny that I kind of assumed something similar.

But he lives in a flat that any family would probably feel at home in.

There are even decorative cushions on the sofa.

Who the hell is this guy?

Another clatter forces me to look up from the soft furnishings, and I find the man in question standing in the middle of his kitchen with a tea towel over his shoulder and a spatula in his hand.

What the actual fuck?

His eyes hold mine for a beat before they drop down to my body.

Nerves slam into me despite the fact he's already seen me dressed in his shirt—and only his shirt—but for some reason, it feels like it's the first time he's really seeing it.

Nervously, I tug at the open neck that slipped low on my shoulder and fold my arms across my chest.

"Come here, beautiful," he says softly, his vicious, cold tone from before long gone as he holds his free hand out for me.

I hesitate, not knowing what to do, but also aware that if I do what I'm told then there's a chance he's going to drag me under his spell again.

"Come on, you must be hungry." A genuine smile curls at his lips, making his dimples show, and my heart tumbles, knowing it's directed at me.

I know it's the wrong thing to do, but my body doesn't seem to be in agreement with my head, because when I move, it's to close the distance between us.

"Good girl," he praises, and despite knowing better, I smile at him, stupidly loving those words coming from his lips.

The second I'm in reaching distance, his fingers curl into the front of his shirt that I'm wearing as he hauls me right in front of him.

His head lowers as he stares down at me, his eyes holding mine until I drag my bottom lip between my teeth.

"You should never wear anything but my clothes," he breathes, making my stomach clench.

Reaching up, he brushes his fingers over my collarbone, making a violent shudder rip down my spine. His eyes flash with understanding, telling me that he's more than aware of how his touch affects me before he pushes the neck of his shirt from my shoulder once more.

"Better," he murmurs, dropping his lips to my neck and giving me the sweetest kiss.

He doesn't pull back straight away. Instead, his lips linger on my skin as he breathes me in.

"Daemon," I moan when he begins kissing along the slope of my shoulder and up my neck.

"I've dreamed of you being here since the day I moved in."

Then maybe you should have spoken to me, I think, but they're not the words that fall from my lips.

"Oh God."

My fingers curl in his t-shirt when his hands find the curve of my waist. My feet leave the floor as he lifts me onto the counter, nudging my knees apart with his hips and stepping between my thighs.

"You shouldn't be doing this," I tell him, although, in contrast to my words, my head falls back, giving him better access as he moves to the other side of my neck.

"I do a lot of things I shouldn't, beautiful. This barely scratches the surface. You're the one who shouldn't be allowing me to do it."

"I'm more than aware," I breathe when his teeth scrape against my skin. But I'm powerless to make him stop. The second he looks at me with those soft, vulnerable eyes, the moment he touches me, everything outside of us fades away to nothing. It's intoxicating. It's addictive.

"I need to kiss him off you, beautiful. The only touch you should remember is mine."

His words are the reminder I need.

"Stop," I say, although my voice doesn't hold the conviction I was hoping it would.

He chuckles, actually fucking chuckles against my neck.

"You don't mean that, Angel. You know you want it just as much as I do. You know that you were always meant to be here, with me."

His hands skim up my thighs, sliding under the fabric of his shirt until he's holding my hips in his firm grip.

"I know you feel it too."

"It doesn't matter what I feel," I hiss, pressing my palms against his chest to get him to back up, which he thankfully does, although only a few inches.

"You didn't run for the front door, Calli. You could have left my bedroom and tried to bolt. You didn't. You found me instead."

My eyes narrow, frustrated to hell that he's right. I didn't even consider turning in the opposite direction and attempting to leave the flat, to run from him.

My first thought was him. What he was doing.

Damn it.

"You know I'm right, beautiful. You want to be here right now just as much as I need you here."

"You're crazy."

"Yeah, I'm pretty sure that's not news to anyone." His lips quirk into the beginnings of a smile at that statement, but something dark sweeps through his eyes.

He rubs at his stubbled jaw before dropping his eyes down my body to my bare, parted legs that encase his hips. His eyes zero in on the juncture of my thighs that's hidden beneath the fabric as if he can see straight through.

Thankfully, my stomach growls and reminds him that we're both currently in his kitchen for a reason.

"I need to feed you," he murmurs, his eyes finding mine once more before he backs up toward the messy island in the middle of his kitchen.

Resting back on my palms, I watch as he works, mesmerised that this dark knight knows his way around a kitchen.

And I discover not long later that not only does he know his way around, but damn, he can cook.

After placing two plates full of poached egg and avocado muffins on the dining table, he comes back for me.

I expect him to help me down, so I squeal in surprise when he sweeps me off the counter and into his arms. He carries me to the dining table where he sits in the chair he pulled out, placing me down onto his lap with his arm locked around my waist.

"We can't eat like this," I argue, struggling against him.

His free hand threads into my hair, dragging my head back so I can see him.

"Keep wiggling your bare pussy against me like that

and it's not going to be breakfast that I'm eating," he groans in my ear, his lips brushing my skin teasingly.

An unintentional wanton moan rips from my lips at the image that pops into my mind.

"You want that, don't you?"

"Daemon," I warn, attempting to slip from his grip once more, but all I achieve is to grind against his very obvious erection.

His lips brush my ear, his hot breath racing down my neck making me shiver, all of which makes my nipples harden against the fabric of his shirt.

"I could lay you out right here on the table and taste your sweet, sweet pussy again. Remind you who you really belong to. Is that what you want, Angel?"

My lips part to reply as my head and body war with how I should respond, but I don't get a chance because his teeth nip my ear, sending a bolt of pleasure shooting through my body, ending at my clit.

"Oh God," I moan as his tongue laps at the sting.

"Tell me you're mine," he demands, his hand sliding up my thigh.

My lips stay firmly shut as he grazes higher, pushing the fabric of his shirt up.

My thighs part shamelessly when his knuckles graze my mound, and he groans as if he's in physical pain.

"How wet are you, beautiful?"

I don't respond, I don't think either of us needs to hear the confirmation of what we already know out loud. He must be able to feel me soaking his trousers as it is.

I suck in a breath, waiting for him to connect with where I so desperately need him, but his touch never comes.

"You need to eat," he says, turning the tables, his voice all business once more.

Releasing me, he reaches around my body for the cutlery and cuts me a piece of his delicious-looking breakfast, spears it with a fork and lifts it toward my lips.

"Eat," he demands.

"I can feed myself, you know," I snap at him.

"I'm aware. Humour me."

"Why should I do anything you say?" I sass.

"Because you know it pleases me. Because you know I'll give you whatever you want for it."

"You'll let me go?" I ask hopefully, although I can't deny the disappointment that washes through me at the thought of walking out.

There is something very, very wrong with me.

He chuckles again, and I curse silently that I can't see the look on his face as he does so.

"I think that's the last thing you want to do right now, isn't it?"

"No. I need to go and—"

"Say his name and you won't be getting anything."

Silence descends as tension crackles between us.

"I'll never forgive you for what you did," I tell him, careful not to use Ant's name. Although I can't deny that there is a part of me that wants to see what it would make him do. But I've probably seen enough of Psycho Daemon to last me a while, especially in the past fuck knows how many hours.

"Yes, you will," he states confidently.

When he moves the fork closer once more and the muffin brushes my lips, I cave and open my mouth so he can continue to feed me.

Holy fucking shit.

I moan in pleasure as my eyes roll back in my head.

Boy can cook.

"Good?" he asks smugly.

"There's no need for arrogance," I mutter, more than used to seeing or hearing that from my brother and his friends rather than from him.

When he offers me more, I don't hesitate to take it this time.

Before I know it, my plate is empty and my cheeks burn, knowing that I allowed him to feed me all of it like I'm a useless child.

"You must be hungry," I say, looking at his still-full plate.

"Fucking starved," he grunts, but instead of reaching for his food, he swipes it aside as he lifts me from his lap and places me on the dining table.

"D-Daemon," I shriek as realisation hits me.

"I told you, if you're a good girl, I'll reward you with what you need."

Grasping the bottom of my shirt, he pulls it apart

harshly, and the buttons holding the fabric together rip off, pinging around the room.

"Oh my God," I gasp, more turned on by that one move than I think I've ever been in my life.

"I have two regrets from Halloween," he tells me, his voice deep and harrowing.

My chest heaves as his eyes feast on my body.

"That I never got to see you—really see you. And that I never took your virginity."

His eyes find mine again and my breath catches at the intensity within them.

He means every word of that statement.

"Every single day since that night, I've regretted walking away."

"You didn't have a choice. They needed you."

"But I needed *you*."

5

———

DAEMON

I stare down at her with her pink cheeks, her heaving chest and hard nipples.

Fuck, she literally takes my breath away, she's so beautiful.

"You could have come to me any time after that night. I'd have understood. But then weeks passed, months, and all I got was a cold shoulder and your basic pleasantries when you had no choice but to be in the same room as me."

"I always want to be near you."

She scoffs, ripping her eyes away from mine. "You could have fooled me. It was as if I dreamed up that night. That it never really happened."

She gasps when I wrap my hands around her knees and spread her legs.

"I never forgot a second of it," I force out as my mouth waters for a taste of her.

"You've barely looked at me since."

"I'm looking at all of you right now, and I can assure you, there's nothing else in the world I'd rather be staring at. You're fucking perfect, Angel."

Her blush brightens, spreading down her neck and onto her chest.

Slowly, she turns her face back to me, her eyes locking with mine before they drop down my body until she's able to see exactly how she affects me.

"Not a day has passed that I haven't thought about you or that night, I fucking swear to you."

Her stare lingers on the tent in my trousers, and she swallows thickly before her lips part.

"Prove it," she whispers shyly.

My breath catches at the challenge in her eyes, my cock jerking with my need to finish what we started all those weeks ago.

"With pleasure."

Releasing her legs, I lean over her, wrapping my hand around the back of her neck and lifting her from the table, crashing her lips to mine.

A deep, hungry growl rumbles in my chest as she mimics my moves, sliding her fingers into my hair and twisting until it hurts. She licks deep into my mouth as if she's been craving this as badly as I have since that night.

I understand why she thinks Halloween meant nothing to me. But I had—have—my reasons for doing what I did.

I had no right dragging her off into the shadows like that. I'd managed to watch her from a distance all these years, but something snapped in me that night from the first second I laid eyes on her despite my best intentions wherever she's concerned.

I was doing what was best for her, and I knew for a fact that it wasn't me.

I still know that, but seeing her laid out beneath him on Friday night...

Fuck.

Anger surges through me, and my need to fucking own her despite the fact that she's mine right now hits me harder than I've ever known.

I was only six years old when I saw this beauty in her.

Six years old when I told myself that one day, she'd be mine.

If only I knew what the next few years were going to hold and how quickly I'd learn that I was never going to be good enough for a girl like Callista Cirillo.

Discovering that was something akin to losing a loved one. I had no idea what it was at the time, but I've since discovered the deep ache in my chest every time I thought about not making her mine was grief.

She might have been living and breathing in front of me, but a part of her—us—died the day I realised she needed a better man.

So I took a step back and watched from the shadows.

I watched her grow. Blossom from the sweet girl to an innocent young woman who struggled to come to terms with the world she'd been born into, while I'd jumped into it feet first a long time before.

I'm dragged back to reality, to her, when her teeth sink into my bottom lip so hard the taste of copper fills my mouth.

"Calli," I groan into her kiss, hardly able to believe she's allowing this to happen right now.

I might be crazy, possessive, impulsive, jealous, and a whole heap of other bad things, but I'm not an idiot. I'm more than aware that she should have run the second I gave her the chance earlier.

I even left the front door unlocked for her.

But she didn't take it. She didn't even try to leave.

My chest swells with the knowledge that she chose to be here.

She chose to be in my flat with me instead of going to discover the fallout from what happened with the Italians on Friday night.

Hell, she's barely even asked me about any of it.

She saw me at my worst. Yet, she's still here.

Needing more, I rip my lips from hers and kiss across her jaw, nipping at her skin. Doing exactly what I said I needed to do earlier and erasing his touch, his kisses, his marks from her skin by replacing them with my own.

Her back arches on the table as I glide my hand up her side, not stopping until I'm cupping one of her breasts.

"Oh God, yes," she moans, her body arching again when I release her neck and take the other in my palm.

"Fuck, you're sensitive," I groan when I pinch both of her nipples and she cries out.

Her grip on my hair tightens and she tugs me forward toward her body.

"What do you need, beautiful?" I ask, wanting to hear her beg for me.

"Your mouth." Her eyes find mine and she tugs on my hair once more, the biting pain making my cock weep. "Please. I want your mouth on me, Nikolas."

"Fuuuck." All the air comes racing out of my lungs.

I hate that name. It's connected to so much shit in my life that I'd rather forget. Hearing it usually makes me murderous. But listening to it fall from her lips as a needy plea...

Fuck.

It does something to me I've never experienced before.

"You're a fucking angel."

Dipping my head, I suck her nipple deep into my mouth, making her cry out my name—my real name—once more.

I groan, the vibrations shooting through her, causing her fingers to twist tighter in my hair.

"I need you, beautiful."

"You don't deserve me," she forces out between her heaving breaths as I kiss down her belly, aiming for that sweet spot between her legs.

"You think I don't know that? But as true as that might be, I'm not sure I can let anyone else have you either."

"That's not for you to— shit," she shrieks when I latch onto her clit and suck it into my mouth. "Oh my God. Fuck. Nikolas." Her hips roll, grinding her cunt right against my face.

Best fucking moment of my life.

Last time was epic, but she didn't know who I was.

This right here... it's made all the sitting back and watching her over the years worth it.

Because she's here. Not because she has to be—she could have easily left—but because she chose to stay.

She wants this.

And for some fucked-up reason, she wants me too.

I lap at her as if I'd die without it, savouring her taste, memorising her cries of pleasure and pleas for more.

Anything you want, beautiful.

Her climb toward her first release is fucking stunning.

I watch from my position between her thighs, her eyes holding mine as she watches, as her cheeks redden and her breathing becomes so laboured she has no chance of controlling it.

"You taste like heaven, Angel. I could eat you forever."

"Fuck, yeah," she groans, her head falling back and severing our eye contact for the first time since she pushed up on her elbows to watch me when I begin to tease her entrance.

Her muscles ripple, trying to pull me in deeper, but I hold back, wanting her to climb right to the edge.

I want her fucking begging for me.

"Did he eat you this good, Angel?" I ask, pulling my mouth away from her, terrified of the answer but desperate to know.

"No," she cries. "No."

She reaches out, grabbing my hair once more and dragging my face back to her cunt.

"Don't stop."

"Tell me what you want," I demand.

"I want your mouth," she repeats.

"My mouth where?" I ask, only a breath away from her swollen clit.

"O-on me."

"Tell me where or you won't get it."

She sucks in a breath, dragging some confidence right alongside it.

"I want your mouth on my pussy, Nikolas. I want you to make me come all over your face."

"Hell, yes," I grunt, giving her exactly what she needs, sucking on her clit once more and plunging two fingers inside her soaked cunt.

"Jesus. So wet for me, beautiful."

"More," she cries, pulling my hair so hard I'm sure it's about to rip clean from my head. It would be more than worth it.

Curling my fingers, I search for that sweet spot that's going to make her see stars as her legs begin to tremble and her moans get louder.

"Come for me, beautiful. Come all over my face."

I flick her clit with my tongue once more as I rub

her G-spot and she falls, crying out my name over and over.

My chest swells, hearing it fall from her lips. My hatred of my real name dissipates with every cry, every plea for more.

I work her until she's spent, her skin flushed, her chest heaving as she fights to catch her breath on top of my solid walnut table.

I can't deny that I've had fantasies of this. Calli has been the feature of many, many different ones over the years, and images of laying her out on any surface of this flat have been right up there since I moved in. I knew in reality that she'd probably never even have a reason to visit.

I never could have ever imagined that I'd get this chance.

Ever.

"Oh God," she whimpers when I finally release her and stand up.

Her eyes find mine and I discover a depth, a fire in them that I never knew existed.

Although I've lusted after her for as long as I can remember, I've always had her up on this pedestal, much like everyone else. She's this innocent princess that none of us dared go anywhere near.

But right now, all of that is gone. The only thing that's staring back at me is desire and need, both laced with hate, fire, and passion.

It. Is. Fucking. Everything.

Before I get a chance to move, she pushes from the

table and practically climbs me like a fucking tree. Not that I'm complaining.

Her legs wrap around my waist, her arms wrap around my shoulders, and her fingers twist in my hair, gripping it hard.

"Calli," I groan, my own arms holding her just as tight as I lift her from the table before her lips find mine and she kisses me, not faltering when she must taste herself on me.

Her kiss is raw, dirty, and messy. Everything I could have asked for.

The heat of her cunt burns me through my trousers, and my need to back her against a wall just to fuck her hard and fast to take the edge off burns through me.

But I can't.

She's not the kind of woman I can lose myself in and just send away before she gets any ideas about a second round or a future.

Up until that night in the derelict building, sex has been nothing but an act. A stress reliever. It's never been anything to really enjoy, to lose myself in, to treasure.

But the second I touched her, everything I'd known before had been forever ruined.

I'd never be able to be with a woman again and be satisfied with the nameless fucking in whatever dark corner I could find for a few minutes.

Everything would always be compared to her and that night—and nothing would ever be good enough.

Fucking magical voodoo pussy, and I haven't even fully experienced it yet.

"Jesus, Cal," I mutter as she drags her teeth across my jaw, her tongue lapping at the rough stubble covering it.

Her lips descend my neck, and a violent shudder rips through my body as I walk us into my bedroom.

"Fuck," I bark when her teeth sink into my skin. "You just bit me," I gasp, looking down at her, wondering who the hell I've got in my arms.

When she finally releases my skin, she's got a little bit of my blood on her lips and a feral, dark look in her eyes that I'm more than familiar with.

Who the hell is the girl who's been hiding under the twinsets and pearls all these years?

"Y-y-y—" I stutter, struggling to find my words and cursing myself for falling back into old habits.

Her warm palm lands on my cheek and she holds my eyes, silently telling me to take a breath.

"Y-you're fucking perfect."

With my hands palming her arse, I lift her a little, capturing her lips in a searing kiss before I lay her out on my bed.

Reluctantly, I release her so I can take in the sight of her lying there, wearing just my shirt, her skin flushed with my hickeys and bite marks littering her body.

Reaching up, I run my fingers through my hair, barely able to believe I'm standing here with her right now.

She sits up and immediately reaches for my waistband.

"Whoa, shit," I hiss when she makes quick work of undoing my belt and ripping open the button, dragging the zip down.

When her fingers curl around the fabric, ready to tug my trousers down my legs, I panic and wrap my hands around hers, stopping her.

Her eyes immediately shoot up to mine, and they narrow in confusion.

"You don't want—" She cuts herself off, swallowing nervously as shame washes through her.

Cupping her jaw, I rub my thumb over her bottom lip.

"M-more than you could ever imagine. I-I-I'm j-just trying to do the right thing," I confess, squeezing my eyes closed tight, because I'm not sure what I'd do if she took the out that I'm offering. But it's Calli. I have to give her one.

"It's a bit late for that, don't you think?"

My eyes pop open at her comment a beat before she drags my trousers and boxers down my legs without any hesitation.

Her breath catches and her teeth bite into her bottom lip as her eyes land on my length.

"Holy fuck," she gasps, studying the metal balls on either side of my dick. "You... You're p-pierced."

"What can I say?" I mutter, kicking my trousers off. "I'm a sadist who gets off on the pain."

"Can't say I'm surprised," she whispers, almost sounding amused.

"Now, where were we?" I ask, wrapping my hand around my cock and running the tip over her full lips. "Did you want to wrap your pretty little mouth around my dick, Angel?"

6

CALLI

He doesn't give me a chance to answer that question. Instead, the second my lips part, he thrusts his hips forward, forcing himself into my mouth.

His taste explodes on my tongue, replacing my own from his kiss, and I hungrily suck him.

Really, I have no fucking clue what I'm doing. But I figure I'm a quick learner and that he'll soon put me right if I do it wrong. I mean, how hard can it really be?

He pulls back and I lick up the underside of him before swirling my tongue around the head of his cock, teasing those two little balls on either side.

Risking a look, my eyes rake up the dark fabric of the shirt he's still wearing until I find his parted lips and then his dark, hungry eyes that bore down into me as if he's imagining all of this. As if I'm not really here worshipping his cock like I've spent my entire life waiting for the chance.

I haven't. But I can't deny it's been something I've thought about more than once since our rendezvous on Halloween.

He got to taste me that night, and I can't say I haven't been curious about what it would be like to return the favour.

Taking him in my mouth again, I sink down on him until I can't take any more. He hits the back of my throat and I have to fight the need to gag.

"Fuck, beautiful," he grunts, his fingers twisting in my hair, holding me in place before dragging me back and setting the rhythm he wants.

I bob up and down on his length, delighting in every grunt and groan of pleasure that falls from his lips as the salty taste of his precum lands on my tongue.

"Angel. Fuck," he barks right before he rips his cock from my mouth, reaches down, grasps me around the waist and throws me back on his bed. "I'm not coming in your mouth. Not this time, at least."

"Th-this ti—" I don't get to finish my question because he crawls onto the bed between my legs, spreading them wide and staring down at my pussy before raking his eyes up my bare body and focusing on my lips.

Reaching out, he traces them with his fingertip.

"Perfect," he breathes before finding my eyes and settling between my legs.

He rubs the head of his cock through my wetness, just like he did that night before he was forced to walk away.

Dropping his forearm beside my head, he leans over me, his nose brushing mine in a tender move that makes my brain misfire.

"Tell me you're still a virgin," he demands, his voice so deep it almost doesn't sound like him. "Tell me you didn't give this away to him when it always should have been mine."

He pushes inside me ever so slightly, but it's enough for my entire body to tense in anticipation for what's going to come next.

My words catch in my throat as I think of Ant, of how we got here.

This is fucked up.

I shouldn't be lying here with Daemon staring down at me like I'm exactly where I belong, when only days ago I was in almost the same position with Ant.

And now he's...

I squeeze my eyes closed and a fresh wave of hot tears threatens to erupt as I think about the reality of what happened Friday night.

"Calli?" Daemon warns, his voice edging on that dangerous tone of his that sends a shiver of fear and desire down my spine.

"I-I... It's yours. He... we never—"

"Fuuuck," he groans as his hips piston forward, his cock spearing inside me and making my spine straighten as my body fights against the unusual invasion.

"Oh my God," I cry as pain shoots through my body.

Daemon's body lowers down on mine, pressing me into the mattress, his hips unmoving as his hand wraps around the back of my neck, tilting my head exactly where he wants it so he can claim my mouth.

He kisses me until the pain has gone and all I feel is the fullness of him inside me and an unignorable need for him to move.

"Nikolas, please," I moan, needing to see the way his eyes flash with desire every time I use his real name.

I've always known that he hates it—it's why I used it to taunt him. But while I was expecting the anger hearing it caused, I wasn't expecting the hunger that crossed his features.

"I need—"

"Trust me, Angel. I've got you."

His hips roll, and although there's still a little lingering pain, mostly it just feels insanely good.

"Oh God," I gasp.

"That would probably offend him, Angel. I'm nothing but fucking Satan."

His lips dip to my neck and my back arches into him, needing more. Needing everything.

"Do you have any idea how many years I've dreamed of this, of having you beneath me, of being inside you?" he all but groans against my lips as his hips continue to move, his cock thrusting inside me in the most mind-blowing way.

"Liar. You barely noticed I existed," I tell him on a gasp as he grazes some deep part inside me.

His entire body stills as my words hit him and he pushes up on his palms, staring down at me with a hard expression on his face.

"W-what?" I ask, suddenly nervous that I'm doing this all wrong.

"Calli," he breathes. "You're the only girl I've ever noticed."

All the air rushes out of my lungs at the honesty in his tone.

His lips slam down on mine. His words, his touch, his kiss, the slow roll of his hips utterly consumes me.

He keeps up the gentle pace for another few minutes before his inner devil starts to take over and he sits up, ripping us apart, wrapping his hands around my hips and lifting my arse from the bed to give him the perfect angle.

"You good?" he asks, but he must read the answer on my face because he doesn't give me a chance to respond before he thrusts forward with more power than I'm expecting.

If it weren't for his grip on me, I'd have shot up the bed.

His lips press into a thin line and the muscles down his neck tense and ripple as he begins fucking me like a man on a mission. He's still wearing his shirt, and I hate that he's hiding a part of himself from me.

I feel like I've seen so much of the real Daemon in the past few hours and yet, he's leaving that one bit as a mystery.

I don't like it.

But as he keeps pounding into me, I have no chance of doing anything about it.

His fingertips dig harshly into my hips, hard enough that I have no doubt he'll leave bruises behind.

"Fuck, Angel. Fuck," he grunts, one of his hands releasing me and skating up my body until it finds a home around my neck.

I gasp, not used to the harsh grip as his jaw tics.

"Mine," he hisses. "You. Are. Fucking. Mine," he grunts possessively, slamming into me with every word.

"Tell me, Calli. Tell me that you're mine."

I'm so lost to him that anything outside of our connection doesn't exist right now, and I find myself crying out, "Yes. Yes, I'm yours," as his grip on both my throat and hip tightens, his cock swelling even bigger inside me.

"Play with your clit," he demands. "I want to watch you come before I fill your cunt with my seed."

My lips fall open at his crass words. I'm powerless to do anything but follow orders, and I find my hand grazing my lower stomach before I press two fingers against my clit.

"Oh fuck," he grunts as I clamp down on him. "Yes. Fuck. Flick that clit, beautiful. Come all over my fucking dick."

I do as I'm told while he stares at my hand as I work myself.

"That's it," he encourages as I begin to reach my

peak. "Yes. Mine. Mine. Mine," he chants, his dark, haunted eyes staring into my very soul. A devilish smile curls at his lips. "And just like that, the angel hands herself over to the devil himself."

His ominous words are the final straw and I shatter, my body convulsing for long minutes as I ride out the best orgasm I've ever experienced, my pussy milking his own release out of him.

"Calli. Angel. Fuck, beautiful. Fuuuck."

His cock jerks inside me, filling me with his seed like he just promised he'd do.

My chest heaves as I stare at him, watching as he rides out his pleasure. It's something of pure beauty as his face pulls tight, his eyes closing as his lips part. It's a moment I could be suspended in forever as my body lies limp on the bed, utterly spent from both of the orgasms he's given me.

But then, he opens his eyes, dark, haunted, dangerous eyes that I chastise myself daily for not recognising the night of the Halloween party, and everything comes crashing down around me.

He releases my throat and lifts his hand to my cheek, cupping it in his warm palm.

"Mine," he whispers darkly as my stomach knots anxiously.

I swallow, trying to stuff down these weird feelings, wishing I could go back to any time in the past hour where he's taken over me so wholly that I've forgotten that anything exists outside this flat.

But the reality is that life has continued outside, and the fallout of the ambush on the Italians' warehouse will have been affecting everyone's lives that I care about. Yet, here I am, rolling around in bed with the guy who shot the good guy I was meant to be spending time with and abducted me, drugged me, tied me to his bed and claimed me as his own.

After a few more seconds, he pulls out and drops down beside me, immediately wrapping his arm around my waist and dragging me into his body.

"You're fucking everything, Calli," he murmurs in my ear, sounding relaxed and sleepy.

And you are certainly something, I think to myself.

There are so many sides to him, more than I think even he's aware of.

The cold, dark Daemon is brutal, terrifying. But the sweeter side of him is... fuck. It's all a massive head fuck.

He nuzzles my neck, breathing me in, kissing and nipping at my skin.

"What's wrong?" he asks when I don't respond or melt into him like I was. "Did I hurt you?"

Yes. But not physically.

"No. I'm fine," I lie. "I just need to use the bathroom."

When I roll away from him, I'm surprised to find that he lets me go.

Pulling his shirt around me, I rush toward the bathroom and look over my shoulder right before I lift my hand to awkwardly close the broken door behind me.

I look back one more time to find that he's lying on his side with his head on the pillow, staring at me with a contentment I've never seen on his face before.

It makes my heart tumble.

I did that. I made that cold, emotionless guy look all soft and teddy bear-like.

But at what cost?

With a small smile, I slip into the room and erect a barrier between us as I suck in a giant breath of air.

As I move toward the toilet, the evidence of what I just allowed to happen slips down my thighs and I cringe. I know I told him that I was on the pill at Halloween, but he didn't so much as hesitate before pushing inside me bare.

Did I just make the biggest mistake of my life?

Knowing that he'll undoubtedly come looking for me if I take too long, I don't linger and just clean up, padding over to the basin.

Not finding any soap, I open the mirrored cupboard in front of me in search of some—only there's a different bottle that catches my eye.

I wash up and then grab the smaller bottle, reading the label of the sleeping pills that have been prescribed to Nikolas Deimos.

I guess it makes sense that anyone with a soul that dark, after all the things he's done, has trouble sleeping at night.

Before I think better of it, I untwist the top and tip four of the small white pills into my hand.

The label says take no more than one, but fuck it. The guy fucking drugged me in his car after shooting my boyf— No. Ant was never my boyfriend. But he could have been. If it weren't for our blood, our families. We could have been everything. Had everything.

Another sob threatens to erupt, but I swallow it down. The time for my inevitable breakdown is coming. But first, I need to get the hell out of here and away from that... that monster.

Dropping the pills into the pocket of his shirt, I finger brush my hair and splash some water on my face.

His eyes are barely open when I step back into the bedroom.

"Angel," he murmurs, holding his arm out for me to rejoin him.

"I'm just going to get a drink. Would you like anything?" I ask, hoping like hell his sweet side won't come out and offer to go and get it for me.

"There's a bottle of Fanta in the fridge. The glasses are to the right of the sink."

Perfect.

With a nod, I spin on the balls of my feet and rush out of the room and set about my mission.

Thankful that he's a good cook, I locate his rolling pin quickly and I'm able to crush the pills on the counter before dropping them into one of the drinks. I stir it, careful not to make too much noise. Once I'm confident that it's dissolved enough in the bubbles, I pick them both up and head back to his room.

"Here," I say, crawling onto the bed and passing him the drink I've laced with his crushed sleeping pills.

My heart thunders in my chest as I wait for him to take his first sip.

He lifts the glass to his mouth, and I swear I actually stop breathing.

But right before the glass hits his lips, he pulls it back again.

My entire body trembles with nerves.

If this hasn't worked, if he suspects anything, I am so fucked.

Totally fucked.

I realise in that moment as he stares into my eyes that letting him take my V-card probably wasn't the stupidest thing I've ever done.

This is.

Because even if it works, when he wakes up, he's going to be gunning for me.

"I don't deserve you," he whispers before lifting the glass once more and downing the lot in one.

If I weren't on the verge of a panic attack then I might even be impressed at his ability to neck a fizzy drink quite so fast.

When he's downed all but the last couple of millimetres, he looks into the glass with his brows pulled tight as I sip at mine.

"That tastes funky. It was a new bottle, right?" he asks.

"Yeah," I say, forcing a smile onto my lips before taking another, bigger sip. "Yeah, I see what you mean," I lie, screwing up my nose and placing my glass on the bedside table.

"Come here, you," he says the second I've released it. Wrapping his arm around my waist, he pulls me against his body and spins me around so I have no choice but to look at him.

Reaching out, he tucks a lock of my hair behind my ear and stares down at me as if I'm about to vanish into thin air.

To be fair, that's exactly what I'm attempting to do.

"I never did tell you, but I love this hair on you. You're so sexy as a brunette."

"Yeah?" I ask, my heart naïvely fluttering at the compliment.

"Everything about you is sexy, Calli. Spent all my life dreaming about having this. Having you beside me."

"Who knew the devil could be so sweet," I whisper, smiling up at him.

"Even Lucifer has a weakness, Angel."

Leaning forward, he brushes his lips against mine, and despite knowing better, I fall under his spell once more.

He drugs me with his lazy kisses and gentle caresses until he rips his lips from mine in favour of a yawn.

"Tired?" I ask.

"Hmm... I haven't had sex in... a while. It's taken it out of me."

"How long?" I ask, hoping that his one-way trip to unconsciousness will allow me to get some truths out of him.

"Before Halloween," he confesses, his eyes already closed as his fingers draw patterns on my thigh. "I couldn't touch anyone else after you. It could only be you, beautiful."

"Why that night? What changed?"

He thinks for a moment, and I begin to wonder if he's fallen asleep, but then his voice startles me. "Because since Emmie and Stella, I've seen something new in you. I've seen a fire. A strength that I didn't know was there before. And I started to believe you could handle me."

"Handle you?" I ask softly.

"Yeah. I'm not a good person, Angel. I've done a lot of bad things. And I'm..." He pauses, and I once again think he's asleep. But when he finally speaks, my heart cracks for the little boy still hiding inside the hard outer shell. "I'm fucked up. I'm not good enough for you, for anyone. I'm broken."

"Daemon," I sigh, placing my hand on his cheek.

There are so many things I want to tell him, but all the words get stuck in my throat.

And when he begins snoring softly, I realise that he wouldn't have heard them anyway.

I wait for five minutes, although as I lie there

watching him sleep, memorising his soft features when he's relaxed, it feels like hours before I finally slip from his hold. All the while, my heart is in my throat when I watch him mindlessly reach for me in his slumber.

"I'm sorry, Daemon. But I can't be yours."

CALLI

My legs move as if I've got the devil himself chasing after me.

Well, to be fair, I pretty much do. He's just currently in no position to be running anywhere. I hope.

My heart pounds so hard in my chest, I swear I can feel it in my ears.

I don't look back.

I can't.

If he's there—if he wasn't as asleep as I thought he was—then I'm screwed. Royally fucking screwed.

I mean, I am anyway.

When he wakes up, he's going to hunt me down like a raging bull, I have no doubt.

I'm just hoping that I'll have had enough time to figure out how to deal with him.

Shit. How do you deal with the devil?

My hands tremble and my legs barely hold me up as I fly toward the lift and my escape.

I have no idea what I'm going to do once I get out of this building. I guess I'll figure that out once the cool spring air hits my bare legs.

All I know is that I can't stop.

I press the call button for the lift, bouncing on the balls of my feet in impatience, not noticing that it was already rising before I pressed it.

I should have noticed.

I should have taken the stairs and run from who is inevitably about to step out of it.

I can add that mistake to all the others I've made this weekend.

"Fuck," I hiss the second it dings, announcing its arrival.

I'm about to bolt to the right, knowing that whoever is in there can't see me like this. If any of them find out... if it's Nico...

Fuck.

But I'm too late.

"Calli?"

I spin back around the second the female voice hits my ears, and I breathe a massive sigh of relief when I find Brianna, Jodie's best friend, standing before me with a cake box in one hand and a bottle of rose prosecco in the other.

"Oh... uh... hey. I gotta—"

I nod toward the now-empty lift and run toward it.

"Are you okay?" she asks, despite the fact that she can clearly see I'm not.

"Yeah, great. You never saw me, okay?" I beg. I have no idea how trustworthy she is, but I really, really need her not to go blabbing to Jodie and Toby the second she gets inside his flat.

"Nuh-uh. No, we're not playing that game."

Before I know what's going on, she's walking back into the lift with me and hitting the button for the ground floor.

"I'm calling an Uber. Where are we going?"

"Home," I whisper, my bottom lip trembling as I realise that she's going to help me escape.

"Uh... here, put it in." She passes me her phone, and with a trembling hand, I manage to get my address in so she can order a car.

"Was Alex really that bad a lay, huh? Did he even get you off, sweetie?"

"What? No. Yeah. Fuck," I bark, dropping my head into my hands as a sob erupts.

"Here," she says, and when I look over she's got a pair of knickers in her hand. "They're new, don't worry. They're my emergency pair."

I stare at her in confusion but decide against asking the details right now.

"And this." She hands me a face wipe the second I've pulled the knickers on. "Keep it together and own it. You fall apart when you get home and away from the waste of space who made the mistake of making you feel like shit."

Finally, she hands me a pair of ballet shoes that are rolled up into a little ball.

"Who are you, Mary Poppins?" I ask through my smothered sobs.

"Nah, I'm just a girl with a few more years of experience with this shit than you. Best advice I can give you? Stay the hell away from any guy who makes you feel as wrecked as you do now."

"It's not that easy," I whisper.

"I know. It never is."

The lift dings, and thankfully, no one greets us on the other side and the Uber is already waiting for us by the entrance.

Bri holds the door open for me and shocks me by jumping in with me.

"Oh, you don't need to—"

"Let's go, man. We haven't got all day," Bri snaps at the driver before popping the top off her prosecco and handing it over.

I eye it suspiciously before she damn near thrusts it into my hands.

"Now, tell me how small Alex's cock really is and I'll laugh right along with you."

I blow out a pained breath.

"It wasn't Alex."

I watch as she thinks about who else lives on the floor of that building and her eyes widen in shock.

"No," she breathes.

A sad smile pulls at one side of my lips before I tip

the bottle up and swallow down more mouthfuls of the bubbles than I really should.

But that's the least of my issues.

Dance with the devil and you're always going to get burned.

I guess the only question is, just how bad is it going to hurt?

I attempt to hold myself together the whole ride home with my arms wrapped around my waist, holding Daemon's ruined shirt tightly around my body.

On the outside, it might look like I'm succeeding, but on the inside, I'm crumbling fast.

"W-what day is it?" I ask as the Uber takes the final turn toward my parents' house.

"Sunday."

I nod, already predicting that to be the case, although wishing not so much time had passed.

Surely, people would have noticed that I've fallen off the face of the earth this weekend. I don't even have my phone. I left it and my bag in Ant's room.

Brianna's concerned stare burns into the side of my face, but I refuse to look up and see the sad look in her eyes that I know is going to be there.

"Th-thank you," I say, finally unwrapping my arms from my body but being careful not to flash the driver. "I'll pay you back for the journey, I just need—" A silent sob cuts off my words, and I quickly slam the door closed before either of them gets to witness me break.

I'm almost around the corner, my door nearly in sight when Bri's voice rips through the air.

"Calli, wait."

"Shit," I hiss under my breath.

Her footsteps crunch on the gravel behind me and in only seconds, she's right at my side.

"You don't need to do this. I'm okay," I argue.

She glares at me, although I still refuse to actually look at her.

"I know you are. But I'd feel better if I got to share the rest of this with you." She holds up the bottle of prosecco that I've already taken a couple of big mouthfuls of.

"That's really not—"

"Who else are you going to talk to about this, Calli?" she asks as I come to a stop outside the entrance to the basement and send up a silent prayer for Dad's over-the-top tech which allows me to enter with my handprint and not the key that is God knows where right now.

Dread sits heavy in my stomach as I consider the possibility of that key falling into the wrong hands. I left it in enemy territory, after all.

"No one," I mutter as I push the door open and walk inside, remembering that Bri asked me a question. "Glasses are in there." I point toward one of the kitchen cupboards as I pass, making a beeline for my chest of drawers to find some clothes before I lock myself in the bathroom.

"I'm going to order Chinese," Bri calls just before the door closes. "Something tells me you need it."

My lips part to argue, but I quickly find that I don't have any words. Instead, a massive lump clogs my throat and red-hot tears fill my eyes once more.

"Thank you," I force out, my voice rough with emotion before the catch clicks closed and I fall back against the door, dropping my face into my hands.

My body trembles as I suck in shaky breaths and images from the past two days flicker through my mind as clearly as if I'm watching a movie.

If only I'd done the right thing and refused to meet Ant on Friday night.

I knew we were going to get caught. I knew we were on borrowed time. But that still wasn't enough to stop me from putting him at risk.

And then there's Daemon.

A part of me is glad that it wasn't Nico who found me. But it's not a very big part.

It could have been Alex, or Toby, or Seb. They wouldn't have freaked out quite as badly. They might have helped me escape. They certainly wouldn't have dragged me out, drugged me and locked me away in their lair. Okay, so Alex might have. But at least he wouldn't have...

"Fuck," I breathe as more and more regrets slam into me.

Finally, I push from the door, let Daemon's shirt flutter to the floor and shove my borrowed knickers to my ankles, wincing at what my life has been reduced to this weekend.

I was already keeping enough secrets from my best friends, and now they're only growing. And I've just dragged Brianna right into the thick of it.

Turning the shower on, I step under the water long before it has time to warm up. My need to wash my mistakes away, his scent from my body too much to deny.

I gasp as the ice-cold water literally takes my breath away, but I force myself to stay there to endure the pain of my mistakes.

Squeezing my eyes closed as the water begins to heat up, images of Daemon sleeping peacefully on his bed fill my mind.

My hands tremble as I vividly remember crushing up those pills and watching him drink them without even questioning me. Guilt assaults me, twisting up my stomach until I have no choice but to rush from the cubicle, drop to my knees and heave into the toilet.

My stomach convulses, expelling the breakfast Daemon fed me a few hours ago. The memories of how sweet he was as he cared for me in his own dark way bring more tears to my eyes.

"Calli?" Bri shouts. "Are you okay?"

My entire body trembles and I rest my brow against the toilet seat, feeling weak and hopeless.

"Yeah," I call back weakly.

"Calli," she warns, aware that I'm lying to her.

Sitting back and wiping my mouth with the back of my hand, I blow out a breath.

"I'm okay." Thankfully, my voice comes out a little stronger this time, almost strong enough to convince her.

"Dinner will be ten minutes," she tells me, but something tells me it's not what she really wants to say.

"Okay, I'll be out in a bit."

"You want me to go and kick his arse into next week?" she offers, making a smile pull at my lips.

The image of her storming over to his and doing just that is too amusing to ignore. Well, until I remember that he's probably still out cold and unable to defend himself.

"It's okay. I can handle it."

It's a lie. A huge fucking lie. When he wakes and comes after me... a shudder rips down my spine.

I thought he was bad that night as he marched me away from Ant and pinned me back against the car. Anger like I've never experienced came off him in waves, but I fear I've barely scratched the surface of Daemon's depravity—and, if his words are anything to go by over the past few days—his obsession.

The things he said to me about being the only girl he's ever seen, about not wanting anyone else since he was six years old.

Pushing to my feet, I stumble back toward the still-running shower and tip my face to the water.

A million and one questions spin around my head,

but the most pressing are around the things he said about wanting me, watching me, craving me.

It was bullshit… right?

He's never so much as looked my way, ever. He barely even spends time with the guys, let alone knows I exist.

Forcing thoughts of him out of my head, I grab my shampoo and set about washing him from my body, too.

I want to say I feel better as I pull on a pair of leggings and an oversized hoodie, but I don't. My head and my heart are still both wrecked over the events of the past forty-eight hours, and it's more than obvious that it shows on my face when I step back out into the main living area of my new basement home.

Bri's smile drops as I walk toward her, my eyes locked on the containers she's laying out on my kitchen counter.

"Please, don't look at me like that. Trust me, I know I fucked up. I don't need to read it on your face."

"Wha— I'm not. No. I don't think— I don't even know what's happened," she argues.

"Pretty sure you've figured out the basics," I mutter, stealing a spring roll and ripping it in half with my teeth.

"Things often aren't as simple as they seem. You've met your family and the people surrounding you, right?" she says, trying to make light of the situation.

"Sadly," I confess, beginning to load up a plate with

more food than I'd probably be able to eat in a week but not giving two shits about being a pig.

Without another word, I walk over to the sofas and lower my plate to my lap, ready to dive in and lose myself in my favourite comfort food.

I never lose Brianna's attention, but equally, she doesn't say any more. She just places a glass of prosecco in front of me and then makes herself comfortable on the sofa opposite me with her own food.

To start with, the silence is blissful, but it doesn't take long before it changes and the need to talk about what I've done becomes too much to ignore.

"You won't tell them, will you?" I ask, my eyes begging hers.

"No," she says instantly, making my whole body relax. "But that doesn't mean I don't think you should tell someone. How long has this been going on for?"

I shake my head, wishing there was a simple explanation for all of this.

"Th-there... there isn't anything going on. This weekend was a one-off." Lie. "It was a mistake."

Her attention never wavers from me. It's as if she's hoping to read all the things I'm not saying in the depths of my eyes.

"Calli, I..." She lets out a loud sigh. "I'm not even going to pretend that I have any clue what's going on here, but from what I've seen, I think you're playing with fire."

I can't help but laugh at her words.

"You think?" I blurt. "Nico will—"

"Need to get over himself. His protective-big-brother shit is cute and all, but fuck, girl. I can't imagine how insufferable that must be."

I shrug. I guess it seems that way to someone who's not in the middle of it. But it's my life, Nico is my brother, and deep down I know he only wants the best for me. And it's all I've ever known. He's an overbearing prick that I got used to a long time ago.

"Unless you're doing it on purpose," she offers.

"What? No. He might be a royal pain in my arse, but I'd never do anything to actually hurt him. Not on pur..." My words trail off as I realise it's a lie.

I've been seeing Ant for months. Sneaking in and out of his room at the warehouse. It may never have been a strike back at Nico, but I've never been under any illusion that he would be happy about it. Hell, I knew that Nico would kill Ant the second he found out, yet I've still been unable to stop.

"I wouldn't blame you if you were. Sometimes, guys like that need teaching a lesson. I'm just not sure doing so right under his feet—literally—is the best way forward."

"Nico is Nico. None of us have any kind of chance at teaching him a lesson. He's stubborn as a mule."

"You got that fucking right," she mutters, making me smile on the outside while my inside cringes hard, knowing that she's been with him, having seen the push and pull they're currently in the middle of.

Silence stretches between us once more as we continue to eat. I want to enjoy it, stuff my face until all

I can think about is how much of a pig I am and how full my belly is. But I can't. Because while thoughts of him continue to float around my mind, my appetite is pretty much non-existent.

"I can't believe you ended up with him. Especially when Alex has been following you around like a little sad puppy for weeks," she finally says.

I glare at her, really wanting to not go there, but fearing she's not going to give me any option now she knows the truth.

"It's complicated."

"Oh, trust me. I get it. Just one question though."

"Fine," I sigh, hoping she means that and isn't going to ask a million the second I answer her.

"Why isn't he here knocking your door down? You ran away, and I don't get the impression any of those boys let anything slip through their fingers like that."

Without instruction from my brain, I look over my shoulder at the external door we walked through, and then the sliding glass panels that look out over the sunken garden beyond.

My stomach knots with anxiety as to whether they're all locked. It's pointless. They always are. But still, the thought of him turning up here after what I did makes my stomach bottom out.

He's going to kill me when he catches up with me.

A bolt of fear strikes through me, but it's quickly followed by something else. Something I really shouldn't be feeling. Excitement.

"Do you want him?"

"That's a second question," I point out, quirking a brow at her.

She rolls her eyes. "Sorry, I just—"

"It doesn't matter what I want," I confess sadly.

Her lips part to ask another question, I'm sure, but thankfully, she thinks better of it.

"I love those makeup bags over there. Have you been making them?" she asks, diverting the questions to my new hobby.

Pushing thoughts of boys that I shouldn't think about let alone find myself anywhere near aside, I focus on the little bit of my life that actually makes me happy right now.

8

CALLI

Reluctantly, Brianna left after Jodie started blowing up her phone, wanting to know who she'd been distracted by. I could see in her eyes that really, she wanted to stay and try to drag some more information out of me, but I wasn't having any of it. As far as I'm concerned, the less anyone knows about the shitshow that is my life right now, the better.

I don't need anyone's judgy eyes or opinions over how I've managed to make some seriously questionable decisions in the past few months.

With my tablet clutched to my chest, I climb into bed as memories of Halloween night come back to me.

The second he touched me, it was like nothing I'd ever felt before.

I want to say that things would have gone differently if I'd known who it was, if I were able to see through the mask and to the danger that was lurking beneath. But I couldn't. I was too drunk, too determined to break out of my innocent little life, and I jumped in without considering the consequences.

I just wish I could regret it. But I can't. Those few minutes in that dark room, even without knowing who I was with... It was everything. The excitement, the recklessness, the desire. All of it brought me to life in a way I'd never experienced before, and I was there for it. Hell, clearly, I'm still fucking here for it, because I fell headfirst into him this weekend despite what he had just done. Despite the fact that he'd barely said two words to me since that night.

I'm a fool. I know I am. Wishing for something that's never going to happen.

We can't be together, I know that.

Not only would we never work, Nico and Theo, my parents, would never allow it.

They all have very solid ideas about who I'm going to end up with, and while Daemon might be an invaluable member of the Family, I know he's not who any of them would put me with to pop out little soldiers for my dad and brother to train.

I let out a pained sigh as I wake my tablet up and log into the secret account I have to message Ant.

My heart pounds and my hands tremble as the app opens up.

I have no idea what happened after Daemon marched me out of his room. All I know is that he shot him. My initial reaction was that he killed him, but as the hours have passed since, there's something inside me that wants to believe he didn't.

Daemon might be a lot of things, but he's not stupid. He'll have known that I'd never forgive him if he did kill him.

But does he care enough?

All the air rushes from my lungs as I stare at our brief conversation from Friday night and find nothing new.

"No," I whimper. "No, please."

Calli: Ant? Are you okay? Please, please tell me you're okay? I'm sorry. I'm so, so sorry.

A tear splashes on my screen as I hit send and just stare, praying it's going to be delivered. That it's going to be read.

But it never is.

Abandoning my tablet, I drop my head into my hands and sob.

M y eyes barely respond when I try to open them when I come to some time later. They're swollen and they hurt. And as I roll onto my back to stare up at the ceiling, I realise that's only the tip of the iceberg, because my entire body aches. My inner thighs pull and my core... that's sore in a way I've never felt before.

My cheeks heat as I remember staring up at Daemon as he thrust into me, claiming my virginity like he actually believed it belonged to him.

I sigh, closing my eyes once more, wishing I could drift back off into the nothingness that sleep offers me.

Unfortunately, I don't get anything close to that kind of peace, because my tablet starts ringing somewhere on the bed.

With a frustrated huff, I throw the covers back and start searching.

I cringe when I find a video call with Stella awaiting me. I have no idea what I look like—probably the back end of a dead rhino—but something tells me that ignoring her will be worse.

Swiping the screen to connect the call, I grunt, "Morning," as I fall back down on my pillows.

"Anyone would think you spent all weekend partying," she says with a laugh.

"If only," I groan, fighting like hell to keep images of what my weekend really was like from my head. "What's up?"

"Nothing. Just checking you're still alive. You kinda went off-grid."

Shit.

"Uh... yeah. I just needed a weekend to myself, you know? I had tons of work to do and—"

"It's totally cool. Things have been a bit... crazy this weekend, anyway."

"Oh yeah?" I mutter, already knowing that she's only going to give me the CliffsNotes of what's actually happened. It seems even my new best friends don't think I can handle the whole truth these days.

"Shit, Cal," she sighs, regret laced through her tone. "It's not that I didn't want to tell you. The Boss said—"

"I get it, okay? It's my life."

"Jodie and Joanne were abducted by Jonas after he escaped, and the Italians helped orchestrate the whole thing."

"What?" I blurt, sitting bolt upright.

"Yeah, I know. It's fucked up."

"Is Jodie okay?" I ask. "Toby?"

"Yeah, everyone is good. Well, aside from that motherfucking cunt and his little Italian friend."

"He's gone?" I breathe, even more relieved than I expected to be at finally hearing that news.

"Yup. We've finally sent him on his one-way trip to hell. Toby blew that house sky high."

"He... he blew up..."

"Jodie's house."

"Christ."

"It's over, that's all that matters. They're gonna set Joanne up in a flat downstairs."

I nod, trying to imagine how they might be feeling right now.

"When did all this happen?"

"Friday night." I swallow nervously as understanding dawns as to why Daemon was in the Italians' warehouse then. "I'm sorry we didn't tell you more. We knew the Italians were involved and that they were potentially watching us. Damien and your dad demanded we all be as normal as possible."

"Normal?" I balk, trying to push past the fact that they'd all lied to me. "If you all started acting normal then they'd know something was wrong."

"Oh, shush you."

"What's happening with the Italians?" I ask, needing something, anything that might help me discover what happened to Ant. It's not like I can just head over there and ask.

"Honestly, I don't really know the details, but the guys went and raided their little hangout on Friday night. Took a couple of their key guys hostage in the hope of delivering a message. I dunno what they're really planning to make it look like they've got the biggest dicks. What I do know is that they all came back looking like they'd been to war."

"They killed them?" I ask, the blood visibly draining from my face, making me wish she hadn't video called me. I might be getting better at hiding things, keeping my secrets, but I have zero game face.

"I don't think anyone died, no. There are going to be a few suffering from the ambush, though, if the amount of blood on the guys was anything to go by."

My lips part as a million questions dance on the end of my tongue about the events of Friday night, but I quickly swallow them all down for fear of giving too much away.

"Cal, are you okay? You look a little... pale." Her

eyes dart around my face and I panic, lifting my hand up to cover my neck. From how bright those hickeys were when I stood in front of the bathroom mirror yesterday, I know there's no way they've miraculously vanished overnight.

"Yeah, I just didn't sleep very well," I lie. Truth is, I slept like the freaking dead. It was probably a mistake. I should be sleeping with one eye open from now on, waiting for Daemon to strike back. I have no doubt he will. He's known as the boogeyman within the Family. The one who is likely to sneak up on you when you least expect it. He's deadly, brutal, the exact opposite of the person you want coming after you in the dark.

My stomach knots and my eyes shoot to the floor-to-ceiling windows which expose me to anyone who might feel like wandering down here. I really should have lowered the blinds before I crashed last night.

The sun is quickly rising, but there are still enough dark corners out there where someone could hide.

A shiver runs down my spine.

Would he risk coming here? Chance getting caught by my dad? By Nico—if he were ever to come back?

"Calli?" Stella shouts, dragging me back to reality.

"Shit, yeah. Sorry."

"You really didn't sleep well, huh?"

I shrug, keeping my hand locked on my neck, suspiciously I'm sure.

"You're coming to school, right?"

"Yeah, I'll be there," I say with a sigh.

"Okay, awesome. Things are going to get back to normal now."

"Really?" I ask sceptically. If Dad and Uncle Damien have a couple of the Marianos locked away somewhere, then I really doubt things are about to get easier.

My stomach turns at the thought of them having Ant. I have no idea if they stormed that place Friday night with targets in mind, but after finding me in Ant's room, I can only imagine that Daemon would have been gunning for him.

"I'll see you at school, yeah?" I bark at Stella before cutting the call and running toward the bathroom.

I stand in the middle of my basement with my heart thrashing in my chest and my hands trembling at my sides. I stare at the door I know I should have walked out of over five minutes ago, but I'm having a real hard time forcing myself to move.

I don't want to go out. I don't want to risk walking straight into him in the hallway, or for him to be sitting in the common room waiting for me.

Sucking in a deep breath, I force myself to move forward and put him to the back of my mind. With any luck, he's still sleeping off the effects of those tablets.

Summoning up some inner strength, I jog up the stairs that will take me to the main house so I can borrow a car to get me to school.

I try not to think about where mine is, or my phone, or anything else I took to Ant's place Friday night.

"Mum?" I call when I get to the top of the stairs, but unsurprisingly there's no response. It's been a long time since I would find her in the kitchen preparing our breakfast and ensuring we got ourselves to school on time, but every now and then, I can't help hoping she might just show her face, to make sure I'm doing what I'm meant to be.

Even Jocelyn is absent this morning, probably off on some insane task that Mum has set her.

I press my hand to the scanner beside the cupboard with the car keys—total overkill, if you ask me, but Dad is all about the security in this place—and scan the black fobs for options. Grabbing the one for Mum's Audi, I swing the door closed, leave a quick note letting her know that I've borrowed it, and head out.

I should probably be worried that admitting to borrowing her car will invite questions about the whereabouts of mine, but really, the chances of her even seeing that are slim let alone her noticing one of her least favoured cars is missing. So I take my chances. I can handle Mum, I think. My biggest issue right now is getting my car and phone back—or figuring out a way to get a replacement—and escaping Daemon's wrath.

It's not until I get to the bottom of the stairs that lead to our front door that I look up and I damn near trip over my own feet.

My car.

I freeze on the spot, staring at my white Mercedes

parked in its usual space, and my brow creases in confusion.

Glancing over my shoulder, I look around for the culprit as dread seeps through my veins.

Someone found my car in Italian territory and brought it back.

Someone knows. Or at least suspects.

"Fuck."

Not having enough time or brainpower to take Mum's key back, I drop it into my school bag and head toward my car.

Pulling the driver's door open, I find my handbag sitting there, waiting for me ominously.

If I'd had the stomach to eat or drink anything since I last threw up its contents, I'd be doing it again as I stare down at the evidence I really don't need that someone knows where I was Friday night.

Feeling anything but prepared for facing anyone, I throw my bag onto the passenger seat and drop down.

After putting my phone on to charge, it quickly lights up with incoming messages.

I start to wonder how Stella and Emmie allowed me to disappear for a weekend, but I quickly discover the truth when I open our chat to find that I never really disappeared.

I scroll back, finding that I've replied to messages over the past couple of days, making it look like everything was good with me. And to my utter astonishment, I've even given the same excuse for hibernating that I did to Stella this morning.

It's nothing more than a coincidence, but it's freaky as fuck.

"Who did this?" I mutter to myself, going back to my inbox to hunt for clues. But there are none. And it only leaves me with more questions than I already had.

It can't have been Dad, Nico, or Theo. They surely would have had something to say about finding my car on enemy soil and my belongings in one of their bedrooms.

Was it Ant? Or someone he trusted to bring it back? Would they be brave enough to drive straight into Evan Cirillo's driveway? I'd like to think not. But why would one of Dad's guys do it and not say anything?

One name stands out in my mind.

Alex.

Recently, we've struck up something of a friendship.

I've barely tolerated Nico's friends over the years, but something's shifted recently. We've found some kind of common ground, and I've discovered that beyond the stupid jokes and innuendoes, he's actually a pretty decent guy.

Not that I'd ever admit that to him.

But something tells me he'd have my back.

He'd want to protect me, I'm sure of it.

There's only one way to find out if I'm right.

I bring my car to life and back out of my space, ready to embark on another joyous day surrounded by the elite of Knight's Ridge.

9

———

CALLI

Thankfully, the concealer I applied more than liberally to both my under eyes and my neck seemed to do the trick, and no one so much as questioned what I'd been up to over the weekend. All more than happy to buy my story about being home, working on assignments and studying for exams.

I was sure that Jerome was going to spot something in our study session together over lunch, but even he seemed oblivious as I kept all our conversation focused on work.

And there was no sign of Daemon all day.

It's not unusual not to see him at school. Unlike the rest of us, he only attends part-time, even that took some convincing and blackmail from Uncle Damien when we were all coming to the end of our time in year 11.

Daemon was more than happy to give up on education and just dive straight into life as a Cirillo soldier. Unfortunately for him, that wasn't an option as far as Uncle Damien and Dad were concerned. In the end, they settled for part-time education, but it was a battle I was glad I wasn't a part of.

I might hate having almost every second of my life dictated by them, but sometimes, I can't help thinking that going along with it just makes life easier in the long run.

Fighting it seems like too much hard work.

Not ready to go home and face the music, and also desperate to talk to Alex, I find myself a seat in the early spring sun after school and watch them all out on the football pitch.

I'm not the only female sixth former sitting around watching the guys, and I can't help but roll my eyes at them as they blatantly check them out.

They're brave, especially the desperate two of the lower sixth girls who sit there openly talking about Seb and Theo. Clearly, no one has told them just how lethal both of my best friends are. Either that, or they're just stupid.

"Take your shirts off," the redhead shouts, and I tsk a little too loudly.

"Problem?" the blonde hisses at me.

"Who, me?" I ask, pointing to myself. "No, I'm good." Movement over her shoulder catches my eye, and I can't fight the smirk that pulls at my lips. "You might want to reconsider who you're shouting at, though."

The blonde stands, her face reddening as she prepares to get into a slanging match with me.

"You're just jealous because they would never look twice at you," she spits. "They— what the fuck," she squeals as her head is ripped to the side and she's given little choice but to drop to her knees.

"Do we have a problem?" Emmie seethes, stepping up beside Stella, who's snarling down at the blonde girl who's now on the verge of tears.

"N-no," the redhead stutters.

"Funny, because I thought I heard you demanding that our boys take their shirts off for your benefit," Stella states.

"W-we were just having fun," the blonde whimpers.

"And they're hot," Red adds, clearly having bigger balls than her friends.

"Right, well how about you go and have fun while watching the rugby team instead?" Emmie suggests. "I think they're more on your level."

Red stares at Emmie, a wicked comeback right on the tip of her tongue.

Wisely, though, she swallows it down and reaches for her friend.

"Come on, Lex. Let's get out of here. They're not worth it."

"That's where you're wrong," Stella says, placing her hands on her hips and glaring pure death at both of them. "They're more than fucking worth it."

The two girls look at Stella and Emmie as if they're

the craziest bitches on the planet. Pride washes through me as I glance between my two best friends. Yes, they might be all kinds of fucking crazy, but they're everything to me.

"Go," Emmie says, waving the two of them off as if they're nothing.

"Anyone else wanna stick their nose in where it doesn't belong?" Stella asks the small crowd of girls sitting at another bench.

A couple of them shake their heads before they all move to grab their bags and skulk away as if they were never there.

The second they're out of earshot, Stella and Emmie fall about laughing before dropping down on the other side of the picnic bench to me, their eyes locked on their guys.

"I'm sure you shouldn't have enjoyed that so much," I mutter, still amused by their little show.

"Scaring the piss out of our classmates? Hell yeah, we enjoy that," Emmie says with a laugh.

I shake my head, my skin beginning to tingle as Stella rips her eyes from Seb and turns her attention on me.

"What's up, baby C?" she asks, her eyes boring into mine as if she'll be able to get the answers she wants.

"Nothing," I lie. "Just thought it would be nice to study out here. I've been locked away all weekend."

My words force Emmie to turn back to me as well.

"We're worried about you, Cal."

"So worried you didn't want to tell me the truth

about what was going on last week?" I quip.

"Cal, that's not fair," Stella argues.

"No," I snap, my fist curling in frustration. "What's not fair is you joining in and keeping me on the sidelines of my own life, my own family."

"Cal, that wasn't—"

"Don't make excuses. You've both told me in the past that I deserve better." Grabbing my bag, I throw it over my shoulder as my frustration grows. "Maybe you should think about that before you blindly put your boys' words before our friendship."

I take off before they get a chance to respond. A part of me is proud of standing up for myself. But there's a bigger part that just wants to crumple into a heap of tears.

All day, I've been looking over my shoulder, waiting for Daemon to show his face and tip my world on its head once more. The pressure of my dangerous decision yesterday is starting to show.

"Calli, wait. We're sorry, just—"

The sound of multiple sets of cleats pounding against the path up ahead drags my attention away from the apologies, and when I look up, I find three sweaty, muddy football players heading my way.

"Everything okay, baby C?" Alex asks, his brows drawing together as he studies me.

Swallowing down the emotions threatening to bubble over, I force myself to hold his eyes, desperately trying to read if he's the one who knows where I was Friday night.

"Y-yeah." I kick myself for not sounding as confident as I wanted to.

"Our girls causing trouble again?" Seb asks beside him.

"Normal stuff," I say, thankfully sounding a little stronger. "Just scaring off a few more girls who think they can run their mouths."

"You know," Alex mutters, "I thought it was meant to be guys who got all possessive and jealous."

"Yeah, well, that might have something to do with the fact you've never had a girl as fierce as Stella and Emmie," Theo points out.

"Uh... not true."

"Bro, we've seen the girls you hook up with. We all know you're a sap for a quiet, innocent one," Seb points out, his eyes alternating between Alex and me.

"Alex isn't fucking Calli," Theo snaps predictably.

"Cous, you need to let that go," I snap, more than fed up with their stupid opinions about who I should and shouldn't be spending time with. And honestly, if he knew who I *had* been with recently, he'd probably change his tune pretty quick, because Alex is a way safer option. It's just sad, I guess, that he's not the one who fires me up inside, despite the fact that he looks practically identical to the guy who does.

I have no idea what it is I see in Daemon that I don't see in Alex, but there's something. Something that just speaks to me on a level I don't understand.

"Just go," Alex says, fighting for me as he often does. "You've got two horny girls waiting for you. Go fuck them in the locker room or something," he mutters before wrapping his arm around my shoulders and spinning me away from them.

"Deimos," Theo warns.

"Fuck off, Cirillo." His hand leaves my shoulder for a beat and I don't need to look back to know Alex is flipping him off. "Come on, baby C. You can tell me all about what's got you so riled up."

"I'm fine," I argue.

He stares down at me, and that one look says more than any words could.

"Really, I am."

"You fancy driving me home? Theo gave me a ride this morning, and I don't think he's gonna be feeling all that charitable right now."

"Sure. Just try not to make my seats smell like sweaty boy."

"Aw, you love it," he says, threading his fingers in my hair and dragging me closer to his body.

"Ew, don't be gross," I shriek, having no choice but to breathe him in, and damn it, he doesn't smell gross at all.

"Go get the car warmed up, I'll be right there," he promises, releasing me and darting toward the door that leads directly into the locker room and to where my brother is probably telling the rest of the team about whatever disgusting activities he got up to this weekend.

I watch him go with a smile playing on my lips, and

the anger that was erupting not so long ago begins to simmer down.

It was irrational. I know that Stella and Emmie were only following orders, orders that I'd have no choice but to follow if they were demanded of me. But that doesn't stop the whole situation pissing me off.

My phone buzzes as I drop into my car. I'm tempted to ignore it, but the possibility of it being Daemon or Ant is enough to have me pulling it from the inside pocket of my blazer.

Stella: We're really sorry. Call me later?

I tap the side of my phone, trying to come up with something to reply with.

Calli: I'm sorry I shouted. I'm just struggling with everything atm.

Stella: I'm here. Whatever you need. x

My heart swells at her words, because I know they're true. Since the first day we met, she's been nothing but supportive. It's why I feel so guilty about snapping at her, at them.

"Turn that frown upside down, baby C. You're too pretty to be sad," Alex says sincerely after throwing his bags into the back of my car and dropping into my passenger seat, stretching his long-arse legs out.

"I'm good," I lie, forcing a smile on my lips.

"Hmm... I don't believe you."

I glance over at him after putting my car into drive, wishing he'd say anything that would hint at him knowing where I was Friday night.

"So, what had you out watching us run around the football field? You're not usually one to join our gaggle of admirers."

"Gaggle?" I ask.

Alex just shrugs. "Shameless sluts, any better?"

I snort a laugh as I pull out of the car park. "About sums them up," I mutter.

"Aw, come on, baby C. You know you wanted me to take my shirt off too," he teases.

My cheeks heat as I'm taken back to last weekend when we gatecrashed Toby and Jodie's little dirty trip away. I was drunk and got caught checking him out. I mean, it's hardly the crime of the century. Any girl would have a hard time not letting their eyes drop when all that toned skin was right in front of them. But that's nothing compared to the memory of how we woke up after I was dared to sleep in his bed.

I shake my head, forcing that image from my mind. I need to focus, and letting those butterflies take over as I remember how his body had reacted to mine that morning isn't going to help the situation.

Is it wrong of me to wonder if being with him would be different from his twin? Hell yes, it is. But I can't deny that now I've had a taste of what I've been missing all these years, I'm all for continuing my exploration.

After all, it's what the guys have done every day of the freaking week for as long as I can remember. Why shouldn't I have my fun? Especially now my V-card has been well and truly shredded.

My stomach knots and my skin tingles as the memory of his burning touch, his tight grip on my hips as he thrust into me fills my mind and makes my temperature soar.

I squeeze my eyes closed for a beat and force myself back to reality.

"Get as naked as you want, Deimos, but don't be expecting the same in return. I'm merely giving you a lift."

"You're good. I wasn't so drunk that I've forgotten about our little skinny-dipping session last weekend."

My cheeks burn hotter.

"Probably for the best you do try to forget," I mumble. "Nico will fuck you up if you so much as think about my tits."

"If that were true, I'd have been six feet under a long time ago."

"You're a shameless flirt, Alexander."

"That may be true, Callista. But something tells me you love it."

I startle when his finger brushes against my ear, tucking a lock of dark hair behind it.

I swallow nervously. I really don't need him studying me too hard. I might have got away with it at school and fooled the girls, and Jerome, but I fear my concealer will only last so long.

"You want me to stop for food?" I offer, knowing that the way into any of the guys' hearts—or flats, so I can keep digging—is through their stomachs.

"What did I do to deserve this treatment today?"

Isn't that the question?

"Nothing. I'm hungry, and I know you will be too, so..."

"Burgers?"

"You got it."

I take the next right and head toward the guys' favourite burger place as Alex calls our order in.

"Don't go anywhere," he says after I pull up outside Burnt Coals, the place that makes the best burgers in the city.

"You're gonna bring back food. I'm not likely to ditch you now."

"Pretend you want me for the burgers all you want, baby C. We both know it's my body that's got your mouth watering."

"You're delusional," I call before he shuts the door on me.

I watch him go, my eyes shamelessly dropping to his arse in his football shorts.

"Fucking stop it," I bark at myself. One roll around the sheets and I'm already turning into one of the whores who follow the guys around with my tongue hanging out.

I don't want Alex. Hell, I don't want any of them.

Or I shouldn't.

Resting my head back, I close my eyes, letting my mind drift back to my time with Daemon.

Every single inch of me knows that I shouldn't have allowed myself to fall under his spell quite as easily as I did.

But it was impossible.

One touch. One whisper in my ear. One slight hint at the vulnerable little boy hiding behind the dark mask, and I'm fucking gone for him.

I can't deny that I've always had a bit of a soft spot for the boy who never fit in. I used to feel bad for him, watching from a distance as the rest of the guys played football, battled on the Xbox or whatever other dumb shit boys did, and he would sit on the sidelines. He was always invited to join in—unlike me—but he hardly ever did.

I've always wondered why. Why he felt he couldn't get involved, be a part of their group.

We all know he was different, that his interests lie in other places, but that didn't matter. He was—he is—a part of them. He just keeps himself on the periphery for some reason I'm still yet to discover.

Because of me?

I shake that thought from my head the second it even lands.

There's no way I had anything to do with it. I'm still trying to force myself to believe those words he said to me this weekend.

He can't have meant them. Surely.

10

———

CALLI

"Where was Daemon today?" I ask, hoping like hell it doesn't sound as suspicious as the words feel as they roll off my tongue.

I was half expecting for Alex to tell me to go to Stefanos' place. The guys keep teasing him for not fully moving yet. And I must admit that being back here after running away less than twenty-four hours ago has me a little on edge.

I really should have thought this through. Much like everything else I've done recently.

"Fuck knows," Alex mutters, throwing another two chips into his mouth.

"I thought he was in on Mondays."

Alex's eyes meet mine over the coffee table separating us as we eat, and my heart jumps into my throat.

"You know as well as I do that he does what he wants."

I shrug, trying to play it off like I don't care.

"Your knuckles look sore," I say, changing tact.

He glances down at his busted hands before reaching for his burger.

"Fucking Italians. They're too hard-headed for their own good."

"What's happening there?"

Alex pauses mid chew.

"Baby C, you know I can't tell you that."

In a low move, I lean forward, resting my elbows on my knees and thrusting my tits together, knowing he'll be able to see straight down my shirt.

"Oh yeah? Because I think you can tell me everything. You're just a pussy who follows orders like a good little boy."

"Calli," he growls, his eyes predictably dropping to my chest. "If you want something, just come out with it. I'm not in the mood for games. I'll give you anything." He winks before biting down on his bottom lip temptingly.

"I just want to know what's going on. Stella said you've got two Italians locked up somewhere."

"Yep. Pair of fucking cunts cried like babies about it, too," he says proudly.

"Who are they? Capos, or..." I push, desperate to find out something, anything about Ant.

"One is. The other is a soldier. Ricardo's cousin, or nephew or something."

I have to fight to smother my reaction.

"I wasn't involved with the planning. Just a part of the execution."

"So I'm assuming they're going to be retaliating at some point soon," I say, impressed by how steady my voice is despite the panic that's raging within me.

"We've got a couple of guys on the inside. We'll know when they're going to strike," he says after swallowing a mouthful. All the while my food sits on the coffee table, mostly untouched.

I lied about being hungry to get up here, and now my appetite is non-existent.

"I sense a warning about looking over my shoulder coming," I mutter.

"We're not about to lock you up, Cal. Although," he mutters, deep in thought, "I'm sure I could keep you more than entertained here for a few weeks." He wiggles his brows at me and I shake my head.

"You're insufferable."

"Insatiable." he grins.

"Jesus. I'm not fucking you," I hiss.

"Did I say you were?" His cheeky smile is all it takes for me to back down. "Seriously though, just keep your phone on and maybe dig out some of that jewellery your dad's given you over the years," he says, his eyes dropping to my chest once more to where my necklace should sit.

I roll my eyes. I'm more than aware that every piece of jewellery I've ever been given by my parents is tracked. It took a few years and the guys turning up when I was least expecting them to figure it out, but I did.

Mostly, I try to avoid wearing it at all costs. But there are times when I have little choice but to take the threats on our Family seriously, and I reluctantly fasten a necklace or bracelet on my body just in case.

Thanks to their refusal to train me up like Stella, I'm basically a sitting duck for any of our enemies.

I'm feeling a little more prepared for that kind of situation since Stella has been working with me at Mickey's and teaching me how to throw a decent punch. And we've snuck out onto the shooting range when the boys have been distracted, so at least I'm half confident that I could take someone down if need be. Not that any of them would allow me to carry a gun.

Sometimes, I hate being a girl in a man's world.

"Can you stop staring at my tits now, Alex?"

"Oh, so now you've got the intel you want, you're putting away the goods?" he mocks. "They're good tits. You should be proud."

I sit back, crossing my legs and folding my arms as I glare at him.

"What? If I had a pair like that, I'd be playing with them all day long."

"Because you don't play with your dick enough," I quip.

"I'd rather you played with it."

"Why am I friends with you?" I mutter.

"I dunno, been asking myself the same question."

"Clearly, you won me over with your wit and

sparkling personality," I say as he picks up his empty plate and takes it to the kitchen, stealing a handful of my abandoned chips in the process.

"Well, yeah. That's obvious."

"Big headed much."

"Not as big as my—"

"Have a day off, yeah?" I laugh, watching him as he puts his plate in the dishwasher and pulls a new can of Coke from the fridge, cracking it open and downing the lot.

I watch with wide eyes, vividly remembering someone else doing that exact thing. Only, when Alex is done he crushes the can and lets out an almighty burp.

"Sexy," I mutter.

"Damn right, baby."

Reaching behind him, he drags his previously sweaty shirt off and throws it into the washing machine beside him.

"And I'm all yours, if you want me," he offers, his hands dropping beneath the counter before he bends over.

"Tell me you didn't just—"

"Fancy joining me in the shower?" he asks, stepping out from behind the island completely fucking naked with just his hand cupping his junk—thank fuck.

"No, thanks. I'm good. I should probably just—"

His phone buzzes on the counter and he

immediately reaches for it, ignoring what I was saying as a frown pulls at his brows.

"Everything okay?"

"Y-yeah, of course. Don't go. We can do that English lit assignment or something, yeah?" He gives me one of his signature smiles which is powerful enough to make almost any girl follow his lead, and I quickly find myself nodding.

"Just put some damn clothes on."

"Nah, I quite like having you looking at me like you want to lick every inch of me."

"What?" I screech. "I am not—"

"You're too easy, baby C. I'll be five minutes."

He takes off and I'm powerless but to watch him walk away, bare arse and all.

"I know you're watching," he shoots over his shoulder.

"Yeah, because your arse is horrible," I lie.

"Sure thing, babe. Take a photo if you want."

The second he's out of sight, I jump up from the sofa and rush toward where he left his phone, praying that it didn't have time to lock.

"Yes," I breathe when I find the screen still illuminated. Another message pops up as I scan the apps on his home screen, but I pay it little mind. My biggest concern right now is finding where Daemon is.

My hand trembles as I reach to open the tracking app, and my heart is in my damn throat as I wait for it to load.

After a few seconds, eleven dots appear on the

screen in Alex's bros and hos group. My heart thumps against my ribs as I scroll up and scan down the list of people until I find his name.

Daemon Deimos: zero miles away: now.

Fuck.

My eyes lift from the screen to the wall of Alex's kitchen that I know connects him to Daemon's flat.

I jump a bloody mile when a crash comes from down the hall where Alex's disappeared, but when I hear no more, I get brave.

Closing down the tracker, I open his messages and find his recent conversation with Daemon.

Alex: Bro, you in school tomorrow?

Alex: Dude, you good?

Alex: Don't make me come and fucking find you.

There's no response, and it makes my stomach knot hard.

Alex: Bro, tell me you're alive.

That final message was sent when we were in the car driving back here.

For the first time since I did it, I'm hit with the blood-curdling fear that I might have overdone it.

The bottle said one tablet. I gave him... four, I think. Shit. I don't even really remember, I was in such a panic to get the hell out of there.

What if I overdosed him?

What if I've killed him?

"Oh shit. Shit. Fuck."

I fight to drag in the air I need as my head begins to spin.

My fingers curl around the edge of the counter as I try to force my legs to hold me up and get myself under control.

The water cuts off down the hall, and I know I need to move. I can't be caught snooping. I'm already in enough shit. Potentially a hell of a lot more than I bargained for when I saw a way to get out of Daemon's flat yesterday. But that's all I wanted. An escape. I didn't want to—

A sob erupts from my throat, pain slicing through my chest at the harsh reality of this situation.

But then, just as I'm about to close down the app and run back to the sofa to pretend nothing has happened, dots start bouncing on the screen.

"Oh my God, oh my God."

The wait for the words to appear takes forever as the sounds of Alex moving about behind me increases. He's going to be out here any minute and I'm going to get caught and—

Daemon: I'm good. Long weekend. Popped a pill and crashed.

"Holy fuck," I gasp.

"If you need someone to talk to, you're more than welcome in my boudoir, baby C."

Squeezing my eyes closed for a beat, I try to pull myself together.

"I'm good without a visit to your herpes-infested bed, thank you very much," I call back, much to his amusement.

Finally, I close down the app and put his phone back to sleep. I cringe that Alex isn't going to see that message alert and will still be worrying about his brother, but there's not much I can do about it right now.

I'm still standing in the kitchen like a spare part when Alex reappears dressed in a pair of grey sweats and a white, skin-tight shirt.

I stare at him with a smirk.

"Nice choice of outfit," I mutter, trying not to blatantly stare at the more-than-obvious outline of his dick through the fabric. "You could have put underwear on, though."

"Why would I do that?" he asks smugly. "You okay?" he asks, his eyes bouncing between mine.

"Yeah, I was just getting a glass of water." I smile sweetly at him, hoping that he'll buy my bullshit.

He studies me for a beat and I hold my breath,

waiting for him to call me out, but he doesn't say anything. Instead, he steps forward. His freshly showered, sexy boy scent hits my nose, and fuck if it doesn't make my mouth water.

I'm so lost in him for a beat that I don't notice that his attention has dropped from my face. That is, until the heat of his fingers burns my neck.

"Calli?" he growls, his brows pinching as he stares at—

"Fuck," I hiss as his thumb brushes over what I know is one of the brightest hickeys I had to fight to cover up this morning.

"Who did this?"

My heart rate spikes, and I have no doubt he can feel it against his fingers that are now wrapped around the side of my neck.

I stare into his concerned and possibly jealous grey eyes, begging him not to do this.

"Alex, please can we not—"

"Who, Calli? Who marked you?" he forces out through gritted teeth.

His grip on me tightens, and it does little to calm my racing heart.

"It doesn't matter. Please, just leave it."

I try slipping from his hold, but he's having none of it. His other hand clamps down on my hip, his grip just a touch too harsh to be friendly.

"What did you really do this weekend, Callista?"

My teeth grind in irritation.

"None of your damn business," I hiss, putting a

little more effort into moving. Thankfully, he lets me go this time and I storm across the room, leaning over the sofa and grabbing my bag. "You have no right to get all judgemental on me. Not after the way you all act, banging different girls every night of the week."

When I glance back, I find him standing in the middle of his kitchen with his face twisted in concern.

"I'm not judging, Calli. I'm just looking out for you."

"Bullshit. You're just as bad as Nico and Theo. It's one rule for you lot and an entirely different one for me. Bunch of hypocrites."

I get to the door and have my fingers around the handle before he speaks again.

"I'm sorry," he breathes a beat before the heat of his body warms my back.

I sigh, not wanting to back down when he's being a dick, but also unable to maintain my irritation. Alex can be such a puppy dog when he wants to be, and it's hard to say no to him when he turns on the charm.

His hand slips inside my blazer and lands on my waist, his touch burning me through my thin shirt.

My gasp rips through the air when he spins me around and presses me back against the door I was about to escape through.

"I promise, I'm not judging you. You can go out there and sleep with every arsehole that exists, if you want." The way his eyes flash with anger tells me that that's not entirely true. "I just..." He squeezes them closed, severing our connection for a second. "Did he treat you well?"

His eyes find mine once more, and a lump grows in my throat at what I find staring back at me.

Why couldn't it have been Alex?

It's not the first time I've asked myself that, and I'm sure it won't be the last.

But while I might agree with the rest of the female population at Knight's Ridge and think he's hot, and sweet, and did I say hot? He just doesn't make me feel the way his other half does.

"Did he make your first time special?"

I bite down on my bottom lip to stop the truth from spilling free.

"Fuck," he barks when I don't respond. "Did he hurt you? Was he too rough? Just give me his name and I'll go fuck him up for you."

Lifting my hand, I press my palm against his chest.

"No, you don't need to do that." Although, I have no doubt that if—when—he discovers the truth, he'll beat Daemon's arse for it. That's if Nico and Theo give him a chance. "He was..." I focus on the more pleasant parts of my time with Daemon. "Sweet."

Alex's thumb grazes my stomach as he stares down at me. His eyes drop to my lips for a beat and my heart lurches in my chest at the prospect that he's about to kiss me.

Thankfully, he thinks better of it and takes a step back, giving me some room to breathe.

"So, that English assignment," he says somewhat nervously, combing his fingers through his damp hair.

I should leave. But the thought of stepping through that door and walking headfirst into Daemon is enough to put me off, so, in the end, I just smile up at him and push from the door saying, "Sure."

11

DAEMON

My body is heavy, my brain hazy as I come to once again, confused as fuck.

Thankfully, when I open my eyes, I find I'm in my bedroom. Although that doesn't explain why I slept like the fucking dead when I usually struggle to get more than a couple of hours a night.

I roll over. It takes every ounce of energy I possess to move my stiff muscles, and I fall onto the other pillow.

Everything is calm for three seconds, then the sweet scent of her fills my nose and everything crashes into me with the force of a breeze block fucking wall.

"Calli?" I call, some stupid, pitiful hope still burning within me that she might still be here despite the reality that I don't want to believe hovering on the periphery of my thoughts. "Calli?" I shout louder, but there's nothing. "FUUUUCK."

Anger, desperation, and panic all collide inside me in a maelstrom that I have no power over.

Despite my lingering exhaustion and brain fog, my body moves on instinct.

I can barely hold myself up as I stumble into the bathroom. I catch myself on the towel rail, damn near burning the skin off my palm in the process.

"Shit," I hiss, wrapping my hands around the basin and hanging my head as it spins as if I've drunk every single bottle of vodka in the world.

My head pounds, my heart aches, and my entire body trembles in anger with my need to find her, to drag her back here, to find a way to fucking prove to her that everything I told her was true.

But she's where she's meant to be.

Out there, living a life without me.

A roar I barely recognise rips from my lips as pain tears through my chest. Desperation, loss, that normal feeling of just not being good enough rages within me as my fingers tighten on the basin.

I suck in deep, calming breaths, trying to get myself under control before I risk looking up and finding myself in the mirror.

I gasp at the unfamiliar face that's staring back at me.

Despite hours of sleep, my eyes are dark and shadowed. My lips are still swollen from her kiss, but it's the bright red scratch across my cheek that makes the pain worse.

Running my fingertip over the scab, I let my mind

drift back to her freaking out in the back of my car. She was vicious, brutal, and beautiful. I've never seen fire in her, and fuck if it didn't bring me to my knees, even if I was the focus of all her hatred.

If we were anywhere else, I wouldn't have gone to the extremes I did. But I needed to get her out of there. I needed both of us away from the others.

I knew it was my chance to keep her to myself for a little bit. Not to convince her to be with me, or to try to make her fall for me. Just to have her here, with me, by my side for just a small amount of time.

I've fought it. I've done everything I can to convince myself that she's not the one my black and tattered heart beats for, but it's pointless.

She's it.

She's all I see. All I crave.

But just look at what it's done to me.

Opening the cabinet in front of me, I stare at the little bottle with the lid barely on.

I didn't need evidence to know what she'd done. I've felt like this before, and I know the reason for it.

It's just always been my fault in the past when I've doubled up in a desperate need to get some rest.

I never thought anyone—Calli—would use them against me.

Does she really hate me that much?

Did she need to get away from me so desperately that the only way she thought she could achieve it was to drug me?

Shame burns through me.

But I don't regret it. Not a single second of it. Because while she was here, even while she was fighting me, I had everything I've ever wanted. I just have to hope it's enough to hold onto, because no matter how much I might already be craving a repeat, something tells me she's not going to accept it willingly.

I stumble back and fall unceremoniously onto the toilet. I drop my head into my hands in the hope that when I lift it again that my mind will have miraculously cleared and that I'll have a solid idea about how to handle this.

As much as I should stay away from her, now knowing that she's in bed with the enemy—literally—means I can't.

She cannot be spending time with the Italians. She just can't. It puts her at too much of a risk. And I refuse to allow her to be in any situation where she might get caught.

Sadly, when I stand once more, I don't feel all that much better.

Dragging on a pair of boxers, I head out to my kitchen for the strongest cup of coffee my machine will spit out and search for my phone.

I find it on the counter beside the mess I left behind while making our breakfast late on Sunday morning.

Waking it up, I find a stream of messages from Alex, and one from Dad, and more than a handful from Isla demanding to know why I'm ignoring her.

"Jesus," I mutter when I take in the date and find that I've been out of it for over twenty-four hours.

How many of those pills did she give me?

The evidence that something was up when she returned with our drinks was more than obvious. I could see that something was off in her eyes, the way she nervously chewed her bottom lip. And then the taste of the Fanta. That wasn't normal. If it were anyone else sitting on my bed wearing only my ruined shirt, then I might have questioned why it tasted so funky. But it was Calli. My fucking angel. I never would have suspected anything of her. Clearly, I've underestimated our innocent little princess. But then I guess, she does have Cirillo blood running through her veins, and the apple only falls so far from the tree.

***

"Holy shit, what happened to you?" Alex asks when I let myself into his flat a few hours later.

Her scent hits me, and it angers me equally as much as it turns me on.

The second I loaded the tracking app and discovered that she was here, mere feet away from me, I nearly forgot about everything and just stormed in to have it out with her.

But that's not how I work. I don't let my hot-headedness take over, and just because this situation involves Calli, it doesn't mean that I can forget everything that makes me the fucking fantastic soldier that I am.

So I waited. And waited. It was fucking painful to do so as images of what the hell the pair of them could be doing just the other side of the wall played out vividly in my mind.

Alex has made his interest in her very clear recently. I always thought it was just a game to rile Nico and Theo up. I mean, that's all it used to be. But something has changed with him. The way he looks at her these days is more meaningful, more serious.

The sight of him doing it makes jealousy like I never even knew existed erupt within me like a deadly volcano.

It's wrong. I have no claim over Calli, and nor should I have.

I came to terms with the fact that she would find another man, a better man than me to spend her life with many years ago.

But Alex? My twin?

That shit hits on a different level.

"Nothing," I grunt, going straight for his coffee machine and making myself another double espresso.

"You look like you just came back from the dead, Bro."

"Fucking feel like it," I mutter to myself.

"So what's going on then?" he asks as I fall onto the sofa and stare down into the mug of liquid gold in my hands.

"No clue. I popped a couple of sleeping pills. I've been out for... a while."

"Daemon," Alex warns, knowing full well I shouldn't be having more than one.

"It's fine. It's been a tough few weeks. I just needed to crash."

He glares at me, and after a few seconds, I lift my eyes to meet his.

I love him more than fucking anything. But fuck, sometimes I also really fucking hate him.

Everything about him is just so... easy. Life for him is so... easy.

The complete fucking opposite to mine. And for as long as I can remember, all I've wanted is to be more like him. To see the world through his rose-coloured glasses. To roll with the punches and not take life too seriously.

But that's not my reality.

While he's all lightness and laughs, I'm the dark, lost soul who just doesn't fit by his side.

All my life, I've had to listen to people compare the two of us.

Why can't I play football like him? Why can't I get grades and succeed at school like him?

It's exhausting, being the second-rate twin. But it's also normal now. I know my place, and I embrace it the best I can. All the while fighting to carve out my place in the Family, to prove my worth and find a future where my grades and academic ability don't matter.

"You need to stop that shit, man. It's not good for you."

"It is what it is. It smells like girl in here," I point out, needing to get to the bottom of my visit.

Alex closes the laptop sitting beside him that he must have been working on when I barged in and studies me once more.

"I was just hanging with Calli. Doing some school work."

I narrow my eyes at him.

"What? Why are you looking at me like that?"

"Nico will gut you like a fish if you lay a finger on her," I tell him, not even cringing at the fact that I deserve that kind of end after what I've done to her.

Part of me is surprised I didn't wake up to both Nico and Theo breathing down on me with their knives poised.

But for some reason, she seems to be keeping everything that's happened between us a secret so far.

What I can't work out is why.

She has no loyalties to me, not really.

And it's not like I've treated her well.

I got her off at Halloween and walked away without another word. Something that really fucking pained me to do. And then there's this weekend.

Why wouldn't she go running to big brother and let him deal with me? Surely it would be easier than waiting around for me to appear in the dead of night to retaliate.

She has to know it's coming.

She's proved time and time again that she's not all that naïve when it comes to me. She's also shown both of us that she's clearly got the ability to handle me, too.

So maybe it's what she wants.

Maybe she's waiting.

Maybe that's why she was here.

She wanted me to find her. To know she was hanging out with Alex. To torment me.

"I can handle Nico," he grunts, pushing his hand through his hair while my gut twists painfully.

"You're serious, aren't you? You're actually going after her?"

He shrugs. "You know me, Bro. I'm not about making plans or taking anything seriously. She's fun to hang out with. We'll see where it takes us. Plus, she's fucking hot, man. You should have come with us last weekend."

"What happened last weekend?" I ask, although I already know I'm going to regret it.

I know they went away, but I haven't heard any of the details, and I learned long ago it was better to just stay off my brother's socials.

"Fucking skinny dipping, man. I swear, her curves are fucking sinful. She grew up good."

My fists curl at my sides and I fight not to let my jealousy show on my face.

"She got naked with you?" I grit out.

"Yeah. Is that so hard to believe? I'm not a complete cunt. She slept in my bed, too."

All the air rushes out of my lungs at his words.

If he notices my reaction, then he doesn't comment. Instead, his smug smirk just grows wider.

"Best fucking night's sleep I've had in forever. I would suggest you try it, but then I'd have to share, and that ain't fucking happening."

I raise a brow at him.

"Again. That ain't happening *again*."

"You're full of shit, Bro," I say, resting back and sipping on my coffee as if all is right in my world. All the while I secretly wonder what it might be like to actually drift off to sleep with Calli in my arms.

"I haven't fucked her, if that's what you're getting at."

I can't deny that relief doesn't flood my veins at that statement.

"Not surprised. If she saw you naked before getting in your bed, she probably decided your small cock wasn't worth the effort."

He flips me off but decides against getting into that argument.

"She's seeing someone, though. She's got hickeys all over her neck."

His jaw tics with irritation at that.

"She's been walking around with a guy's marks all over her throat, and Nico's just let that fly?"

"Nah, she'd done a pretty decent job of covering it up. I just got a little closer than everyone else."

My blood boils at his comment, but I keep my reaction locked down.

Calli has every right to hang out with Alex. She can

spend time with anyone she wants. As long as they're not Italian.

I might want to stake my claim on her, but I know it'll never happen.

She'd be better off with a guy like Alex anyway. Someone who can make her laugh, treat her right.

Not a cold, dark arsehole like me who dreams about locking her up and keeping her for myself.

12

———

CALLI

The second I pull up at home, my skin tingles as if I'm being watched.

My heart jumps into my throat as I sit there looking, waiting.

Now I know he's awake, I'm on full alert.

He's not going to let what I did slide. There's no way. That's not how Daemon works.

My hand trembles as I reach out to cut the engine, my unease only growing.

The house beside me is in darkness. Both Mum and Dad's usual cars are absent from the driveway.

We might be in the city still, but the Cirillo land is vast, and if someone were to get to me here, no one would ever hear me scream.

Knowing I can't sit in my car all night, I gather up my bags and push the door open, swallowing down my fear.

I can handle Daemon.

What's the worst he's going to do? Tell me he owns me and fuck me again? Pretty sure there are worse things in life.

Sucking in a deep breath, I take off around the side of the house, my eyes scanning the darkness in preparation for him to jump out at me.

The bushes beside me rustle, making my heart rate spike, but as the wind blows my hair, I assure myself there's no one there.

Until there is...

"Oh my—" My heart jackhammers in my chest despite the fact that I knew it was coming.

A warm hand covers my mouth, cutting off my scream before my feet leave the floor and I'm pulled against a hard, familiar body.

His scent fills my nose and a sob erupts behind his hand.

"Unlock your door," he growls in my ear, and I do so without hesitation.

In only seconds, we're in my basement and I'm released.

"Ant," I cry, throwing myself at him, wrapping my arms around him, holding tight.

He grunts as we collide, but the fact that he might be in pain after getting shot by Daemon barely registers through my relief.

"You're okay," I breathe, nuzzling my cheek against his chest, letting my tears soak into his shirt.

"I'm so sorry, Calli. If I had any clue that—"

"Shh, it's okay," I assure him, looking at his battered

face through blurry, tear-filled eyes. "I know you didn't know. And I'm sorry too. I was so scared that he... th-that y-you were—"

"I'm okay, Sunshine." He forces me back and my arms drop from around his body as he cups my cheeks in his hands and lowers down to stare into my eyes. "I'm okay. It would take more than a bullet to my shoulder to keep me away from you."

"Ant," I sigh, swooning at his words. I try to fight it. I can't fall under his spell right now—it's too dangerous. "You shouldn't be here," I tell him, wrapping my hands around his forearms as he continues to hold me.

"I needed to see you. Needed to know you were safe."

"I'm okay. Daemon wouldn't hurt me," I say with a wince. He might not hurt me physically, but he's more than okay with drugging me, tying me to his bed, and shredding my heart to pieces.

"What happened? Where did he take you?" He searches my eyes for the answers. "I know you haven't been here. I waited all day Saturday for you to show."

"He took me to his place. Hid me from the others," I partly lie.

"And he didn't hurt you?"

"No, Ant. He didn't."

All the air rushes from his lungs, cascading over my face in a minty burst as he accepts my words.

Releasing my face, he wraps his arms around my body and drags me back into him.

"Fuck. I've been so worried about you. Did he tell anyone else?"

"I-I don't think so. I don't know. Fuck. I'm so glad you're okay."

I hold him tighter, relieved that Daemon didn't do what he so easily could have on Friday night.

"I can think of worse ways to go. My last memory would have been your pu—"

"Don't say it," I half cringe and half laugh. "God, that was mortifying."

I plant my forehead in his chest, wishing I could forget about the moment Daemon crashed into the room while Ant was about to dive between my legs.

"I'm sorry I allowed anyone to find you like that. I thought we were safe."

"It's not your fault."

Stepping out of his embrace, I glance over at the windows. If anyone were to look inside...

"We should go somewhere else. If my dad comes home or..." *Daemon comes to find me,* I think silently.

"Your dad's busy."

Dread twists up my insides, and it must show on my face.

"Shit, no, it's nothing bad. I just know he's dealing with the fallout of Friday night. Peace talks or some shit, I don't know. I haven't got involved."

"I hate this," I mutter, walking toward the control panel on the wall and lowering the blackout blinds just in case.

He shouldn't be here. It's dangerous. I might be

able to block out the world and lock the doors, but that doesn't mean he's safe. For all I know, Dad's already seen him on the security cameras and is heading back to kill whatever guy is brave enough to come down here.

"What if you've already been seen?" I blurt, letting my thoughts out.

"I haven't. Trust me, Sunshine. I'm not going to get you in any more trouble. I fucking promise."

He closes the space between us and catches my hand in his.

"Fuck, I've been so worried about you," he says cupping my jaw and lowering his brow to mine. "I had all these crazy thoughts running around my head about what they would do to you if they knew."

"My family wouldn't hurt me, Ant."

"Physically no. But they have more than enough power to control you. To stop this. Us."

"There can't be an us."

"I know. Fuck, I know. But it doesn't stop me from wanting it."

Pain slices through my chest as if my heart is being ripped in two.

Before I get a chance to come up with a response to that, his lips find mine and I'm powerless but to lose myself in his tender kiss.

It's soft, gentle, loving, and everything I should want a kiss to be.

But I can't deny there's something missing.

The edge of darkness, the touch of pain. The thrill

is there, of knowing I shouldn't be doing this, but it's not the same as it has been with Daemon.

That being said, as he pulls my body against the length of his, I push all thoughts of the man who abducted me, drugged me and bound me to his bed from my mind and lose myself in the sweet guy who's done nothing but care for me since we first met.

If the situation were different, he'd be the perfect guy. One I would happily bring home to meet my parents and introduce to my friends. But I can't. It's already a miracle that he survived Friday night. I can only assume that Daemon decided to spare his life, because even I know he's a better shot than that. He was almost at point-blank range—there's no way Ant would be standing here right now if Daemon wanted him dead.

I guess the only question is, why isn't he?

Ant walks me backward until my calves hit my bed. He lowers me back and I go happily until he grunts in pain.

"Shit, are you okay?"

"Right now, I'm fucking perfect," he says, crawling over me the second I'm laid out beneath him.

His hand slips under my shirt, holding my waist, but he doesn't make a move to push it any higher, seemingly just content to kiss me.

"I was so scared he'd punish you for being with me," he mutters, kissing across my jaw and down my neck.

"He's not like that, not with me." I cringe at my words, but I can't deny that they're true.

"I still don't trust him with you, even if you are a Cirillo."

"Ant, don't," I moan. I don't need any reminders of all the reasons he shouldn't be here right now, all the reasons why I should be sending him away.

But I can't. I'm too fucking relieved that he's here, that he's alive, and I'm too lost in his kisses.

I arch off the bed, my own hand slipping inside his hoodie, my palm grazing his abs.

Needing more, I reach for the zip running down the middle of his body and pull on it.

The second I see the bandage covering his chest and wrapping around his shoulder, I pause.

"How bad is it?" I ask.

"It's fine. Just hurts a bit," he confesses, sitting up straight and looking down at me with longing in his eyes.

"A bit."

"Yeah." He pushes the fabric from his shoulders and throws it to the floor, gifting me the sight of his bare torso.

Sitting up, putting us chest to chest, I brush my fingers over the fresh bandage.

"He could have killed you."

"It would have been worth it."

"No," I say, gripping his chin between my fingers. "Don't say that. Don't ever say that."

His dark eyes hold mine, the rich brown almost black as he stares at me.

"But it's true. I really like you, Calli. I just wish—"

"I know," I breathe, slipping my hand around the back of his neck and resting my head on his non-injured shoulder. "You should go," I whisper regretfully.

"I shouldn't have even come. But I can't stay away."

A sob erupts in my chest and I hold him tighter in the hope it'll stop me from falling apart in his arms.

"I just need tonight, Sunshine. Please. I just need..."

He lowers me back to the bed and falls onto his side, pulling my body close.

"Just give me this and then..." He swallows roughly. "I'll try to do the right thing."

He emphasises the word 'try', and while I might agree with him with a silent nod, I know it's never going to be enough for him to walk away.

Our legs tangle together and I let go of all of my concerns about what happens when the sun rises, just giving myself over to this sweet guy who is risking it all to spend time with me.

13

DAEMON

Darkness surrounds me as I lean back against the tree trunk, my short nails digging into my palms. The pain from it barely scratches the surface of what I need right now, but it's all I've got aside from the piece tucked into my waistband. I'm not stooping to those levels. Not yet, anyway.

The second I saw him step out of the shadows and wrap his hand around her mouth, I wanted to do what I probably should have done on Friday night and put a bullet straight between his brows.

But once again, I didn't.

And why?

Her.

I've never spared anyone's life before. But for some reason, when I pulled that trigger, I'd subconsciously already lowered my aim from his head, knowing that she'd never forgive me if I'd blown his brains out right in front of her.

I could have done it later in the night when I went back, but still, I spared him.

I watch them through the window in the door which she has no way of blocking.

I know, because this isn't the first time I've sat up here and watched her when she thinks she's hidden from the rest of the world.

It's beyond fucked up. But I'm long past caring.

I need her.

It took me a long time to find the right tree and the perfect branch that would give the best vantage point, but it was worth it.

Their legs tangle together on her bed, and I have to fight to stay still and not overreact.

She's not yours.

The only time she gets up from the bed is to visit the bathroom, and when she emerges she's wearing her pyjamas. Not the sexy kind, either—a long-sleeved t-shirt and a pair of trousers.

I can't help the smirk that pulls at my lips.

He might be inside with her right now, but she's keeping a barrier between them. It's everything I need to know.

I sit there until my arse is more than dead, the lights in the basement before me have gone out and my vision of them has been severed.

I should go home.

My body aches and my head still spins from the strength of those pills.

But I can't leave.

I can't walk away, knowing that she's inside with him.

Hopping out of my favourite tree, the leaves on the ground beneath my feet rustle as a plan forms in my mind.

Slipping inside her basement is easy. Calli might have happily taken over the space that Nico previously used as his party pad, but she never thought about changing the permissions on the biometric scanner to keep us out.

I guess she's never had a reason to think we'd want to invite ourselves in.

How naïve of her.

As much as I want to say this is my first time slipping inside in the cover of darkness, it's not.

There have been a couple of times since she moved in that my need to be close to her has overridden my common sense.

The first time was purely curiosity to see if I could get in, without the risk of moving through the house to get to her.

The second and third, not so much.

In the dead of night while she's sleeping, I'm able to indulge myself in the fantasy that she could be mine. I'm able to pretend, to run my knuckles over her soft skin, to tuck her hair behind her ear and listen to her calming breaths.

I'm sure for anyone else, lying beside her when she's so calm and peaceful would send them to sleep right alongside her, but I'm not anyone. I'm the devil, consumed by the darkness that sleep eludes unless I'm seriously running on empty and I've knocked back a pill. Or two.

At least it assures that I can enjoy indulging in my addiction without the risk of getting caught by someone who would kill me for invading her privacy.

I work at my best while hiding in the shadows, and my obsession with our now not-so-innocent little princess is no different.

The silver moonlight that streams in through the one uncovered window illuminates the space enough that I'm able to see the way Ant holds her while they sleep.

It should make me happy that she's turned her back to him, but it doesn't. Not with the way his arm is locked around her body like she belongs to him and her arse is tucked up right against his crotch.

My chest aches as I stand there at the end of the bed, watching them.

You should have killed him, the little devil that takes up most of my subconscious says.

Maybe I should have.

Although, it wouldn't be my shoulder she would be crying on if I had.

No. I need to come at this differently.

I need to figure out his angle, because there's no way he'd take a risk like this. There has to be a reason for his interest in her.

Or does there?

Her power has me forgetting everything I've always

told myself I couldn't do. Maybe she just tangled him up in her hypnotic web like she has me.

If I were the enemy, would I walk away? Or would I be exactly where he is right now?

I don't even need to pacify myself with an answer.

The fact that I'm standing here right now is all the evidence I need.

Calli shifts, a quiet moan rumbling deep in her chest. One I remember all too well from when she was sleeping in my bed. I take a step back, slipping into the shadows.

With the contents of my foraging in my hand, I step into the bathroom and silently close the door behind me.

Holding the branch with dry leaves in front of my face, I pull my lighter from my pocket and flip it open, letting the orange light of the flame illuminate the room.

My own reflection catches my eye in the mirror, my face lit up like a demon behind the glow of flame as I hold it to the bottom leaf.

A smile curls at my lips as it catches, and adrenaline shoots through my veins.

Goodbye, Antonio Santoro.

In only a few seconds, every leaf is burning, smoke billowing from the top of the branch. Moving to the middle of the room, I hold it under the smoke detector, and not a heartbeat later does the alarm start blaring, quickly followed by the sprinkler system Evan had installed when they renovated the house a few years ago.

Ice-cold mist rains down on me as I put my fire out and stalk toward the window to get rid of the evidence.

"Oh my God," Calli squeals from the other side of the door.

"Oh shit," Ant barks.

"You need to leave. What if they know you're here? What if this is a setup?"

I can't help but smile at her suspicions.

That's it, Angel. Question that motherfucker's motives. I know damn well I am.

"Wait. Are you suggesting that—

"No, Ant. Not you. Them."

"Fuck. I'm so sorry. Are you going to be okay?"

"Yeah, just go."

My phone buzzes in my pocket as I'd expected.

Evan: I need someone to check out my place. Fire alarm has been activated.

Daemon: I'm a few minutes away.

Evan: Calli is home alone. Make sure she's safe.

"You fucking got it, Boss," I breathe.

"Dad, yeah. I'm fine. Yeah. I'm going to head up

now." Her steps thunder up the stairs before a door slams, cutting her off from me.

I wait a couple of minutes as the water continues to soak both me and the bathroom before I shoot back another message.

Daemon: Everything looks fine, Boss.

Evan: I'll call off the fire brigade. Head inside to be sure though.

Daemon: Sure thing.

Suddenly, I'm plunged into silence and the water stops spraying.

Moving to the door, I wait, my pulse thundering in my ears, for her to return.

Was soaking Evan's entire house an over-the-top way of getting rid of Ant and raising his suspicions? Yeah. Do I give a fuck? Not a single fucking one.

"Fucking hell," Calli sighs

My phone buzzes again and I lift it from my side.

Nico: You need me to come over, man?

I smile at the fact that everyone else bar me is asleep right now and less than prepared to jump into action.

Daemon: Nah, man. It's all good.

Nico: Calli can crash here if she needs to get out.

I smirk. Oh yeah, that's not happening.

Daemon: I'll keep you informed. But everything looks good. Must have glitched.

"What the fuck am I meant to do now?" Calli cries. "Isn't life already shit enough?" she asks no one.

Dropping my phone back into my pocket, I push the door handle down and pull it open.

She doesn't notice me. She's too busy standing in the middle of the basement, staring at her bed in disbelief.

I step up behind her, moving silently in the darkness before I make myself known.

She doesn't have time to scream as I cover her mouth with one hand and wrap my arm around her waist, pinning her back against me.

"I hope you're not still wishing you were in that bed with him, Angel."

She wiggles against me, but all she achieves is grinding her arse back against my quickly-growing cock.

"I fucking love it when you're all wet for me, beautiful."

I lick a line from the neck of her t-shirt all the way to her ear.

"You taste so fucking good. I could eat you all night."

She moans against my hand, her back arching when I suck on the sensitive skin beneath her ear before lapping at my bite, just like I would elsewhere. She damn well knows it too.

"He didn't get you off again, did he?" I tease. "It seems I have impeccable timing when it comes to you."

She groans again, her jaw moving beneath my hand in her attempt to say something. Or bite me. I kinda hope it's the latter.

My hand on her mouth remains locked in place. My arm that's holding us together, however, moves.

Splaying my hand against her stomach, I tuck my fingers under the damp fabric of her top and push it higher.

"You should take these off. You'll catch a cold," I whisper.

A groan catches in her throat as my hand cups her breast, squeezing less than gently before I find her hard nipple, pinching until she cries out.

"He left you wanting, huh, Angel?"

She tries shaking her head, but it's not very successful.

"Those Italian cunts aren't man enough for the job. You want a real man, you don't need to be looking at the enemy."

I tease her, tugging her nipple until she's

whimpering and shuddering in my hold as her release just from this alone edges closer.

"Did he leave you this desperate, Angel? Or is that me?"

Finally, I let my hand drop from her mouth, immediately wrapping my fingers around the hem of her shirt and ripping it from her body.

"I hate you," she seethes. "I fucking hate you."

"Yeah," I agree, cupping her tits in both my hands and pinching her aching nipples between my fingers. "I can feel it. Gets you fucking wet though, doesn't it?"

"The only thing wet right now is the entire fucking house."

A laugh rips from my throat.

"Pretty genius plan, right? I'm glad you're impressed."

"I'm not fucking impressed. Everything I own is soaked."

"It'll dry," I say, peppering kisses along her shoulder. "Have you been waiting for me, Angel?"

"No," she hisses. "I'd hoped those pills had killed you."

"Ouch," I growl. "But I think we both know that you don't mean that."

"Don't I?"

"You came to Alex's place earlier in the hope of checking on me, didn't you?"

"N-no. We did homework."

"Is that right? From what I heard, he got close enough to you to see these," I say, circling my tongue around one of the hickeys I left on her throat. "He wants you."

"Yeah," she agrees. "I think I might go for it with him, too."

"Twins and an Italian. I think I like this side of our sweet little Calli."

Dropping one hand down her body, I tuck my fingers into the waistband of her trousers.

"Daemon," she moans, bucking back against me.

If she wanted to fight me right now, she could. It doesn't escape my attention that her arms are hanging limply at her sides as I take my time exploring her body.

"Tell me about this fantasy then, Angel. You want Alex and me at the same time? We could, you know. We've done it before."

All the air rushes out of her lungs at my confession.

I'm not surprised it shocks her. As far as anyone knows, I'm not very good at group activities. But things with Alex are different. We've shared everything from the day we were conceived. Just because we don't hang out together with the others all that often, it doesn't mean that we're not still close. That we don't like sharing.

"No," she admits. "I'll just take him. You can watch from the sidelines, if you want."

She shrieks when I spin us, pushing her back against her kitchen counter and forcing her to lean back over it.

"You're funny," I breathe, getting so close to her

that my nose almost brushes hers. "Careful, Angel. You've chosen the wrong person to play this game with."

"I didn't choose to do anything with you, in case you've forgotten," she snaps. "If I knew it was you on Halloween then…"

"Then what, beautiful? You wouldn't have let me eat you until you were coming all over my face?"

"No. I'd have run in the opposite fucking direction. You're the devil, Nikolas, and I have no intention of dancing with you."

A growl rumbles in my throat at her use of my name. I should hate it. I do when it rolls off anyone else's tongue. But everything about her is different.

"You're a beautiful liar, Angel. You might not have known the truth, but you wouldn't have turned me away that night. Especially when I got down here."

I push my hand inside her trousers once more, cupping her pussy.

"This was made for me. And only me. It's why that Italian fuck hasn't had a taste. He knows it belongs to someone else. Someone who's just waiting to blow his fucking brains out."

"W-why didn't y-you?" she stutters when I press my finger between her folds, grinding against her clit.

"Now isn't that the million-dollar question," I mutter. "Maybe I just like picking you up after he's failed to make you scream. Tell me, Angel. Did he just come over here tonight to tuck you into bed and cuddle? "

"Fuck you. It's n-none of your business why he was here tonight."

"So," I say, dipping lower and pushing two fingers inside her. My mouth waters as her heat and juices cover my fingers. "You started with Alex, driving him crazy and leaving him with blue balls, from what I can understand. Then you moved on to your little Italian friend, and now you're here with me—the devil—with my fingers buried in your cunt. You're not the innocent little princess everyone has you pegged as, are you, Angel? You're a fucking tease."

"No, Alex is my friend."

I can't help but laugh. "Is that the line he's spun you? He wants in here, Angel. You're forbidden, and he wants a taste of that fruit to find out if it's as sweet as he believes."

"You're wrong. He cares," she argues.

"And Antonio. Does he care, too? Or is he playing you? Is he only hanging around because he has no choice? Is he saying all the right words, making you fall, making you believe every single word he says when actually, he's making you his snake?"

"No," she cries as I curl my fingers deeper.

One of her hands lands on my shoulder while the other wraps around my forearm as if she's about to drag me from her body.

Slim fucking chance of that now I'm knuckle-deep.

"He's not playing me."

"How confident are you? Really?"

"He's not," she states forcefully. I almost believe her. Almost.

"And then there's me. My little seductress has no idea that I've been walking around with a hard-on for her for years."

Releasing her hip, I collar her throat, pushing her back farther. One of her legs lifts, wrapping around my waist, giving me better access to her.

"Nikolas," she cries, her eyes widening as her voice hits her ears as if she didn't mean to let it free.

"Oh, Angel. You have no fucking idea what you do to me."

"Y-you need to leave. You need to leave and never look back."

"We both know that I'm not going to do that, don't we? I've tasted you now. I'm going nowhere."

"What if I want Alex? Ant?"

"Want them all you like. Fuck them if you have to. Just know that you're mine. Every single inch of you belongs to me, and every time you go anywhere near them, they're one step closer to death. I'll only let you play around for so long, Angel, before I reclaim what was always meant to be mine."

"You're delusional."

"I'm a lot of fucking things, Angel. But deluded isn't one other them."

y back arches against the damp kitchen counter beneath me as Daemon's burning hands press against the inside of my thighs, spreading me wide, and his tongue swipes up the centre of me.

This wasn't meant to happen.

I was with Ant. He was being so sweet and—

"Fuck, Nikolas," I cry, my fingers twisting in his hair, holding him in place as I grind against his mouth as he sucks my clit, driving me higher and higher.

I should have known something was up the second that alarm started blaring. I should have known the devil was going to be behind it. Maybe, subconsciously, I did. Because when he stepped up behind me, I didn't freak out half as much as when Ant jumped out at me earlier. It's like some part of me knew he'd come for me.

I just didn't think I'd end up laid out on my kitchen counter, getting eaten like I'm his favourite meal.

"Oh God," I whimper, my release building, my need for him growing. "More, I need more."

He groans, the deep rumble flowing through me and pushing me even closer.

"I n-need—" But I snap, my demands cut off as I scream his name, my release slamming into me and making my entire body jerk on the counter with the power of it.

Pleasure washes through me in wave after wave as I try to suck in the air I need.

I gasp, my brain coming back to me, and I wake up sitting upright in bed, my skin flushed, my chest heaving, and a delicious pulsing between my legs.

"Holy shit." Did I just... "Fuck."

Dropping my head into my hands, I replay those images that just seemed so real in my mind as my temperature begins to lower. My eyes shoot to the kitchen counter where he had me laid out for him. But he never let me fall. He brought me to the edge time and time again as his cruel words filled my ears, and then he vanished into the night.

"Shit, shit, shit."

I fall back onto my pillow, my dry pillows, and something startles me when it hits my cheek.

"What the—" I pick up the small piece of paper, my brows pulling together as I study it.

It's a... it's an origami bat?

My heart picks up speed as I stare down at it, my

mind racing as I try to figure out what was dream and what's reality.

Placing the bat down on my bedside table, I swing my legs over the side of the bed and look around. Evidence of the sprinklers going off is everywhere, and it makes my heart slam in my chest, thinking that my dream might just have been a repeat of reality. No wonder it all feels so real.

I find my phone on the floor in the middle of the room, a small puddle beneath it. Lifting it up, I dry it on the pyjamas I'm wearing, ones I didn't put on when I first got changed when Ant was here, and I wake it up.

I've got a whole stream of messages from Dad checking in and making sure everything really is okay. But it's the one from Daemon that makes my heart jump into my throat.

Daemon: Keep looking over your shoulder, Angel. You haven't seen the last of me.

A rush of desire floods me before I curse myself out. That threat shouldn't be tempting to me. I should want him gone. But I fear that all I'm going to be able to achieve is to fantasise about when he's going to pop up and 'punish' me again for drugging him. If what happened last night can even be described as a punishment.

It's not until I sit at my kitchen counter with a coffee that I finally look at the time.

"Oh fuck," I gasp, jumping back up and racing toward the bathroom. Not that it'll do much good. I'm already late.

***

"What the fuck happened last night?" Nico barks as I race toward the girls' locker room after school for our gymnastics class. I'm late after our study session ran long, and I really don't have time for his bullshit.

Tugging my shirt up higher on my throat in a pathetic attempt to hide the marks from his prying eyes, I suck in a deep breath and turn to face him.

"Nice of you to show your face and find out for yourself."

"It was the middle of the fucking night. I was wrecked."

"So much for protecting me against all the horrors in the world," I mutter, my eyes rolling so hard they hurt.

His lips part to argue, but he quickly decides against whatever was about to fall from his lips.

"You need to decide what line of this whole overbearing, overprotective big brother thing you lie on, Nico. You can't try to control my life one second and then not care if I burn to ashes in a house fire the next."

"Dad said you were fine."

"Not the point, dickhead," I hiss.

The reality is that I didn't want him anywhere near the house, or my basement, last night. But that is not the point.

He tries to make out that he's all that in the brother department, throwing his weight around and making sure I only do what he wants me to do, yet he's not there when I could potentially need him.

"You're a hypocrite," I snap. It's not the first time I've said those words, and I'm sure it won't be the last. "How many girls was it last night? Is that why you couldn't come to my rescue?" I cringe at my own words.

"I didn't have—"

"Baby C, there you are," a booming voice calls down the hallway, making my stomach tumble.

"Deimos," Nico growls, already predicting what's about to happen.

Alex's arm wraps around my shoulder and he pulls me into his body, dropping his lips to my ear.

"You okay, baby? You didn't reply to my messages."

Hiking my bag up higher on my shoulder, I twist out of his hold and glare at him.

"What?" he asks. "I was worried when I saw the group chat this morning."

"You are aware that if there really was a fire, I'd have been left to deal with it alone last night, right?"

Obviously, it's not true, and I'm overreacting to their lack of action last night, but I can't help it.

"Daemon said—" Nico starts but cuts himself off when my glare turns deadly.

Thanks to Ant and Daemon—hell, Alex too—I'm a headcase. My emotions are shot, my nerves are frayed, and I have no idea which way is up. That means my go-to reaction to everything is to overreact and snap at everyone.

I wish I could be more level-headed about it all. Maybe I will be in a few days, once things settle down.

"Shit, Cal," Alex said, rubbing at the back of his neck nervously. "I slept right through. Think you wore me out when you came over." His smirk grows when Nico growls in anger.

"You were at Alex's place last night?"

"I'm over this. Both of you just get out of my bloody way." I barge past Alex, shoulder checking my brother when he just stands there glaring at him with that annoying bloody muscle in his temple pulsating. "I already know you didn't have company last night," I shoot over my shoulder. "You're never this much of an unbearable prick when you've got laid."

"Oh bro, she's got your fucking number," Alex howls.

Thankfully, I miss Nico's response as I push into the locker room and get surrounded by pointless girl gossip.

"Calli, what's wrong?" Stella asks the second she looks up from securing her sports bra and finds me standing in the middle of the room like I don't belong.

"N-nothing. Just Nico being his usual wanker self."

"He's been like a bear with a sore head all day, especially seeing as you've avoided everyone like the plague."

"I'm not feeling very sociable," I mutter.

"What's wrong? I thought the fire was a false alarm."

"It was... I just..." My eyes burn with tears and a lump forms in my throat.

"Shit, Cal." Stella rushes forward and wraps her arms around me as I fight not to fall apart in front of the bitch squad that is the gym team.

"I'm okay," I whisper once I feel a little stronger. "I'm just exhausted. I've got a basement to clean up, and Nico is an arsehole."

"Can't argue with that last one," Stella says lightly. "But you don't need to do your place alone. Wanna blow this off, grab some food and Emmie, and go and get started?"

"No, I can't ask you to—"

"Callista Cirillo," she growls, a warning in her tone that I have no choice but to take seriously.

"Miss Peterson will be pissed."

"Fuck her. You're more important. Plus, it'll give us a chance to talk. Something tells me you've been avoiding it since last weekend."

"I-I haven't. I—"

"Calli," she breathes. "Don't lie to me."

I sigh, not wanting to keep running from everyone and hiding how I feel.

"Things have just got a bit on top of me recently."

"I'm sorry," she says.

"It's not your—"

"We've had so much shit going on that we've neglected you."

I shake my head. "I'm used to—"

"No. Just no. Just because that's how the guys have already treated you, it doesn't mean it's right, and I'm sorry."

She takes a step back and looks around at the rest of the squad, all of which have paid us zero attention. Might have something to do with the fact that my best friend is a bad-arse who has punched more than one of them at this point and generally proved time and time again how she's so much better than every one of their elite arses.

"Let's go, before Miss Peterson appears."

Throwing a hoodie around her shoulders, she pushes her feet into her trainers and gathers up her bag.

"Have you got your car?" she asks as we slip out of the locker room and head down the now thankfully empty hallway.

"Yeah."

Stella reaches for her phone and starts tapping away before she turns to me and says, "Emmie is in."

A smile pulls at my lips as the realisation of just how badly I needed some time with my girls hits me.

The need to tell them the truth about what's been going on burns through me, but I know I can't. I can't breathe Ant's name to them. If anyone else were to find out and the gossip were to spread, he could be dead before the sun sets. And as for Daemon. Well... I guess we just keep pretending that nothing happened there. I mean, we've been doing it since Halloween, so it shouldn't be too hard.

Only now, he's not ignoring you.

I want to share with my girls, and tell them that I finally lost my V-card. But at the same time, I'm not ready for them to know.

Stella takes the lead and drags open my driver's door before I get a chance to get close, but I don't complain. I'm more than happy not to have to focus on anything right now.

I expect her to head straight back to my place, so I sit up a little straighter when she takes a turn I'm not expecting.

"Where are we going?"

"Meeting Emmie and getting you something I think you desperately need."

To run away?

"Oh yeah?" I ask, curious to know what she thinks I'm missing right now—aside from my common sense, obviously.

The second she takes us toward Reaper territory, I have a very good idea of where we're heading. The café in question has quickly become Stella and Emmie's favourite place in the city to hang out and stuff their faces with more sugar than I'm sure they should consume in a month.

I've only been here a couple of times with them,

and I can't argue that Stella's right. It is exactly what I need.

I spot Emmie's bike a few spaces up as Stella parks and we climb out.

She steps up beside us after pulling her helmet off and tucking it under her arm, and together, the three of us walk into the waffle shop.

The second we step inside, my stomach growls loudly with the sweet scent of the sugar, and all eyes turn on me.

"Regretting forgoing lunch now?" Stella asks with a knowing smirk.

"I just didn't want to deal with people," I confess. The thought of having to sit in the middle of the group and probably be forced to listen to Nico's shit was enough to have me running for the sanctuary of the library.

"We get it," Emmie says, nudging me in the shoulder as we head for the booth at the back of the small café. "They're a lot to take at times."

"Just them?" I ask lightly.

"You love us and you know it. Imagine what your life would be now if we never crashed into it."

Simpler, I think as we slide into the seats. But that's not what falls from my lips. "I don't want to think about it. My life sucked before you two appeared."

"That's what we like to hear," Stella says with a laugh. Plucking the menus from their holder, she passes them over as if we're actually going to read them.

"So what's new?" I ask them, hoping to turn this

around on them, but the second both of their stares burn into the top of my head, I realise I'm shit out of luck with that.

"Nothing. For once, life is calm. Toby is happy, Jodie is going to be okay."

"What about Sara?" Last I heard, she was still in a coma after the fire in Lovell.

Stella blows out a sad breath.

"Pretty much still the same. Jodie keeps reporting that she's making progress, but she's still asleep and they don't really know what's going to happen."

"Shit, that's…"

"Yeah," Emmie mutters sadly as a depressing silence hangs over us.

"Everyone else is good, though," Stella says, forcing some lightness into her tone. "So that only leaves you."

"I'm fine," I say for what feels like the millionth time in the past two days. "I'm just tired."

"We're not idiots, Cal," Emmie says. "We know something is up with you, and we know it's more than just being left out of what was happening last week. Talk to us, please," she begs.

"I-I—" I start, but I quickly discover that I can't muster up any words. I can't tell them about Ant. I can't tell them about Daemon. Guilt tugs at my insides as I look between the two of them, pleading with them to just drop it. To change the subject.

Thankfully, the waitress comes over to take our orders, giving me a few extra minutes to come up with an answer.

Not that it helps.

By the time she walks away again, I'm still sitting here with my stomach in knots and my heart in my throat.

And Stella's next words don't make the situation any better.

"I saw you, you know," Stella says quietly, her eyes boring into mine as I suck in a sharp breath.

"Oooh... what have you been caught doing, baby C?"

"Don't call me that," I snap, my heart slamming against my ribs as I wait for her to reveal what she's seen.

"Someone was creeping out of our building like a naughty little princess last night," Stella teases.

The sigh of relief that wants to race past my lips is almost impossible to hold back as I realise that what she's seen is the least of my crimes recently.

"Alex and I were working on an English lit project. There's nothing to get excited about."

"But that's where you're wrong, Cal," Emmie says, her eyes glittering with excitement. "If you were in Alex's flat, then someone was probably very, very excited. That boy has it bad for you, girl."

I want to argue, but then I remember being pressed up against the door as he gazed down at me, his eyes focusing on my lips.

Jesus. I'm so deep in shit right now.

"There's nothing going on with me and Alex," I argue.

"Yet," Stella adds with a smirk. "I know it's probably the wrong thing to say, given the situation with big brother and all, but I think you two would make a cute couple. And I know he's a bit of a whore, but I reckon he's got skills."

"He does, from what I've heard," Emmie confirms. "Two girls were talking in my art class the other week—"

"Stop, please, stop," I beg. I'm already forced to listen to more than enough of that shit from the guys. I don't need it from my girls, too.

"What? I'm just saying. Losing it to him would be preferable to many, many others."

Ripping my eyes away from their grins, I'm distracted as someone familiar walks into the café and looks around.

"It could be worse. It could be someone like that," Stella jokes.

"You know who that is, right?" I ask, amused that she can be so observant most of the time yet Jerome's presence completely passes her by.

"Uh... well from his uniform I'm assuming he's someone I should know but... nope."

"That's Jerome," I point out. "His dad is a soldier."

"No," Emmie breathes, her eyes drinking him in.

He's cute, in a really put-together, quiet, nerdy way. Not at all Stella and Emmie's type if their boys are anything to go by—and from my recent experiences, I'll happily say he's not mine, either.

He's calm, quiet, serious. The complete opposite of the bad boys we're surrounded by on a daily basis.

And he's good company. He doesn't stick his nose in where it's not wanted. He's just... a friend.

"Do not tell me he's going to follow suit. They'll eat him alive." Stella shrugs.

"I have no idea," I say honestly. Whenever we spend time together, I always get the impression that he doesn't want to talk about that stuff, and to be quite honest, neither do I, so we both just... avoid it.

"I guess every crime organisation needs an IT nerd. He could fit right in," Emmie quips.

"Don't judge. He's actually quite sweet."

They both stare at me like I've lost my mind.

"What? I've known him all my life. We've had tons of classes together. He's actually my study partner for maths. He's—"

"Boring?" Stella offers with a snort.

"You're mean."

"I know, I'm sorry. But it's just more evidence that you should let Alex pop that cherry. A nice guy like that would never hit the right spot."

"Amen to that."

I sigh, looking back over at Jerome as he pushes his glasses back up his nose, his eyes locked on the menu as if he's scared of looking anywhere but.

"Do you think he's here alone?"

"Why, you wanna invite him over?" Stella asks.

"Hell no, you two would scar him for life. It's just kinda sad if he is."

The waitress delivering three fully loaded salted caramel waffles and hot chocolate drags our attention away from Jerome. I eye my food hungrily, my mouth watering and my belly growling.

"God, I need this," Emmie moans, making Stella snort. "What?" she asks.

"You sound just like that when you're begging for Theo's cock."

"I do not."

"You so do."

Shaking my head at them, I grab my fork and dive in.

"Oh my God," I moan.

"And that's how Calli will sound when she's begging for Alex's."

"I'm not sleeping with Alex," I mutter. "Oh look," I say, thankful to get the heat off me as a woman I recognise walks through the front door.

"Is that his mom?" Stella asks as the woman slips into the booth with Jerome after dropping a kiss on his cheek.

"Yeah. Iris is lovely."

"Can you imagine any of our guys having a waffle date with their mum?" Emmie muses.

"Toby would," Stella announces. "He'd do anything for this kind of sweetness."

"I bet Alex would too," I say, regretting it instantly when they both turn their stares on me.

"See, you know him better than you're trying to let on."

"I don't," I sulk. "I just know that Gianna is awesome and that he'd have no issues with hanging out with her."

"She's right," Emmie points out.

Thankfully, I manage to steer the conversation to school, classes, and our upcoming exams.

"You ready for next year?" Stella asks me.

"Nope, not in any way," I say, lifting my mug to my lips for another sugar hit.

"You sent in all your applications though, right?"

"You know I did. I just... I dunno. I don't think I really want uni."

"There's nothing wrong with that," Emmie assures me.

"You've met my parents, right?"

"Barely."

I sigh, hating all this weight that's pressing down on my shoulders right now.

Their expectations are exhausting. Good grades, a respected university, a worthwhile degree, a worthy husband and as many little boys as possible that I can force out of my vag to continue the empire.

I guess it doesn't sound all that awful. Life could certainly be worse, but that doesn't mean I'm happy about what my future holds right now.

I want to make my own choices. Not that I know what they would be right now. I just know I want them. I want control over my life, and it just constantly feels like it's slipping through my fingers like sand.

"You guys ready to head out?" I ask, sliding my mug

back while my stomach churns a little. I may have overdone it a little on the sweet treats. Or it could just be dread that I've got to go through everything in my room and see what that idiot ruined when he decided to pull that stunt last night.

"Yeah, I'm riding my sugar high nicely right now," Emmie announces.

"Let's go then."

I slide out of the booth and alert Iris to my presence.

"Calli," she calls, a wide smile curling at her lips.

Walking over, I plaster my own smile on my face.

"Hi, how are you? Hi, Jerome."

He glances up at me, and I swear his cheeks heat at my presence despite the fact that he spent most of the afternoon in the library with me.

"We're really good, sweetheart. I love your new hair."

"Oh, thanks. Mum's not all that thrilled about it," I mutter.

"It really suits you. Don't you think, Jerome?"

I'm sure if I could see through the table I would have watched her kick him in the shin.

"Uh... yeah. It looks... beautiful."

Someone behind me coughs to smother their laughter. I'd put money on it being Emmie.

"Th-thank you," I whisper, squirming on my feet and more than ready to get away.

"I must get in touch with your mum, see if we can organise a family meal again. It's been too long."

I mutter some kind of agreement before Stella steps up beside me.

"Hi, I'm Stella."

"Doukas, right?" Iris asks.

"The one and only." She grins wide, her eyes shifting between both of them—not that Jerome really looks up from the table.

"It's so nice to finally meet you. I've heard so much."

"All good, I hope," Stella teases. "We're sorry to be bores, but we need to steal Calli away. We're just having a break before we go and study."

"Oh, of course. You guys go and do your thing. We're doing the same, actually. Jerome is feeling the pressure of his upcoming exams too. We understand."

"Thank you. See you soon," I say in a rush before being dragged out of the café by Stella.

"Jesus, what the hell was that?" Emmie asks once the door is firmly closed behind us. "He's like... I don't even know."

"Smothered. He's the baby of the family, it's always been the same," I explain. "If you get him alone, he's not actually so..."

"Pathetic?" Stella helpfully suggests.

"He's a nice guy, he's just being crushed by his family and their expectations of him."

Something I understand all too well.

15

DAEMON

I let out a pained sigh as I fall back on my sofa, throwing my arm over my eyes to block out the light.

My head is still fucking fuzzy from those pills, and my need to be with her again is almost too much to ignore.

I'd hoped she might reach out this morning. Have something to say about the fact that I got her riding that very fine edge of her release last night before I disappeared into the darkness almost as fast as I'd appeared.

The sounds of her frustrated cries still ring out in my ears now.

My cock swells as I think about her on top of her kitchen island, finishing herself up with thoughts of me filling her head.

Pushing my hand inside my sweats, I squeeze the base of my dick, my own irritation with myself growing.

I wanted her so badly last night. As her taste coated my tongue and filled my mouth, all I could think about was making her scream and feeling her cunt squeezing down on me, letting her feel every single brutal stroke of my cock thrusting deep inside her.

I startle when my front door slams shut a second before a female voice hits my ears.

"Honey, I'm home."

Quickly rearranging myself so she can't see my obvious boner, I listen to her light footsteps get closer to me.

"Oh no, what's wrong? Not killed enough gangster dickheads today to sate your twisted need to become the grim reaper?" Amusement laces her voice, and I can't help the smirk that twitches at my lips as I lower my arms and blink at her.

Her blonde hair is pulled back from her face, her makeup is as on point as ever, and while she might only be dressed in a hoodie and a pair of jeans, her put-togetherness makes me cringe.

"You're funny, I," I mutter, watching as she stalks over to my sofa and glares at my feet until they move.

Dragging my aching body up, I rest back in the corner and pull my legs away.

The second her arse hits the cushion, she turns to me with her nose wrinkled in disgust.

"You need to go shower."

"Thanks, I. It's great to see you too," I quip.

"You know I love you, D. But you stink, and you're covered in blood."

I shrug. The blood part isn't exactly unusual.

"Who were you fighting?" she asks, her eyes finding each bruise and cut I've been left with.

"Alex."

"Should have known," she says, rolling her eyes.

My smile grows as I remember planting a good couple of solid punches to Alex's jaw and cheek. He's hurting way more than me right now, there's no doubt. The amusing part is that he has no idea why I went so hard on him today.

He just assumes I'm having 'one of those days' where I want to rip the world apart more than I usually do.

But it's not that at all.

It's her. My angel.

And every time I find out he's got close to her, it's going to get worse.

Because she's mine.

She can humour him, fill his dirty little fantasies all she likes. But we both know that when it comes down to it, it's going to be my bed she's warming.

"Go wash that stench from your body and I might just order us food."

"Deal." I hop up before turning back to her, twisting my fingers in her hair and dropping a kiss to her brow. "You're the best, Isla."

"Ew, get off me you dirty, sweaty boy," she squeals, her nails digging into my forearm in an attempt to make me release her.

"You love it and you know it," I tease, finally releasing her hair.

"Pfft, you know nothing, little boy."

"Oh, so those bruises around your neck are from some sweet and innocent nerd, huh?"

Her hand lifts to her throat and her brows pinch in confusion.

"I-I don't know what you're talking about."

My laughter fills my flat and I march toward my bedroom, discarding clothes as I go, and then into the shower.

I let it run hot while I wash, and then I turn it down to its lowest setting and just stand there until I can take no more.

No matter how cold it gets, how much my teeth begin to chatter, my boner never wavers.

My need for her is too strong.

But I refuse to wrap my hand around myself and succumb to the desire.

It would be unfulfilling, anyway.

Everything short of being inside her would be.

"Food's here," Isla calls through my bedroom, her voice floating through the ajar bathroom door.

I sigh, tipping my head back to the ice-cold torrent that's rushing over me.

Isla's been my saving grace over the past few years.

She's older than us, already at uni, and living her best life. But it's not always been that way for her.

Her father is a soldier.

Her brother was a soldier.

I remember the night he died as if it were yesterday.

I shouldn't have been there. Dad told me to stay away. But I just knew deep down something was going to go wrong on the job they were heading out on.

Some stupid motherfuckers from the other side of the city decided it would be a good decision to hop into our territory and start selling fucking smack.

Bad fucking move.

Dad set up the raid on their compound, but something was wrong. I could feel it.

And I turned out to be right when they walked straight into a war zone.

That was the night I perfected my aim with a sniper rifle.

I snuck out after Dad had left and managed to break into a building opposite that had a half-decent vantage point over the courtyard where I was convinced all hell was about to break loose.

I remember watching Drew hit the ground, and I could see the guys who did it turning on Isla's father next.

The adrenaline that shot through me as I made that kill was like nothing I'd ever felt before.

No one knew where the fuck I was. Hell, they didn't know who I was. But I was there, I was helping. And it was all I wanted in the fucking world.

Alex was asleep when I got home. He had no idea that I'd even snuck out. When Dad returned though, he knew. It was the first time I'd seen real pride shining in his eyes. And it meant every-fucking-thing.

I'd spent my life being the second-rate twin. The dumb one, the unathletic one, the dark one. Suddenly, I had a reason, a purpose, and while we might have lost Drew that night, there was no doubt that I'd saved us loads of lives.

That night changed the course of my future. Thank fuck.

Finally, Dad listened to me about not wanting to do sixth form like I knew the others were excited about. I couldn't think of anything worse than another two years in full-time education.

I may not have got out of it entirely, but the deal we struck was a million times better than what I was heading toward.

And that wasn't the only thing that changed. After Isla learned I was the one who saved her daddy's life, we struck up an unlikely friendship, and something about our bond has lasted.

Honestly, I have no fucking clue what she sees in me. But she tells me often that I help make this life we live more bearable. Fuck knows how, it can't be my sparkling personality. But fuck if I care when just my presence seems to make her happy. After living a life where my walking in the room had the opposite effect, it's a nice change.

After dragging on a clean pair of sweats and t-shirt, I let my nose lead the way, the scent of tomato sauce and melted cheese getting stronger with every step I take.

A laugh falls from my lips as I round the corner into my kitchen and find Isla sitting at my island, pulling a slice of pizza away from her mouth, strings of cheese stuck to her chin and sauce on her lips.

"Remind me again why you're single?" I ask, pulling out the stool beside her and dragging my own box over, flipping the lid and letting the tempting scent waft over me. "My favourite," I muse, as if she'd order anything else.

"After that comment, I shouldn't have bothered."

"You're not brave enough." Pulling a slice of my own pizza free, I sink my teeth into it and groan.

Flaming hot. Just like the depths of hell.

The heat of the chilli flakes hits my tongue, and I quickly devour the rest of the slice, craving the pain.

"So, was there any reason why you beat the shit out of Alex?"

"More reason than I usually have?" I mutter around a mouthful.

"Okay, let me guess... it's about a girl."

I glare at her over my next slice, my brow creasing with just how fucking transparent I apparently am.

"When have we ever fought over a girl?"

"I dunno." She shrugs. "But something has been off with you for a while. Something I haven't been able to put my finger on. And the only thing that makes sense is that it's to do with a girl."

"Can you stop psychoanalysing me?" I growl. "You

know I hate that shit. I'm not a fucking uni assignment."

"Thank fuck. Something tells me I'd miss my deadline, because it would probably take a lifetime to really crack you open."

My eyes narrow at her.

"I'm not that fucked up, I."

"Sure," she says, shooting me a grin. "So are you going to deny it, or..."

Rolling my eyes, I humour her with half-truths about the situation. She'll be like a dog with a bone unless I give her something.

"Alex is going after someone he shouldn't."

She considers my words for a few seconds.

"And you're what, trying to protect this girl's virtue? How very... noble of you."

"I'm just trying to do the right thing."

"Sure. I guess I'd better start calling you Mother Teresa then?" she quips, her brow lifting in amusement. "Or you could just tell me the truth."

"That is the truth. And it's not about the girl." Lie. "It's about Alex. He's making a mistake, and I want to see him realise it before he ends up in the middle of something he can't get out of."

"Right."

"You want a drink?" I ask, my mouth burning up and my eyes threatening to start running if I keep eating that pizza so fast.

"Sure. I will get to the bottom of this, though."

"There's nothing to get to the bottom of, I. I'm just

looking out for Alex. So what's going on with you? Those marks courtesy of someone serious?" I ask after placing a beer beside her.

Yeah, my best friend might be a girly girl, but when she's with me, she's just one of the guys, only with a more tempting body. Not that I'd ever go there. There has never been, nor will there ever be anything like that between us.

"Pfft, I don't do serious and you know it."

"Someone's going to make you change your mind eventually, I."

"They're going to have to be something really fucking special. You know I have no desire for the whole married-with-kids bullshit my parents want for me."

"I know, I know. But you deserve someone decent. Your hookups are dickheads."

She laughs, humouring me as if we haven't had this conversation a million times.

"So are you the pot or the kettle this time, D?"

I shake my head. "I ain't like that, and you know it."

"Fucking faceless women to get your kicks? Yeah, that's exactly what you're like. You don't have to sugarcoat anything for me."

"Nah, I haven't been with anyone like that in ages."

My eyes fly to hers as shock renders me speechless. I did not mean to say that out loud.

Lifting my hand, I rub the back of my neck.

"Keep talking. I fucking knew there was a girl."

"No," I backtrack. "I've just been too busy, and no one is really doing it for me."

"So you weren't thinking about her when I came in then? She wasn't the reason your sweats were looking suspiciously tight."

"Nothing to tell."

"You're such a bad liar. Maybe I should just call Alex," she taunts, pulling her phone from her hoodie pocket. But I know she's calling my bluff. She wouldn't ring him. The two of them have some weird love–hate thing going on that I've never really got to the bottom of.

"Go on then. Although he's probably too busy nursing his wounds."

"Or maybe the girl who's got you so twisted up in knots is doing it for him. Kissing his boo-boos and rubbing it all better." She wiggles her brows at me, and I smile. Although all the while, I'm dying inside at the image she just painted.

16

CALLI

"Callista, are you down there?" Mum's shrill voice calls.

It's pointless. She'll have seen my car parked outside when she remembered that this is where she lives, and obviously, I'm not up in the house. Where the hell else would I be?

Both Stella and Emmie groan at the sound of her voice. Neither of them knows her all that well—they've never had a chance—but they've learned a lot through me.

I used to feel guilty bad-mouthing her, because things could be a lot worse. I've always had a home, food, clothes, more money than most and all the privileges that come with it. But I'll stand by my opinion that my mum was not made to be a mother. I don't think she's got a maternal bone in her body.

Nico and I were mostly brought up by nannies.

Multiple nannies, because most couldn't put up with Mum's ideals for how she wanted us to be looked after. She might have been hands-off with us, but that didn't mean she wasn't opinionated. Much like she still is now.

I shoot a look over my shoulder at my girls, but I don't need to say the words that are on my tongue. Instead, they immediately jump into action, hiding the evidence of my new hobby as Mum's footsteps descend the stairs.

The second her head appears, her eyes scan the room before landing on me and she tuts disapprovingly.

I'm wearing a pair of booty shorts and a cropped hoodie. In my own home.

"Really, Callista? You look like you should be in Lovell, wearing that."

"Good evening, Mrs. Cirillo," Stella says, attempting to defuse the situation—not that I'd ever say anything back to her. I'm not brave enough.

"Estella. Emmie," she greets through clenched teeth.

"They're just helping me tidy up after last night."

"Did Jocelyn not come while you were at school today?" she asks, referring to our housekeeper, also known as the long-suffering woman Mum bosses around on a daily basis. I can only assume she pays her a shit load of money, because there can't be any other reason she'd stick working for the tyrant.

"I left her a note to let her know that she should

focus on the rest of the house. I thought you'd want it perfect before returning."

Mum smiles at that, but her nose is still turned up at the state of my room.

"Right, well, I suggest you get this sorted out or I'll be sending her down here tomorrow to do it for you."

"That won't be necessary."

"Have you eaten?" she asks. To anyone else, it might seem that she asks that because she cares. But then she follows it up with, "You're looking skinny and pale. I'm going to talk to Jocelyn about your diet."

"I'm fine, Mum. And I'll be up in a bit to grab dinner."

Both her brows shoot up at my choice of words, but thankfully, she chooses not to say anything more on that.

"By the way, I've told Selene you'll babysit the kids on Friday night."

"Right," I mutter. "What if I have plans?" I ask, disgruntled.

"Cancel them," she says with a dismissive shrug that makes my blood begin to boil.

It's bullshit, I don't have any plans. But that's not the point.

She nods as if my silence is me agreeing, and she heads back up the stairs without another word leaving her lips.

It's not until the door shuts on the floor above that I release the breath I was holding.

"I don't like her," Stella mutters. "And I hate that you feel like you have to hide all of this from her."

"She was hiding it from us until a few hours ago," Emmie points out.

"Yeah, about that," Stella says, turning to me with one of the hoodies I've designed and printed in her hands.

"I just needed something to take my mind off... life. I'm just messing about with it all." It's the same argument I've used since they followed me in and found everything I've been working on for the past few weeks drying all around the room.

"This needs to be more than a bit of fun, Cal. It's incredible."

"You should set up an Etsy shop or something. Maybe you can earn enough of your own money to move away from Cruella de Vil," Emmie suggests.

"As if they'd allow that. The only reason I'm going to be able to move out is when I've got a perfectly suited soon-to-be husband to move in with."

"That's bullshit," Stella spits.

"You don't need to tell me that. The fact that they let me move down here is a minor freaking miracle."

"So I'm assuming Alex isn't a worthy suitor for you?" Emmie asks.

"Honestly, her standards are so high, I don't think anyone is going to be worthy."

"Have you ever brought a boy home?" she asks, although I'm not sure why she bothers. She must already know the answer.

"I try not to bring you two here when I know she might show her face. I'm hardly going to subject a boy to that."

"Nico has no idea how easy he has it, does he?" Stella asks, folding the hoodie up and moving over to the next one. "I'm going to need one of these, by the way." She holds up the navy fabric against her chest, and Emmie laughs as she reads the text across the front.

Not your average princess.

"Have it. I basically designed it for you. You too, Em."

"I'm not wearing anything with the word 'princess' on it and a fucking crown," she sulks.

"Fine, what about this one?" I rummage through the pile I've already folded until I find a black, long-sleeved shirt with *Underestimate me, I dare you,* scrawled across the front.

"That's more like it," she says with a smile, reaching out with grabby hands to take it. "Thank you."

She quickly strips out of her school shirt and drags it over her head.

"Goes perfectly with my resting bitch face, don't you think?"

"You're an idiot," Stella laughs. "She's right about Etsy, though. You could totally sell all this."

I shrug. "Maybe. We'll see. I've already got enough on my plate. This has just been an escape."

"It might be the answer to your questions about your future."

"I'm not sure locking myself down here and making hoodies and stuff is going to pass the Cirillo expectations of me somehow," I mutter sadly. If my parents were like either of theirs, then I'm sure it could be a possibility. Unfortunately, that's not my reality.

"You should do design and business, if that's a thing. Learn everything to get this up and running."

"I wish," I mutter. "Nothing short of my standard business degree will do."

"But you don't want to do it."

"You don't need to tell me that," I argue.

"Just fail your exams. Do another year at Knight's Ridge with us. Double up on art and design and force their hands."

"At the rate I'm going, I might not have to try too hard."

"Calli," Stella sighs. "Don't be so hard on yourself. You're gonna do amazing."

"Amazing in their eyes or yours?"

"Fuck them, Calli," Emmie spits. "We don't give a shit about their standards. And you shouldn't either, although I know that's easier said than done. This is your future, your life."

"And, you're eighteen soon. You don't need to listen to a word from them."

"I'm sure they'd find a way to make me," I sigh sadly.

Stella's phone thankfully cuts through the heavy silence that follows my words, quickly followed by a loud, "Yes."

"What is it? Seb finally seeing results for those dick growth pills he bought?" Emmie asks so seriously I can't help but snort.

"What?" Stella blanches. "You both know as well as I do that Seb doesn't need any support in that department. I'm one happy girl."

"Kill me," I mutter.

"Aw, sorry, baby C. No more dick talk, we promise."

I roll my eyes at Emmie and turn my attention back to Stella.

"So what is it really?"

"A surprise for next week."

"Oh, they got back to you?" Emmie asks excitedly, clearly aware of what Stella's been up to.

"Yeah, and it's all ours."

"Fuck yeah. It's going to be awesome."

"Anyone wanna tell me what's going to be awesome?"

They both turn to me, wicked smiles playing on their lips.

"All you need to know is that you've got to clear your diary for the first few days of the holiday. Apparently, we're going to have a spring heatwave and we're going to make the most of it in style."

"I'm gonna need more than that," I mutter.

"Nope. Just know that it's going to be the best few days of our life, and—"

"And, if you play your cards right with Alex, maybe you could—"

"Tell me you haven't planned a 'let's get Calli laid party'," I beg.

"Nope, it might just be a happy coincidence."

"He's so hot for you, and a few days away might just be what you need. After all, it got you in his bed last weekend."

"I'm not giving Alex my V-card." Because I've already handed it to the devil.

"We'll see. You're gonna need the hottest bikini you own. Fuck it, we should go shopping. Get a few new things that will really drive our boys crazy."

"And my brother?" I ask, lifting a brow.

"It'll be almost as entertaining watching him finally blow his lid as it will be watching Alex drool over your hot-as-fuck body."

"You two are trouble."

"With a capital T, baby."

***

"All finished, sweetie?" Jocelyn asks, coming over to take my empty plate.

"It was amazing, thank you," I say appreciatively.

"I hope you made the most of it. Your mum's made changes to your diet from tomorrow."

"Oh God, now what?" I ask, dreading what stupid thing she's read online this time that will fix my complexion and make my brain more efficient.

"Nothing too crazy... yet. Wider variety of fruit and veg mostly. More fish."

I try to hide my distaste, but I fail. Jocelyn knows as well as I do that fish isn't my thing.

"I'll find ways to make it work." She winks at me and my smile curls up as I think of the little secret treats she's been leaving for years in my bedroom.

If Mum ever found out, she'd probably string Jocelyn up for it, but that doesn't seem to faze our resilient housekeeper.

"I don't know how you do it," I say. "Surely you could get a better job somewhere else."

"It's not so bad, Calli. Sometimes it's better the devil you know."

"I guess," I mutter, hopping off my stool and heading for the fridge for a lemonade.

"Enjoy that. You're on water tomorrow."

"You're kidding?"

"Sadly not."

"I need to move out," I hiss, cracking the top of the can and dropping a kiss on Jocelyn's cheek in thanks.

She's been with us since Mum decided that Nico and I didn't need nannies anymore. She's in her mid-fifties, I think, and is basically the kind, gentle grandmother I never had.

No matter what she's doing, her white shirt is always pristine, her trousers perfectly pressed, and there's never a hair out of place in her chignon. I more than understand why Mum likes having her around.

She's the image of perfection even thirty seconds after scrubbing the floor.

"You can't go yet. Who will I have to talk to?"

My heart aches for her. As far as I know, she's never married and her only son died not long before she started working here. She's lonely, that's more than obvious.

"I'd take you with me if I could," I assure her.

"One day, sweetie," she promises like she always does. We've talked at length before now about how she'll follow me to my marital home and help me raise those little soldiers Dad is so desperate for. Knowing she's willing to stand by my side is about the only thing that seems bearable about it all.

"Are you sure you don't need me to give your room the once over? I'm sure those sprinklers made a right mess over all your... things."

"It's all under control," I assure her. "I've got homework to do, but if you get lonely, you know where I am."

"Thank you, sweetie. But I'm almost finished up if you don't need me."

"Go and enjoy your evening. You never know, tonight might be your lucky night," I tease her.

"Pfft." She waves her hand at me. "I'm too old for all that now, young one."

"Never. You just need to find the right... inspiration."

"You, Callista Cirillo, are almost as bad as that brother of yours."

I laugh at her faux stern expression as she thinks about Nico and his antics.

"I won't be offering up my friends' services to you, don't worry."

Her cheeks flush bright red as she recalls Nico's offer one morning when he refused to keep his mouth shut about exactly what his previous night entailed.

"Go do your work, young one. And maybe check the bottom shelf in your wardrobe later." She winks at me before I slip away.

I lock the main door to the basement. It won't stop anyone if they really want to get down here, but it makes me feel like I'm taking at least a little bit of control over my life.

I'm too lost in my own head to notice anything as I hit the bottom of the stairs and step into my basement, heading straight for the wardrobe. But I only make it a few steps when the shock of a person sitting on my bed makes me scream bloody murder.

"Whoa, it's just me," he says, holding his hands up in surrender and scooting to the end of the bed.

"What the hell are you doing here, Alex? And what happened to your face?"

"Oh, this?" he asks, pointing to himself. "It's nothing, baby C. You should see the other guy."

Shaking my head, I swerve the bed and continue toward my wardrobe to see what Jocelyn has hidden for me.

"It was Nico, wasn't it?" I guess, based on the short conversation we had outside the locker rooms earlier when it seemed like Alex was gunning for a fight by taunting him.

"Some of it, yeah. The rest was Daemon."

I pause dead at hearing his name.

"Daemon? Why?" I ask, unable to not take that bait.

I spin around and glare at him.

He has the decency to look a little guilty.

"Dunno. He was pissed about something. I helped him vent." He shrugs as if it's nothing. "Personally, I think he needs to get laid." All the air rushes out of my lungs without permission. Thankfully though, Alex doesn't seem to notice. "I think he's going through a dry spell."

"Why are you here, Alex?" I hiss.

"Well, firstly to apologise. I'm sorry for suggesting in front of Nico that anything happened between us last night. He's just too easy to wind up, but I should have thought better of it."

I stare at him, refusing to let him see that I accept that apology. Hell knows I've done enough over the years to make Nico blow his top. I just hate it when they all end up turning on each other and ultimately hurting each other. They might all drive me to the edge of insanity with their possessive, over-the-top bullshit, but I still don't want them in pain.

"And..." I prompt when he stops, his eyes focused on my bare legs instead of my face. "I can cover up if you're incapable of thinking straight."

"Uh... shit. Fuck. Sorry." Lifting his hand from his

lap, he combs his fingers through his hair, dragging it back from his face.

For just a beat, with his desire-filled eyes and busted face gazing up at me, I almost think it's Daemon sitting before me.

"I was at home working on my English assignment, and it was boring as fuck. I hoped that maybe we could pick up where we left off last night. A problem shared is a problem halved, right?"

He smiles at me but quickly winces when his lip splits open again, a droplet of blood trickling down his chin.

"Have you even cleaned them up?" I ask with a sigh.

"It's nothing I can't handle, baby C. I'm a big boy." He winks at me, and I can't help but blush. Damn it.

"Let me get the first aid kit," I mutter, spinning on my heels and heading for my bathroom instead of my hidden sweet treat.

I gather up what I need and head back out.

"Seriously?" I ask, marching back out and finding that Alex has made himself at home on my bed. His trainers have been kicked off and abandoned on the floor, his shirt next to them as he waits for me.

"What?" he asks innocently. "I promise to be the best patient you've ever patched up."

"Well, seeing as I've only cleaned Nico up before, that shouldn't be a challenge. He's a fucking baby."

Alex barks a laugh as I place the kit on the end of the bed.

"Does that hurt?" I ask, nodding toward the angry wound on his upper arm.

"Nothing I can't handle."

"Play the big man all you want, but one of the things I do know about that night in Lovell is that you went running to Mummy to patch you up."

"There's nothing wrong with wanting the best nurse in the country to patch up my boo-boo," Alex states proudly.

"Sure. Sit on the edge then and I'll— ALEX," I squeal as his giant hands wrap around my waist and I'm hauled off my feet and deposited over his lap. "Oh no, I'm not—"

"Keep wiggling and things are going to get a lot... harder," he growls.

"Jesus Christ," I mutter, my body instantly freezing.

His hands drop lower once he's confident I'm not going to bolt. He rests them on my hips, his skin burning through my tiny shorts.

"Go on then. Clean me up, baby."

"I think your mind is entirely too dirty to clean up," I mutter, reaching for the kit.

A growl rips from his throat as I move over him, and I have to bite back a grin. I might not want to take this further with him, but I can't help loving the power that comes with my position right now.

"Was it necessary to take your shirt off?" I ask innocently, all the while my mind wondering what it would be like to sit with Daemon like this.

"Just making all my best features work for me."

"And you think your abs are the best thing about you?"

"Of course not. The best bit I kept hidden... for now."

"You're a nightmare."

"You love it. Bet you're wet as fuck for me right now, baby C."

"Really?" I ask. "You came to work, remember?"

"Ow, motherfucker," he barks when I press an anti-bac wipe to the cut in his eyebrow.

"It's okay, baby. Be a big boy for me."

"Oh." He thrusts beneath me, ensuring I don't miss exactly what he's hiding. "You have nothing to worry about there."

My phone dings on the counter in the kitchen and I ignore it while I finish up, refusing to look Alex in the eyes.

The second I'm done, I hop up from his body and damn near run away. He chuckles behind me, and it makes my teeth grind in irritation.

It's annoying me that he's playing this game. But it's infuriating me more that I'm not even sure if it's a game anymore.

It's obvious that he wants me. I didn't need to feel... him beneath me just now to know that. But then, this is Alex we're talking about. He's almost as big a man whore as my brother, so I have no doubt that he'd be hard if anyone's pussy was sitting right above his dick.

I let out a sigh as I dump my rubbish in the bin and

open a cupboard in search of drinks, or more so an excuse so that I don't have to look at him.

"What's wrong, baby C?" Alex asks, sensing that something is up.

"Nothing," I hiss, hating that I sound like an overly emotional teenage girl.

The sound of him shifting around on my bed hits my ears, but I refuse to look up and see what he's doing.

"Don't give me that bullshit. Tell me the truth."

"It's this. You," I snap.

"Whoa, I said don't lie, not don't sugarcoat," he jokes.

My eyes find his with an irritated huff.

My phone pings again, and in my need to remove myself from Alex's penetrating stare, I move toward it.

"Why are you here, Alex?"

"To do our English assignment."

"And that involves you having your shirt off, why?" I mean, it's no hardship looking at him half-dressed but that's not the point. Having him here looking so much like... No. I slam those thoughts right now.

He shrugs.

"Are you actually serious with all of this, or are you just doing whatever you can to rile Nico up?" I ask, gesturing between us.

He hesitates, and it's all the answer I need.

"You can leave if you're only here to play games. I'm not interested in your cock-measuring contest with the boys."

"No, that's not... This isn't what—"

Finally, I pick up my phone and my stomach drops into my feet, Alex's words drifting off to nothing.

Daemon: Careful, Angel. You seem to be forgetting who owns you.

My gasp rips through the air, my hand trembling as my grip on my phone tightens until it hurts.

"What is it?" Alex asks, but I'm too lost to my panic to be able to respond.

He's watching.

Without thinking, I walk toward the wall of windows. The closer I get, the more my skin prickles with awareness.

But I don't see anything.

It's almost dark, the last of the sun peeking through the trees, sending orange-tinted shadows dancing all over the garden and vast patio beyond my little haven.

"Calli?" I barely hear Alex's voice or his footsteps as he closes the space between us. "Calli?"

Giving up on finding him in the shadows, I spin back around to Alex. My hackles are up knowing that not only is he potentially here with an ulterior motive, but that we're being watched too.

"Let's just get this assignment done. Then you can

go home." I don't mean for it to come out as harshly as it does, and I hate that it makes hurt flicker through his features, but it's too late now.

All the good that had come from waffles with the girls has been firmly obliterated by my mum and the Deimos twins.

17

DAEMON

"Where the hell are you? I told you to be here an hour ago," Dad growls down the line not two seconds after I started my car and the call connected.

My grip on the wheel tightens, my knuckles turning white as I squeeze my eyes closed, the image of Calli sitting on top of Alex the only thing I can see.

"I'm on my way," I grit out, desperately trying to keep my cool.

Losing my shit with Alex in the ring earlier was one thing, but if I allow Dad to see any weakness in me then I'm fucked.

He expects me to act a certain way, to put on a cold hard front and not cave to my emotions.

Usually, it's not something I have a problem with, seeing as I don't give a fuck about most things in my life. But Calli is an entirely different story.

And seeing her grinding down on Alex...

The call cuts without him saying another word, and I smack my hand down on the wheel.

"Fuck. FUCK," I bellow, my fury refusing to stay bottled inside.

I sit there for another ten seconds, giving myself a talking to, forcing images of them together from my head before I finally put my car into drive and pull out onto the street.

Seeing her with Alex hits so differently from seeing her with Ant.

Finding him between her legs on Friday night was like a punch to the gut, but deep down I knew that even if he did get a taste of her, it could never last. No one would allow it, and if by some miracle it did get serious, something tells me that before long Ant would turn up dead and put an end to the whole situation.

But Alex...

If there is something between them, if he cares for her even half as much as I do despite not allowing myself to have her, then they could be a possibility.

Evan and Cassandra would approve... well, maybe. He's not exactly the perfectly well-behaved Greek boy I'm sure they want for their little princess. But he's a hell of a lot better than Ant, and I'd imagine more preferable than me.

I might have spent all these years watching her from the shadows, convincing myself that she would be better off with anyone but me. But could I stand by and watch her fall in love with Alex?

I shake my head as the car in front of me suddenly

slams on his brakes, causing my heart to jump into my throat.

I just about manage to stop in time before a dog struts out from the front of the car as if nothing ever happened.

"Fucking stupid mutt," I mutter to myself. "Go then," I hiss when the driver in front hesitates to get going again.

By the time I pull up at the old warehouse in the woods on the outskirts of the city where I know Dad is waiting for me, every single muscle in my body is locked up tight and my fingers are cramping from the wheel and my need to put them to better use.

Alex might have helped me take the edge off earlier, but since then, he's unknowingly woken the monster within me that constantly battles to get out.

"About fucking time," Dad barks as I push through the door to the viewing gallery we've got on our prisoners.

There are three Italians strapped to the chair beyond the glass. All broken, bruised and bloody.

One of them was Jonas's contact who helped him escape from our basement and damn near killed his mistress and daughter, and the other two are the ones Dad took from their compound on Friday night. Ones we're hoping to get more details out of about Ricardo's takeover plans.

But so far, they haven't squealed any more than we already knew from our rat on the inside.

War is imminent, and while we might be ready for

it, we sure as fuck would like a little more information on when exactly they're planning to hit us.

"I'm here, aren't I?" I growl, stuffing my busted knuckles into my trouser pockets.

It's not like him finding me with war wounds is unusual or unexpected, but I really could do without the lecture right now if he finds out that Alex and I have been fighting. He might encourage us to spar, to improve our skills, but he wants our aggression to be kept for work. For us to be able to channel our anger toward those who deserve it. AKA those cunts barely clinging to life beyond the windows.

There was a time that I never would have spoken back to him. All our lives, our father and grandfather have been these larger-than-life mafia capos. Dangerous enigmas that I craved to be yet was told I'd never achieve.

I was never deemed worthy by either of them.

I was too small, too weak, too stupid.

I believed them too. Believed that Alex was the only one who would ever make my father proud. I mean, it may still be the case. He's the only one who'll achieve anything academically. I stand little chance of passing my exams in a few weeks' time, even less seeing as I spend all my free time either obsessing over the girl I can't have or working in the hope that just for a few hours of each day I'll be able to think about something else.

"You look like you're out for blood," Boss points out as Dad continues to glare at me for talking back to him.

"What do you need?" I hiss, my fists curling with my need to unleash fury on those motherfuckers and finally get the answers we need.

"One of them dies tonight if we don't start getting answers," Dad finally says.

"Fine by me."

Shrugging off my jacket, I throw it onto an empty chair and undo my cuffs. After rolling up my sleeves, I give my father one last look before I push through the door.

The scent of their combined bodily fluids hit me the second I step inside the room.

There's nothing in here bar an old table that's been sprayed with blood more times than I can count and dirty concrete floors and walls.

A pained groan rips through the air, the stench of piss getting stronger as they watch me walk toward the table to choose my first weapon of choice.

Grabbing a pair of pliers, I spin around, meeting each of their eyes for terrifyingly long seconds. Terrifying for them, of course. The only thing they'll find in my dark grey orbs is excitement and bloodlust.

I think of my girl, the one that I'll never be able to claim as my own other than in my head, and I step up to the weakest looking member of the trio.

"One of you won't see the sun rise tomorrow. Although," I mutter, looking around for the non-existent windows, "that shouldn't really be an issue for you. Are you missing it?" I ask. It's a rhetorical question, and thankfully they seem to understand that.

"You must be really regretting going up against us now, huh?"

They're all mute as I pace in front of them, passing the pair of pliers back and forth between my hands.

"So, which one of you is it going to be? Or did you want me to choose?"

Again, no one says anything... until I come to stop in front of the wrecked-looking one again and a whimper spills from his lips.

"Aw, look at that. Your boy is trying to protect you from my wrath by putting himself forward."

As quick as a whip, I pull my arm back and swing the heavy instrument in my hand toward his head. It collides with a sickening crunch before blood sprays everywhere, covering both of us.

Wiping my hand down my face, I clear the warm liquid away.

"Dirty motherfucker," I spit while he sits limply in his chair.

"Right, gentlemen. We've got a fun-filled night ahead of us. I hope you slept well."

Exactly as I promised, when I finally walk out of that room, I only leave two men breathing behind me.

They might have finally given us some fresh information, but it was still nowhere near as much as we knew they were hiding.

Only Dad stayed behind to watch all of my show, and he looks up from his laptop screen with tired eyes.

"You done, boy?"

He doesn't so much as blanch at the amount of blood covering me. But then, why should he? This has been his life longer than it has been mine. And he's stood by me, watching me work my magic more times than I can count since he first put me in front of one of our enemies when I was... eleven, maybe, and told me to do whatever it took to make him talk.

I did.

It was the first time in my life that Dad looked at me with anything but contempt and disappointment.

"You haven't been at school this week," he says when I don't respond, as if I'm not aware of that fact.

"I've been busy."

"That wasn't our deal."

"We're about to go to war with the fucking Italians."

My words don't have the effect I was hoping for as he sits back in his seat and folds his arms over his chest.

"Failing wasn't a part of our deal, Daemon. You fail and you'll be starting back there full-time in September, like you should have done to begin with."

"That's bullshit," I spit. "I don't need fucking A-levels for that shit." I throw my hand back in the direction of the two passed out and one dead guy behind me.

"Right now, maybe not. But you've got a bright future in this Family, boy."

"That's funny," I scoff. "For years you seemed to believe I was useless. Worthless."

"Your skills just needed harnessing. But that doesn't mean you won't succeed at Knight's Ridge."

"Whatever," I mutter, storming toward the door.

"I'm not joking around here, Nikolas."

My steps falter, all the air rushing from my lungs as the name I despise hearing falling from his lips rattles around my head.

Just that one word from him makes me feel like that young, useless kid he used to accuse me of being.

Sucking in some strength—strength that that little boy never possessed—I hold my head up high and walk away from him.

My heart thrashes in my chest, my hands trembling as I make my way back to the car.

We're in the middle of nowhere out here, and there's nothing to hear but my own demons and insecurities.

I've got no chance in hell of passing my exams. I barely scraped through last year, but I've been more absent than not this year, despite Dad's jibes and protests. Anything more than a fail is impossible at this point.

"Fuck," I hiss, dropping into my driver's seat and resting my head back.

My head pounds, my eyes burn for sleep that I know will never come, and my muscles ache from laying into those cunts quite so hard.

There's only one thing that relieves it all, and

before I know what I'm doing, I've put the car into drive and I'm heading back toward the city.

Toward my angel.

My intentions were pure. Well, as pure as my fucking intentions ever are when it comes to Calli.

I was going to slip inside, sate my need for her by watching her sleep like I've done countless times before since she moved down here. Hell, I even managed it when she was living upstairs and we'd come around to hang out with Nico. They never noticed any of the times I slipped away when they were distracted, or made an excuse to head up to the main house, because the idea of anything happening between Calli and me, the mere thought that I could have liked her, was absurd. If it were one of the others then Nico probably would have questioned them, accused them of doing something they shouldn't. But it's me. And I don't seem to be subjected to the same line of questioning. I shouldn't mind. But it's just another harsh reminder that I wasn't one of them. I might have been invited to the parties, but I wasn't really a part of their group.

I suck in a breath before I press my hand to the scanner. The click of the lock makes my stomach knot. Deep down, I was worried she might have asked someone to change the permissions after last night. I can't help the smirk that curls at my lips. She wanted me to come back. She's practically begging me inside.

My cock swells as I pull the door open. Her sweet scent engulfs me, and it's almost enough to remove the stench of death from the past few hours from my nose.

The sound of an owl hooting in the trees is cut off when I close the door behind me, and only the sound of Calli's soft snores replaces it.

The fear was very real as I drove over here that she wouldn't be alone. The thought of slipping inside and finding her tucked up in bed with Alex made my blood turn to ice. But one quick check of everyone's trackers, and I knew she was alone.

Silently, I cut through the room until I'm standing right above her. She's got her covers pulled right up to her neck so I can't see what she's wearing, but I've learned over time what her favourite things to sleep in are, and I'd put money on her being in a vest and knickers beneath those teasing sheets.

My teeth sink into my bottom lip as I watch her, my fingers twitching to reach for her, to feel her soft, warm skin against my rough, blood-coated fingers.

A fire burns deep within me with the need to mark her, to dirty her up, to see her painted in the red of our enemies.

My chest rumbles with a deep, hungry growl, and I close the space between us, my need taking over the few rational thoughts I might have when it comes to my angel.

I rip the covers from her body, my eyes feasting on the inches upon inches of skin I reveal as she moans in her sleep, reaching for the covers she's lost.

I dive on her before she gets a chance to wake any further, wrap my hand around her mouth and pin her body to the mattress with my thighs over her waist.

She thrashes beneath me, her eyes flying open and a scream vibrating up her throat, smothered by my hand.

Pure hatred oozes from her eyes as she stares at me in horror, but under that, it's impossible to miss the desire she tries so hard to fight.

She might like to pretend I'm nothing, that I'm not even in the room at times, but I know that deep down, she remembers every single second of our time together. And she wants me. She craves it. Her eyes and her body beg for it, even if her head and mouth are on a different page.

18

———

CALLI

My heart thunders in my chest as his dark, evil eyes stare down at me with wicked intent flickering within them.

My nostrils flare as I try to suck in the air I need.

He brushes his fingertips down the side of my neck and my entire body jolts as sparks shoot through me. The delicate touch is so gentle compared to the brutal man before me. Lifting one arm that's lying uselessly on the bed, I wrap my fingers around his forearm, unsure if my intention is to stop him or encourage him.

His body is covered in dark, dried specks of blood.

It should terrify me. But I've been a part of this life long enough, even if I have been kept away from the worst of it. Nothing the guys or our fathers do scares me now. I can't say it's always been that way, but in the past few months, I've come to realise, embrace even, that this is my life. Standing out on the firing range with a gun in my own hand as Stella instructed me on how to do it probably helped.

I felt invincible with that weapon clutched in my hand. And I'm sure it was just a small rush compared to what the guys get when they go running into enemy territory, taking out those who wronged us.

His fingers continue to trail lower, his eyes following them as they brush over the swell of my breast.

My breath catches as my chest begins to heave.

A warning rumbles in my throat, but it has little impact as he circles one finger around my nipple.

"Did you make yourself come after I left last night?" he growls. The order he gave me before he left me on my kitchen counter crying his name and shamelessly begging for more repeats in my mind.

My eyes widen. I can't tell him no. I might not have touched myself. But when I woke this morning...

He shakes his head and tsks in disappointment.

"I thought you were a good girl, Angel. You shock me at every turn." His voice is rough and deadly, and it only makes me burn hotter for him.

He left me wanting last night. If he was trying to prove how much I craved him despite his fucked-up actions over the weekend, then he definitely got what he wanted as I writhed and begged for him.

You're a shameless slut, Callista, I chastise myself.

But it's Daemon. There's something about him that makes me lose my mind in a way I don't with others. With Ant, with Alex, there's always some kind of wall stopping me from going too far. But all rational thoughts seem to fly right out the window when it comes to my devil boy.

He shatters my walls, crashes through the image of innocence everyone likes to paint of me, and he does nothing short of bringing me to ruin for him.

"Your body craves me, doesn't it, beautiful?" he groans, desire deepening his voice before it completely changes, ice cutting through the heat. "Do you react this way with them?"

I shake my head—well, as much as I'm able to while pinned beneath his unforgiving grip.

"Were your nipples begging for my brother's touch just like they are for mine now?"

"No," rumbles in my throat as he drags the fabric of my vest down, exposing me to him.

The cool rush of air that assaults me only makes my nipples harder, more desperate for the touch he's denying me.

He blows a stream of cool air over my heated skin and my back arches off the bed.

"They think you're so innocent, huh? But we know the truth, don't we? You're not just an angel. You're my dark, dirty, delicious angel."

"Daemon..." His name is nothing more than a moan as he sucks his bottom lip into his mouth.

"You're not even scared, are you?" he asks, glancing down at himself.

My eyes hold his, begging him to remove his hand so I can respond.

"Scream and you'll be punished," he warns, reading my demands.

The second his hand moves, I hiss, "I'm not scared of you."

He chuckles darkly as he presses his palm to the mattress above my shoulder and dips his head. His tongue circles my nipple and my brain damn near backfires at his teasing touch.

"You're mine," he growls, his possessive tone only making my heart beat harder.

"I'm no one's," I argue, determined to hold my own.

He laughs once more.

"You didn't let Alex touch you, did you?" My lips purse. He doesn't need the answer. Clearly, he already knows. "Were you thinking about me while he was trying to tempt you?"

"No," I state, lying through my teeth.

"And what about Ant? Has he snuck in today to pay you a little visit? Am I getting everyone's sloppy seconds again right now?"

My arm moves before I'm even aware of it. Reality comes crashing down around me as my palm collides with his blood-splattered cheek. His eyes flare as pain shoots down my arm.

"Oh, Angel. Must you tease me?" he whispers so quietly it makes my stomach tumble into my feet.

"What the hell are you doing?" I squeal when he wraps his hand around my throat and hauls me from the bed. "Daemon?" I demand as he marches for my bathroom.

The second we're inside, he slams the door closed and locks the door. Then he turns on me with a feral, unhinged look in his eyes which I can't deny sends a bolt of lust-laced fear straight through me.

He prowls forward, a dark, dangerous cloud surrounding him.

"What's wrong, Angel? I didn't think you were scared of me."

I swallow nervously. "I'm not."

"So is there another reason you look like a rabbit caught in headlights right now?"

He steps closer, and before I know he's done it, he's backed me into the shower, caging me in with his solid body.

His eyes are darker than the dead of night, his nostrils flaring with desire, and his chest heaving beneath his black shirt.

It's covered in blood, I know it is. But I still can't find it in myself to be horrified by the state of him. Especially when it's impossible to ignore the way his cock is straining against his trousers.

I did that.

Me.

I affected the guy who prides himself on being cold, detached, and uncaring.

And he wants me something fierce right now. I can practically taste it in the air between us.

"Nikolas," I breathe as my back collides with the wall and he doesn't stop prowling toward me.

His jaw tics as I call him that, his breath catching.

"I'm not scared. But I think you're a coward."

His brows pinch in confusion a beat before his anger takes over.

"Wrong," he spits, suddenly reaching down and pulling something from his ankle.

"W-what are you doing?" I ask, my eyes darting between his and the knife he's just pulled.

"I killed a man tonight, Angel," he tells me, his voice flat and cold. "I tortured him until his body couldn't take it anymore, and I watched as the life drained from his eyes."

My breathing is so loud it's embarrassing as I stand there watching him, listening to him confess his sins.

"I spared the other two. For now. But by the time I left that room, they were unconscious from the sheer amount of pain and suffering I unleashed on them."

"Did you get the information you needed?" I ask, forcing myself to stay calm.

Daemon might be unhinged, but he doesn't do anything for no reason. The men he's talking about will have deserved it.

"Not enough, no."

"Maybe you shouldn't have killed one then," I state.

He presses the point of his knife against his palm, and I startle.

"W-what are you doing?"

His eyes lift from watching the blade and they find mine. He stares at me from under his lashes, dark hunger bleeding from him.

He steps closer again, not moving the knife from his hand.

"Since walking out of that building, there's only been one thing I've been able to think about."

My head spins as I wait for him to confess.

"I want to mark you, Calli."

Oh shit.

"I want to paint you in my blood. Make you mine."

"Y-you're c-crazy," I stutter.

"That's not news to anyone, Angel."

One second, he's standing before me with his knife poised and ready, and the next he's sliced the thing straight across his palm and it clatters to the floor.

"Daem—" His name is cut off as the length of his body presses against mine, his bleeding hand lands on the side of my neck and his lips slam down on mine.

I don't move for a second or two, but then he hooks one of my legs up around his hip, grinding himself against me.

His kiss is brutal, demanding, and I fucking drown in it.

Nothing about him is gentle as his teeth nip my bottom lip and tongue, his fingers digging into my arse as he holds me against him and his other hand touches me everywhere, doing exactly as he craved and painting me in his blood.

My body burns hotter than I've ever known, my

release surging forward faster than I'm sure it should from just grinding against him.

"Nikolas," I moan when he finally rips his lips from mine in favour of kissing, sucking, and biting down my neck.

My head falls back against the tiles. The fleeting thought of making him stop before I have to spend all tomorrow morning trying to cover up his marks is soon forgotten when he takes my vest in his hands and rips the thing clean in two to save pulling it over my head and breaking his kiss.

"Oh God," I moan as his hands cup my aching breasts.

Glancing down, I find exactly what I was expecting—red stains tainting my skin, just like they are his. Only mine doesn't belong to the enemy, just the devil.

My knickers go next, practically disintegrating under his touch.

"Fuck, you're beautiful," he growls, dipping lower and sucking on the sensitive skin of my breast before finally taking my nipple in his mouth.

My fingers curl in his hair, holding him in place as he drives me crazy. His eyes hold mine the entire time, watching every one of my reactions and eating up all of my cries and pleas for more.

"One day," he growls, "I'm going to make you come just like this."

"But not now?" I ask, sounding like nothing more than a desperate whore.

He chuckles, standing back up straight and denying me of any more torment from his maddening tongue.

He doesn't respond. Instead, he lifts his palm and runs his tongue up the length of the cut and then wraps his hand around the back of my neck, pushing his tongue into my mouth and letting me taste his blood.

"Oh God," I whimper.

This shouldn't be so good.

I should be disgusted, appalled. But all I can think about is getting more of him.

I lick deep into his mouth, my hands slipping up his shirt before I drag my nails down his abs, making him growl into our kiss.

"Need you, Angel. Need your fucking mouth on me."

Everything south of my waist clenches in desire at the image his words paint in my head.

Ripping his lips from mine, he stares deep into my eyes, his fingers twisting in my hair until it starts to burn.

"Get on your knees, Angel."

I gasp as I hit the hard floor beneath me and come to a stop directly in front of the massive tent in his trousers.

"What the fuck are you waiting for?" he barks, dragging me closer, forcing me to rub my nose up the length of him.

My mouth waters and my pussy clenches at the thought of tasting him again, of feeling him at the back of my throat.

"Angel," he groans, causing a wave of power to rush through me.

He's such an enigma in our group. The one no one really knows how to take, how to handle. He's dangerous, brutal, terrifying. And yet here he is, totally at my mercy.

Reaching for his waistband, I make quick work of getting it open and dragging both his trousers and boxers down over his hips.

I might have seen him before, but still, that doesn't stop me sucking in a shocked breath at the size of him, along with that silver piercing that seems to call to me.

Is that why he felt so good?

No. That was our connection. As unlikely as it is, something magical seems to happen when we collide, and I'm quickly becoming addicted to these stolen moments he keeps springing on me.

"Fuck," he barks when I wrap my fingers around the base of him and lick the tip. The taste of his precum floods my mouth, and it only serves to make me hungrier for him.

"Not so scary now, huh?" I mutter, looking up at him through my lashes.

The sight of his abandoned knife not far from his feet catches my eyes.

Ideas float around my head, ideas that I'm sure he would love.

The sadistic fuck seems addicted to a good helping of pain.

Suddenly, the stories I've been horrified by that

Stella and Emmie have happily told me seem to make more sense.

I bite on my bottom lip as I wonder if I'd be able to go through with it. Marking him in such a permanent way.

Claiming him.

The thought makes my heart rate turn damn near dangerous.

"Whatever it is you're thinking right now," he says, reaching to grab my chin and forcing my eyes back up to his, "don't forget about it."

Before I get a chance to respond, he pushes the head of his cock past my lips, cutting off anything I might have wanted to say to him.

The power I thought I had down here was just an illusion, because I don't get a chance to take any control of the situation as he thrusts in and out of my mouth, making me hold onto his strong thighs to stop me crashing to the floor with every punch of his hips.

Where's that innocent, naïve little princess now, huh? I think to myself as I take everything he has for me.

Just as his cock starts to swell, his grip on my hair tightens and I'm ripped back, his cock slipping from my lips.

"Wha—"

"I'm not finishing in your mouth, Angel. I dream about being so deep inside your cunt that you'll always remember I've been inside you, and I'm not letting this end any other way."

My feet leave the floor and my back slams against the cold tiles.

"If you've been dreaming of having a sweet guy who will give you the world and treat you like you're made of glass, then you're about to be disappointed, Angel."

"N-no, I don't—" My words are cut off as he slams inside me.

"Knew you'd be fucking dripping for me just from sucking my cock, beautiful," he groans in my ear as he stills for a beat.

I can't help but smile. He might claim to be brutal and only take, but that pause, no matter how brief, shows me that it's bullshit. He cares. He cares more than I'm sure he's even realised he lets on.

"Oh shit," I cry out when he finally pulls out before slamming back into me so deep I have no idea if I love it or hate it.

His fingers grip onto my arsecheeks leaving me with no doubt that I'll have his marks there as well as on my neck for days to come.

"Fuck," he grunts. "Your cunt just flooded. What were you thinking about?"

I hesitate—not because I don't have an answer, but because his punishing thrusts render me useless.

"Y-you," I finally force out. "M-marking me."

"Fuck, yeah. I'd write my name all over your beautiful skin if I could. You're mine, Callista. Mine."

I claw at his shoulders, wishing he'd shed his shirt

right alongside me but too lost to his brutal thrusts to even consider doing anything about it.

One of his hands leaves my arse and he slips it between our bodies, finding my clit and pinching it hard.

"Oh fuck. Fuck," I cry.

"Your pussy... fuck, Angel. I don't deserve this kind of pleasure."

"Yes, yes." I'm meant to be telling him that he does, but I'm not sure it comes across that way as I race to the finish line. "Nikolas, fuck."

"Come for me, Angel. I want to feel you milking my own cum right out of me."

"Yes, yes," I chant again as if it's the only word I can remember as I fall into the most intense release I've ever experienced. And he's right behind me, roaring loudly into the crook of my neck as his cock jerks inside me, filling me just as he promised.

"Oh God," I pant, barely able to drag in the air I need as my head falls back against the wall.

"Fucking perfect," Daemon mutters, his eyes taking in every inch of me as he lowers me to my feet and takes a step back.

His attention on my body makes me look down, and I gasp at the state of me. Blood covers my pale skin as his cum begins to slip down my thighs.

Reaching out, he drags his fingers up my leg until he's curling two of them inside me, pushing it all back inside as if it belongs in me instead of him.

Aftershocks shoot around my body as he teases me.

I'm too lost in the heady sensation to notice him press his hand to the shower control. I soon know what he's done when ice-cold water rains down on both of us, immediately soaking Daemon's clothes.

"Daemon, what the hell are you—"

My words falter as he reaches for my sponge and the bottle of shower gel on the side.

"Cleaning you up."

"I thought you liked me dirty," I quip.

His eyes flare with heat, but he doesn't stop what he's doing.

After lathering up the sponge, he moves closer, getting farther under the spray of the shower, and lifts it to my shoulder. He meticulously cleans every inch of me. The soothing circles he rubs against my skin are at complete odds with his brutal touch not so long ago, and just like everything with this enigma of a man before me, it makes my head spin.

Inch by inch, he washes away the blood he marked my body with.

His touch is hypnotic, but when he pulls his hand away and I catch a glance at the wound across his palm, everything comes crashing down around me.

I reach for him and pull his hand between us so I can look.

"We need to clean this up," I say softly.

In a move that makes my heart tumble, he snatches it back and curls it into a fist.

"It's fine."

His eyes hold mine and the dark resignation within

them tells me all I need to know about what's going to happen next.

"Don't, please." The words fall from my lips without instruction from my brain as I take a step toward him.

But it's pointless. He's slipped his cold, hard mask back into place, and I already know that there will be nothing I can say to change the decision he's made.

"I'm sorry."

19

———

DAEMON

The second I slam my front door behind me, I begin stripping out of my sopping wet clothes. It's easier said than done, especially when my cock swells the second I think of the girl I left behind in the shower.

She begged me not to go.

But I could hardly stay.

I'd used her to sate the anger and uselessness my dad had reignited in me, and that wasn't fair.

She's not my toy to play with and discard the second I fear she might just see more to me than I'm willing to show. And despite my claims, she's not my girl, either. Nor should she ever be. She deserves better than me, more than I'll ever be able to offer her.

With my clothes in soggy piles behind me, I step into the bathroom and come to a stop in front of the basin.

For the longest time, I don't lift my eyes from the taps. I can't. I'm too terrified of what I might find staring back at me.

Disappointment. Regret. Guilt.

Sucking in a deep breath, I force myself to look up.

My breath catches at the pathetic man staring back at me.

No wonder my father said what he did, thinks what he does.

My eyes drop to my body. Thanks to my shower with Calli, most of the blood and dirt from my hours with those three snakes has been washed away, leaving me with nothing but the scars of my past haunting me.

"You're too weak for this life."

"You'll never be the soldier we need you to be."

"You're not strong enough. Brave enough. Clever enough."

My father and grandfather's words ring out in repeat in my head as the evidence of them stares back at me.

I shower and fall into bed, my body on autopilot as I battle the demons in my head.

But unsurprisingly, I don't find any solace. Instead, I spend the few hours until sunrise staring at my ceiling, wondering if she was able to curl up and go back to sleep after her little midnight visitor.

When my alarm blares, I'm still lying in the same position I fell in. Only at the sound, I close my eyes.

I might hate it, but I've got to listen to Dad and go

to school if I want any kind of future in the Family. But it fucking pains me to do it.

I silence my alarm and swing my legs over the edge, ready to start what I already know is going to be a painful motherfucking day.

My phone starts ringing when I'm in the bathroom, showering once more in the hope it'll help clear my head, but even the thought that it could be Calli—it's not, I already know she'd never call after the way I left —isn't enough to drag me out to look until I'm good and ready.

I quickly discover that I was right not to run, because I find a missed call from my father.

I'm debating calling him back or just flat-out ignoring him when it rings again.

Only this time, it isn't Dad. It's worse.

"Boss," I growl, putting the phone to my ear.

"I hope you're getting ready for school, kid."

"Of course," I mutter, anger swirling within me that Dad's stooped so low as to call in the boss.

"I've spoken to Mr. Davenport and we've put extra sessions in place to ensure you get all the support you need in the lead-up to your exams. I've also spoken to Theo, and he said that he'd—"

"No," I bark, refusing to accept fucking tutoring off Theo.

"Daemon, we all just want to help."

"I'm fine. I can handle it myself."

"You've only got a few weeks. Now isn't the time to be too proud to accept help."

"I've got it under control," I growl, hoping like hell it's the truth.

"Right. Well, you're off duty while you make that happen. And if you don't, I'll stand by your father's wishes and ensure you're re-enrolled for September."

"Boss," I groan.

"You're a fantastic soldier, Daemon. An asset to our Family. Sometimes, we just have to jump through a few hoops to get where we want to be."

I mumble my agreement, but I don't think he realises that passing these exams, even if I have fewer than all the others do, isn't just as easy as jumping through a fucking hoop.

The second I hang up, my phone goes flying across the room, colliding with the wall that connects my flat to Alex's, and I roar out my frustration with the world into the silence of my home.

My phone dings, clearly not busted enough to no longer work.

Stalking over, I pick it up and stare at the screen.

Alex: You okay, Bro?

"Just fucking perfect."

Ignoring him, I stuff my phone into my pocket and head out for the strongest coffee I can make in the hope it helps get me through whatever bullshit Davenport has organised for me.

I t turns out to be back-to-back, one-to-one support sessions around my regular classes.

By lunchtime, I'm so close to walking straight out of that goddamn school I can barely see straight.

My head spins, the dull ache behind my eyes only getting worse with every passing second, and to top it all off, I'm fucking starving thanks to my lack of breakfast.

"Daemon, wait up," a familiar voice calls from behind me.

"What?" I bark, not bothering to look back.

"Dad said—"

"Fuck what your dad said, Theo. I don't need your help."

His concerned stare burns into the side of my face, but I still refuse to look at him.

"I never said you did. I'm sure you're more than capable of doing this yourself. But if you want a study partner or anything, just know I'm here," he says, softening the blow.

"I wouldn't keep your phone close for that call."

"The offer is there, man. And it can be between us."

"I said, I don't—"

"Right, got it. You going to the restaurant? Missed you this week, man."

Finally, I glance over at him, my brows damn near hitting my hairline at his words.

He's destined to be a part of the Family, but he'll end up working our accounts or something equally as safe and boring.

Ignoring the green-eyed monster that makes me want to drag her out of the room and lock her up somewhere only I can see her, I march up to the table as if everything is right in my world.

Movement by the door catches my eye, and I find Alex standing there with the black eye I gave him the night before, glaring death at me as I lower my arse beside Calli as if I haven't got a care in the world.

His jaw tics in annoyance.

Sorry, Bro. She's mine today.

She stiffens the second my shoulder brushes hers, and I have to fight the smirk that wants to curl at my lips, knowing that I'm affecting her.

"You look rough," she states loudly, turning all attention my way.

Dangerous, Angel. Very dangerous.

"Bad night?" Seb asks, concern pulling at his brows.

"You know how it is," I mutter, reaching for my fork, more than ready to dive into the array of food on my plate.

"Up all night studying, weren't you, D?" Theo says snidely as he sits opposite me.

"Something like that. I certainly learned a thing or two." I shoot a look at the girl next to me, whose hands are balled into fists beneath the table.

"So you've made progress?" Theo asks.

"Getting there. I think my intentions are starting to be understood."

"Good. Anything we can do to prevent the inevitable?"

A ripple of tension goes around the room. All of us —well, possibly not Calli, as everyone likes to keep her in some kind of protective bubble—know that war with the Italians is imminent.

Thankfully, the conversation turns to football, something I have less than zero interest in. The person beside me, however...

Finishing my food, I push my tray back and turn to Calli, one of my own hands dropping beneath the cover of the table.

"You ready for the holidays, baby C?" I ask, using the guys' name for her instead of my own.

"Hell yes," she says with a grin. "Weeks without having to see all you arseholes every day," she quips.

"Ouch, baby," Alex complains, clearly listening to every word we say. "I thought we had a good thing going on with our study dates."

"You sure seem to enj-joy it." She stutters as my little finger brushes her thigh, dragging her skirt up where no one can see.

"Oh, hell yeah I do," he smirks. "We're on again for tonight, right?"

Her breath catches when I get higher.

"Not tonight, playboy. It's cheer."

"Damn, Deimos. Even your buddy's sister is

turning you down now. That's a new low, even for you," Toby laughs, the last one of our group to appear.

"Tobes," Theo announces, standing up to welcome him back after the hell he's just lived through with Jodie.

With everyone's attention on him, it allows me a little space to tease my girl some more.

"You look a little tired yourself, baby C," I whisper. "Disrupted sleep?"

Her lips press into a thin line as she glowers at me.

"You need to stop."

"Aw, but watching your cheeks turn pink is too much fun."

A growl rips up her throat as my wandering fingers finally make it to the edge of her knickers.

She gasps, jumping back on the bench seat so violently that she almost tumbles off the back.

"Calli?" Stella questions, her brows pulled together at her friend's weird behaviour.

"S-sorry. I... uh... I thought I saw a spider."

Calli's face only glows brighter as all eyes turn on her.

"I-it wasn't," she confirms.

"Anyway," Nico says, thankfully brushing his sister's oddness under the carpet. "What's the weekend plans? It's the start of the holidays, someone must have a banging party on the cards for Friday night."

Theo, Seb, and Toby all glance at each other suspiciously.

"What? What am I missing?" Nico sulks like a child, as if he's being left out of something exciting.

"We're going on a triple date Friday night."

"A triple date?" Nico repeats, his face twisting, but I'm not sure if he's offended or amused by the prospect.

"Find yourself a decent, serious girl in the next two days and you're more than welcome to make it a quadruple date. I'm sure Brianna would be more than up for what we have planned."

"Fuck off, that ain't happening," he scoffs, much to everyone's amusement.

"Exactly, so you're gonna need to find someone else to delight with your presence," Toby says with a smirk.

"Cal, what about you? Heard of any decent parties I've accidentally not been invited to?"

Calli's eyebrows shoot up in shock. "Me? When have I ever been invited to a party without you?"

"Now, I'm hoping. I'm not spending the first night of the holiday at home alone."

"I'm sure you could find someone willing to put up with you," Calli mutters.

"Nah, he's already shown the girls in this postcode that he can't get them off for shit. They've all gone looking elsewhere."

"Fuck you, Alexander. Fuck you. When was the last time you had a girl screaming your name when she wasn't running away in fear?"

Alex's eyes shoot to Calli, and my blood turns to lava at the thought of him touching her.

My grip on her thigh tightens until she squeaks in warning.

"You're a fucking dick," Alex mutters.

"You two really need to get laid," Stella helpfully points out. "You're right cranky douchebags."

"Well, you would be if your only option for Friday night was hanging with your kid sister," Nico growls, getting my back up.

"I could think of worse things," I say, without meaning to let the words out loud.

"Sorry, Bro," Calli says before Nico gets a chance to respond to my comment, "I'm booked up, babysitting the brats." She shoots an amused look in Theo's direction. "You're more than welcome to—"

"Jesus. When did my life get so boring?"

"Careful what you wish for, man. We're on the cusp of shit getting real exciting," Theo warns.

Silence falls over our group as the stark reality of the situation settles over us.

"Right. Well, now we've discovered that Nico has no friends, I'm out," I say, noticing the teacher I'm meant to be having a lunchtime maths session with heading toward the exit.

I squeeze Calli's thigh again, wishing like hell I could lean in and kiss her before pulling my tray closer, ready to leave them, but Calli's soft voice stops me.

"What's wrong?"

I have to do a double-take at the concern that's pulling at her brows.

My stomach knots with the way she's looking at me. As if... as if she... cares.

The heat of everyone else's attention burns into the side of my face, forcing me to recover.

"I'm out," I repeat, ripping my eyes from her as if her words meant nothing and walking away.

20

CALLI

I watch Daemon walk away with a heavy heart.

There's something different about him today.

And while I might have turned up to school with the intention of ripping him a new one for the way he left me standing in the shower last night, the second he dropped beside me and I saw the defeat in his eyes, everything changed.

It shouldn't have. Deep down, I still want to be mad. But there's something about his aura today that stops it.

No one else seems to notice, and as he gets farther away from our group, their conversations start up again as if he was never here.

I sit there for as long as I can, but in the end, my concern gets the better of me.

I make my excuses about going to study in the

library for a bit and head off without anyone batting an eyelid.

I have no idea where he might have gone. Probably got in his car and left, from the look on his face and the tension pulling at his shoulders as he walked away from our table, but that's not going to stop me from searching.

I head toward the library like I said I was, but I take the long way around, looking into every classroom as I go, hoping he might be hiding in one of them.

But there's no such luck.

That all changes when I give up and push through into the library and head toward my favourite quiet corner.

Most people don't usually venture down here unless they're having private tutoring sessions on the other side of the tall bookcase I tuck myself out of sight behind.

My steps falter the second his deep, frustrated voice hits my ears.

"This isn't going to make a difference," he snaps, his tone lethal. I can't help but feel a little sorry for whoever is on the other end of his irritation. I hope to hell it's a teacher who can hold their own and not a kid who's offered to help. Not that I really think Daemon would accept anything from another student.

He keeps his... issues as quiet as possible, preferring to ignore their existence in the hope that everyone else does the same—or better, doesn't notice.

I guess this explains the attitude when he left the table.

"You keep putting too much pressure on yourself to get it right. Take it slower. Trust the process," a deep voice replies, and I breathe a sigh of relief that it sounds like a teacher. Any kid probably would have already run screaming by now. Daemon can make even grown men question their life choices with just one look, let alone teenagers.

"I have taken it slow. I've been at this for damn near two fucking years."

Someone lets out a heavy sigh. The teacher, I guess.

"Let's try this a different way."

I make myself comfortable, not because I want to listen, but because this is my little slice of heaven in a place that's filled with white noise and bullshit.

I pull my phone and my AirPods from my bag, but before I put them in, I check my messages. There's nothing from Ant. I know us cutting ties is how it needs to be. It's the right thing to do. But it still hurts. Pushing thoughts of him aside, I grab some homework I was given this morning that I need to make a start on.

I keep one eye on the end of the aisle, waiting for Daemon to leave in the hope that I can catch up with him.

Five minutes before the bell, I pack up and kill my music. The sound of Daemon's irritated grunts quickly replace it.

"You can fight this as much as you like, but we will make it happen."

"Doesn't sound like I have a lot of choice," he snaps. "Because if I don't..." His words trail off as my heart jumps into my throat.

If he doesn't what?

I quickly shove everything in my bag and make my way to the end of the bookcase, ready to intercept him.

Mr. Perkins appears first, looking thoroughly exasperated, and I can't help but feel for him. Dealing with Daemon must be draining. Hell knows I'm still feeling the effects of our rendezvous.

I wait until his shadow emerges before me, then I step out, blocking his exit.

It takes a second for his eyes to lift from the floor, and when they do, they're filled with shock.

Until it morphs into something much more terrifying.

Anger. Undiluted, red-hot anger.

His hand lifts, his fingers wrapping around my throat as he forces me back into the shadows.

My back slams against the wall, my bag falling from my shoulder and crashing to the floor.

"What the fuck are you doing?" he snarls, leaning in so close his nose almost touches mine and his scent floods my senses.

"I-I—" I stutter, unable to get my brain to function enough to formulate an answer.

"Did you follow me?"

"Uh..." I hesitate, because yes, in a way I did. But only out of concern, and I found him by accident.

"Why? To laugh at me? To find something you could use against me?"

"What?" I ask, finally finding my voice. "No. Never. I wouldn't do that."

"Then why are you fucking here?"

His dark and deadly grey eyes burn into mine, his fingers tightening on my throat as my entire body trembles, adrenaline shooting through my veins.

"I-I..." Swallowing, I give myself a second to get a grip. "I was worried, so I left the restaurant to see if I could find you. I didn't. But this is where I come to..."

"Come to what?" he growls harshly.

"Hide," I whisper.

"What the fuck have you got to hide from?"

"Aside from you, obviously?" I quip, earning myself another scowl. "I didn't sit here listening to your session. I put my AirPods in. But that doesn't mean I'm not concerned."

"I don't need your fucking concern, Angel."

"No, you just want me covered in your blood and full of your cock. Nothing else matters, right?" I throw back. Hurt twists up my insides, but I refuse to allow it to the surface.

His jaw tics, his teeth probably grinding to dust behind his pursed lips.

"What's going to happen if you don't pass these exams, Daemon?"

He stares at me for so long that I don't think he's going to answer me, but then his lips part. But I don't get anything like the kind of response I want.

"None of your business."

I shake my head at him, not willing to play this game with him while he's got his walls built up so high.

"Fine," I hiss. "Keep your fucking secrets and deal with your issues alone."

"It's what I'm used to."

"I remember a time when it wasn't," I shoot back, thinking back to when we were six and I found him in the den he and Alex had made at the bottom of their garden after he'd had an argument with Stefanos.

"That was a long time ago," he says, pain flickering through his eyes at the memory.

"You can talk to me, you know. Whatever it is, I can—"

"You're right," he snaps, cutting off my offer of help. "I only want you when you're full of my cock."

I gasp at the coldness in his confession, my heart splintering despite the fact that I know that I shouldn't care.

Whatever this is between us isn't serious. I'm just not sure I needed such a brutal reminder of that.

"Get your fucking hands off me," I hiss, forcing as much venom into my tone as possible.

My nails dig into his hand as I fight to drag his fingers from my throat, but he doesn't move or even attempt to loosen his grip.

Curling my other fist, I slam it into his shoulder as hard as I can.

"I said let go," I demand.

But he's not having any of it, and instead of taking

a step back, he closes the space between us. Pressing his hard body against the length of mine, he crowds me against the wall, ensuring I can't focus on anything but him and the anger that radiates from his every pore.

"Nikolas, what are you—"

His lips slam down on mine, stealing my words and my breath.

I resist for as long as I can, but when his tongue sweeps across my bottom lip for the second time, I act on instinct and kiss him back.

It's not until a growl of desire rumbles deep in his throat that reality hits me.

I sink my teeth into his bottom lip, and he pulls back with a feral look in his eyes.

"We're done here," I state, managing to slip out from between him and the wall.

Hitching my bag up on my shoulder, I walk away until there's a safe distance between us.

"When you're ready to apologise, or talk, or accept help or... Whatever. You can come and find me. And if I'm in a good mood, then I might just make time for you."

"You might?" he growls.

"Yeah, because right now, you don't deserve it."

I walk away with my head held high despite the fact that my heart is in shreds as the sound of his growl of frustration hits my ears, a beat before a gut-wrenching thud that can only have been his fist colliding with something.

Fuck him. Fuck him and his dark, stubborn, sexy—

"Fuck."

I expected to be woken in the middle of the night by the devil, but when I came to the next morning, I was surprised not to have received a visit.

But there was nothing. No evidence of him letting himself in and doing whatever the hell he does while I'm sleeping. Although the feeling that I had been watched at some point still made my skin prickle, as if I might find him hiding somewhere if I looked hard enough.

Until I stepped into the bathroom, and there, in the shower, exactly where I stood when he walked away from me on Tuesday night was his calling card. The small origami bat.

That's all I saw of him all day, aside from his back as he walked out of the common room the second I entered, as if he was too scared to look at me, face me.

I want to say that it didn't hurt, being dismissed quite so coldly. But it did.

I wanted him to talk to me. To confide in me. After all, we were already keeping huge secrets together. What's a few more between us?

I tried to put it behind me and focus on school, on everything I still needed to do in order to be prepared for my exams, but that's easier said than done.

"Do you have everything you need, Calli?" Selene asks as she walks into the kitchen, looking as glamorous as ever. If you didn't know she was the wife of a mob boss, then it wouldn't be hard to believe.

"We're good, thank you," I say my eyes flicking between Atlas and Larisa, who are sitting at the breakfast bar, working their way through activity books.

"Okay, well, as usual, order yourself whatever you want for dinner. And if anything goes wrong, I've got my phone."

"It's all under control, Selene."

"Thank you, Calli. I really appreciate you taking the time to help us out."

"Anytime," I say honestly. And I mean it. I really don't mind babysitting my cousins, I just prefer it to be my decision and not to have it dropped on me by my mum, who doesn't think I have anything better to do with my life.

"You're a good girl, Calli. We shouldn't be much later than midnight."

With a kiss on each of her children's heads, she walks toward the front door, calling up to Rhea, their eldest daughter who's hiding in her room.

Dragging a stool between the two of them, I set about helping with their sudokus, dot to dots, and word searches.

Before I know it, over an hour has passed and I'm convincing them that they need to head up to get ready for bed.

I place an order for mine and Rhea's favourite Chinese dishes, knowing that she'll emerge from her room to hang out once the other two are in bed. And after a few minutes, I head up to make sure they're doing as they're told.

I'm still sitting with Larisa, reading, when the doorbell rings almost thirty minutes later.

I check in on Atlas on my way to the stairs to find he's already out cold, and then I knock on Rhea's door to tell her the food is here before going to get it.

"Delivery," a happy voice sings as I pull the front door open and find Alex standing there with our dinner.

"Uh... didn't realise you had a job as a delivery driver. If you want a tip then I guess—"

"Fuck the tip. I'll take a kiss, though."

"Alex," I growl.

"What? It's only fair. Without me, you'd be going hungry right now."

"Or the guy you stole this off of on your way here would have handed it over instead and been happy with a fiver for his trouble."

"Pfft, what's he really gonna do with a fiver, anyway? A kiss from you can be wank bank material for months."

"You're gross."

"You want it?" he teases, holding the bag out of my reach. "You know the terms."

"Fine." The sound of Rhea's footsteps thunders down the stairs behind me as I lean in.

Alex's eyes light up, but a beat before I find his lips, I dart to the side and plant my kiss on his cheek.

"Thanks for the friendly service. Maybe stick to killing people in the future though, Deimos."

I grab the bag and move to shut the door, knowing that he's not going to allow that to happen.

"Whoa, whoa," he says, stepping into the hallway. "I came to hang and keep you company."

"Not necessary. Rhea and I are having a girls' night in."

"I'm down." He rubs his hand down his face. "My skin could do with a face pack. And my nails..." he says, inspecting them. "Pretty sure they've still got some cunt's blood under them from—" I sense Rhea step up behind me a beat before Alex swallows his words.

"Hi, Alex," Rhea says, her voice a little higher than I'm used to.

I turn around and find her cheeks glowing as she stares at him with a coy smile playing on her lips.

Oh boy.

"Are you coming to hang out with us?" she asks, hope pouring from every word.

"Hell yeah. What colour do you wanna paint my nails?"

She giggles, and Alex winks at me.

Jesus. Because his head needed to be any bigger.

They both head to the living room, Alex snatching back the bag of food.

"So what chick flick is first up?"

"Ugh, chick flick?" Rhea groans, making me laugh.

"We usually watch something a little more... grown up than that."

"Oh, like what?" Alex asks as they disappear around the corner.

By the time I've gathered plates and got us all drinks, the two of them are deep in conversation about the latest *Fast and the Furious* film. Alex is relaxed with his feet kicked up on the coffee table, while Rhea sits cross-legged facing him, soaking up every word that falls from his mouth.

"Get it out then, Deimos," I say—meaning the dinner—and instantly regretting my words.

"Callista, there are kids in the room," Alex says with an amused smirk.

"I'm not a kid," Rhea sulks. "I'm almost fifteen. And I know exactly what you guys were all doing at fifteen." She raises a brow at Alex, looking sassy as hell.

Theo is gonna bust a nut keeping this one in check over the next few years. They think they've had a hard time with me, but they're gonna have to step up their game.

"Fair play," Alex mutters. "But I gotta warn you, growing up too quick ain't all it's cracked up to be. Better to stay sweet and innocent as long as possible. Ain't that right, baby C?"

"I'm not getting involved," I mutter, lowering the plates to the coffee table.

The allure of food is enough to drag Rhea off the sofa. She drops to her knees beside me and quickly reaches for her favourite dish, piling it onto her plate.

Alex catches my eye over her head.

'She's cute,' he mouths.

'Behave,' I warn silently, making a knee-weakening smile spread across his lips.

Jesus Christ. Rhea's going to get her heart broken.

"You not eating, Alex?" she asks, sitting cross-legged on the floor while some shoot 'em up plays on the TV. Something I suspect she chose to impress our guest.

"You guys didn't order for me."

My brows shoot up. Alex never ever turns down food. He really is trying to be a gentleman tonight.

"There's plenty. Get down here," I say, unable to bear him watching us eat when I know he's dying for some.

We sit on the floor stuffing our faces until my arse hurts and I can no longer feel my legs. I have no idea what the film is about—we're too busy laughing and joking about life and school. And Alex seems to be playing some kind of game to see how quickly he can make Rhea blush, something he's earned more than a few jabs in the ribs for.

But it's fun, and it's allowed me to laugh in a way I didn't realise I was so desperate for.

"I need to pee," I say as I come down from the high of another laughing fit.

I've got tears in my eyes and my stomach muscles hurt, but it's so good.

I'm barely able to control my legs as I stand to full height and crash into Alex, using his shoulder for support as I wait for the feeling to come back to my legs.

"You need a hand?" he offers.

"To use the bathroom?" I quirk a brow at him. "No, I think I've got it."

Gathering up some of the empty tubs, I make my way through to the kitchen, abandoning them for later before heading down to the bathroom.

My skin tingles as I step back into the hallway, as if I'm being watched.

Ignoring it, I push forward. And it's not until I've got my fingers wrapped around the handle, about to let myself in that I realise I really should have put a little more thought into that feeling.

My heart jackhammers as a hand wraps around my throat and a long, hard body presses against me, forcing me inside.

"Daemon, what the hell are you—"

My words are cut off when he pushes me back up against the door and slams his lips down on mine.

My hands land on his chest, less than gently, as I try to push him off me.

But his weight is too much, and eventually, I have no option but to give in to what we both know is inevitable.

A loud growl rips up his throat when I finally cave and return his kiss, licking deep into his mouth and accepting everything he's offering me as his body continues to crush mine, his cock hard and insistent as he grinds it against my stomach.

"What are you doing?" I breathe when he finally releases my lips in favour of my neck.

"Reminding you who you belong to," he groans against the sensitive patch of skin beneath my ear.

"I'm not yours, Nikolas," I argue.

"We'll see."

"Oh, shit," I gasp as his hand dips under my dress and pushes into my leggings.

A growl rumbles in his throat as he drags his fingers through me, finding me wet and ready.

"I really hope this is for me, Angel."

"Oh God," I whimper as he circles my clit.

"Tell me, Angel. Is this for me... or him?"

I bite down on the insides of my lips to stop me from answering.

When he realises, his movement stops, making me cry out in frustration.

"Tell me, or I'll send you back out there dripping wet and desperate."

My eyes narrow in anger.

"I'm sure he could finish the job," I taunt. It's a low blow, but that seems to be where we've fallen in this little game we're playing.

"Don't fucking push me, Angel. You won't like the outcome. And I think there's a set of young eyes out there who probably wouldn't appreciate it if I carried you out and fucked you over the coffee table to make a point."

"No," I cry in panic.

"Right, so tell me. Is this for me..." He pushes his

hand lower, dipping two fingers inside me and bending them just so. "Or him?"

"You," I cry. "It's for you."

A devilish smile pulls at his lips as I make that confession.

His fingers don't stop as his eyes flick between mine and my swollen lips.

There are a million questions on the tip of my tongue and even more reasons why I shouldn't be letting this happen. But none of them are enough to stop me.

My final words to him the other day in the library still stand, and I'm more than aware that he's here through pure jealousy and not because he wants to talk about anything. But still, as he plays my body as if it was meant for him, I'm powerless to stop him.

"Fuck, I need you," he groans, threading the fingers of his free hand through my hair and claiming my lips once more.

He drags me from the door as if I'm nothing more than a rag doll before ripping his lips from mine and forcing me to stand over the basin.

"Eyes on me, Angel," he demands, dragging my head up so I have no choice but to look at him standing behind me in the mirror.

My breath catches at the darkness surrounding him. His eyes are black, his lips full and parted as he tries to catch his breath.

I did that.

Something crackles between us as we just stare at each other in the silence of the bathroom.

I know I need to get back out there, that they're going to come searching for me soon, but I'm ensnared by this complicated and dangerous man.

Our connection is finally severed when he flips my dress over my back and drags my leggings and knickers down my thighs.

"When you walk back out there, it's going to be with my cum dripping out of you, Angel, reminding you just who you belong to while you laugh with my brother."

"Oh God," I whimper as he swipes the head of his hard cock through my wetness.

"You got that? You're mine, Callista. You're my angel, not his."

"Yes, yes," I cry, desperate for him to stop teasing and push inside me.

I need the sting of him filling me, stretching me open until I swear I'm going to rip in two just for him.

"Please, I need—" My words get stuck in my throat as he finally thrusts forward. His hand in my hair ensures I don't crash straight into the basin. He holds me exactly as he wants me, keeping our eyes locked as he ruts into me hard.

"Can't get enough of this, Angel."

"Th-then you sh-should stop being such a..." His brow lifts as I fight to get my words out. "Arsehole, and y-you might get—"

Crack.

My arse burns with the force of his slap and I scream out, my pussy clamping down on his length, making him growl.

"Fuck," he grunts. "Fuck."

He spanks me again, and a scream rips from my lips.

Not two seconds later, my heart jumps into my throat when my name echoes through the door before Alex knocks.

"Are you okay?" he asks, concern lacing his voice as my eyes widen on Daemon's in the mirror.

He tilts his chin, instructing me to handle this situation.

Swallowing down my panic, I suck in a deep breath.

"Y-yeah, I'm fine. I'll be right out." Thankfully, I sound almost normal as I call back.

"Cal, are you— yeah, okay. I'm just getting us more drinks."

He lingers at the door for a few seconds, as if he's not convinced by my words, but eventually, his footsteps start moving away from us.

Daemon's movements begin increasing once more.

"W-we can't," I whisper, my heart trying to pound right out of my chest at coming so close to being caught.

"Like fuck we can't," he grunts, hips thrusting forward as his hand releases my hips in favour of letting his fingers strum my clit until I have no choice but to fall over the edge.

My teeth sink into my lips until the copper taste of blood fills my mouth as I fight to keep any verbal reaction inside.

Daemon twists his fingers in my hair, pulling until it burns and I'm dragged upright.

His mouth latches on to my throat, his teeth sinking into my skin as his cock swells inside me.

A deep rumble erupts from his throat, his dick jerking violently inside me as he lets go.

"You're mine, Angel. And if you let him get anywhere near you tonight, he's going to know. You smell like me, you're full of me, you're covered in my marks."

My chest heaves, his words making my head spin.

"He's going to hate you," I whisper, unable to look away from him in the mirror.

"I don't care."

21

DAEMON

My skin prickles with her attention as my lie sours on my tongue.

"Bullshit," she spits.

My hand trembles against her hip and I pray to anyone who'll listen that she can't feel it.

She can already see deeper into my soul than anyone else. She already knows too much.

It's one of the many reasons that should have kept me away tonight.

I tried to do the right thing.

I sat my arse on my sofa, surrounded by fucking textbooks and everything I should have been doing. But I couldn't focus.

Instead of maths, my head was full of her.

I knew she was here—she'd let that slip the other day at lunch—and the temptation to sneak in and surprise her was burning through me hotter than it should have.

I had every intention of heading over to keep her company, assuming the kids had gone to bed.

I didn't have a clue about kids. I barely even remember being one myself, if I ever was, but I told myself that waiting until past ten pm would be safe and I headed over.

The last fucking thing I expected to find after I parked down the street and walked into the boss's driveway was Alex's car next to the one I rescued from the Italian's warehouse. I'd left Calli tied to my bed to ensure she'd still be there when I got back from covering her tracks.

Fury coiled in my stomach as jealousy dripped through my veins, quickly poisoning me from the inside out.

The image of them curled up on the sofa together watching a film, drinking, laughing...

I've seen first-hand how close they've become, and while I might not have done anything about it so far for fear of Alex, anyone, finding out the truth, I don't fucking like it.

She's mine. The light in all my dark. The angel to my devil.

The fucking air I need to breathe.

"I see you, Daemon. I see more than you think, and I know you love your brother something fierce, even if you don't want to show it."

My teeth grind at her words.

"It's why you didn't just storm in there and announce your presence. It's why you didn't let yourself into my basement the other day and drag me from his body. You don't want to hurt him."

"No," I argue, my cock softening and slipping from her body.

She spins around the second I stumble back, her eyes boring into mine.

"I see you, Daemon. You can't hide from me."

My chest heaves as I stare at her, terrified that she might just be right.

I've given her more of me than I have anyone else, but I fear she may have managed to bury even deeper than I thought.

When I don't respond, she changes tack.

"You need to leave."

"W-what?" I stutter, not expecting those words to fall from her lips.

"You need to leave. I need to clean up, and you're not going to stand there and watch me."

"And what about Alex?"

"What about Alex? You snuck in, knowing he was here. I assume you had a plan for that," she snaps, her fire making my cock begin to swell again.

She enthrals me when she's quiet, watching what's going on around her and gets lost in her own head. But when she lets that fire burn, I quickly find myself falling deeper under her spell.

My lips part, but I quickly find that I have no words.

"Go walk out there and spend the night hanging

out with us, if you want," she suggests. "Rhea's going to bed soon. We could—"

"Don't," I growl. Really, I have no idea what she's about to suggest, but the images that pop into my head aren't ones we need to discuss.

I might not have put a stop to what's been growing between the two of them, but that doesn't mean I'm going to encourage it in any way.

"Just... don't."

A smile curls at her lips as she studies me.

"Jealousy looks good on you, Nikolas. Who knew you were capable of such feelings."

My teeth grind and her smile widens.

Damn her for knowing exactly what buttons to press to get a reaction out of me.

"What do you expect, when the girl who should be mine is out there playing games with not only my twin brother but also our enemy?"

"I'm not playing games with— No," she interrupts herself. "I'm not getting into this with you now. I don't owe you an explanation for any of it. Especially when you refuse to talk to me. Just leave. We're done here."

"Fine. But I won't be far away. Don't do anything stupid."

Her nostrils flare at my warning, but she refuses to speak the words that are right on the tip of her tongue.

Instead, she just backs farther into the corner, giving me easy access out.

"I'll see you soon, Callista. Don't do anything that's going to need to be punished. Or do. Whatever."

I slip out of the room while she stands there, silently fuming, hoping that I'm not about to walk headfirst into my brother.

I wouldn't put it past the poor, lovesick sap to be at the end of the hall, waiting, worrying that something's wrong with Calli.

Thankfully, he's not, and I can hear his laugh coming from the living room where they were all hanging out when I first let myself in the back of the house.

Pulling open Damien's office door, I slip into the dark room, leaving it ajar so I can watch her when she finally emerges.

I don't have to wait very long before the door just a little down the hall opens and her soft steps pass me.

Her heavy sigh makes me smile.

Following her, I come to a stop on the other side of the wall to hear Alex's reaction, because after what we just did, there's no way she's walking back in there looking as composed as she did walking out.

"Calli, what's wrong?" Rhea asks, her soft voice full of genuine concern.

"Calli?" Alex's deep voice hits me in the chest.

"I'm okay," she says, her voice light as if she's trying to play it off.

"You've been gone ages, and you look—"

"I think I had a reaction to something I ate," she explains, making me shake my head. Although, I can't deny the pride that swells within me.

I should probably be worried that she's able to lie so easily to him. To cover her dirty tracks so smoothly, but I'm not. I already know her darkest secrets, and I fully intend on discovering any others she has before long, too.

"Shit, come and sit down," he encourages. "Do you need anything? A glass of water?"

"No, I'm okay. I think it's passed."

"A cuddle on the sofa it is, then. You know, I've always fancied myself as something of a doctor."

"You hate blood," she points out.

"Only my own," he argues, and I don't need to look around the doorframe to know that he's pouting.

"Ugh," Rhea complains. "You two are annoyingly cute."

My heart begins to race as I consider Calli caving to his offer of a cuddle.

Taking a huge fucking risk, I lean forward, desperate to see what's happening on the other side of the wall.

I don't need to lean far.

My breath catches in my throat as I stare at my girl in my brother's arms.

My fists curl, my nails digging into my palms hard enough to draw blood as my pulse races and my jealousy burns hotter than ever.

How can't he smell the sex on her? Smell me on her?

Is he that fucking lovesick and delusional?

As if she knows I'm here, her eyes meet mine in the

glass unit I'm watching them in, and all the air rushes from my lungs.

She smiles. The little fucking minx smiles.

She knows exactly what she's doing, despite the fact that she told me only minutes ago that she's not playing games with Alex.

She may have told him that she's not interested, but as she leans into his side, she's giving him a very different idea. Even if her reasons for doing so aren't to lead him on but to torture me, to try to force my hand into admitting what I want outside of our stolen moments in the dark.

"Rhea," Calli warns. "I think it's bedtime, don't you?"

Rhea huffs like a petulant kid, and I stand there a little longer, expecting her to argue. But to my utter shock, she just gets to her feet and begins moving toward me.

"Shit," I hiss, needing to find a hiding place and fast.

I dart toward the under stairs cupboard and just close the door before her footsteps hit the wooden floor of the hallway.

My head spins and my blood rushes past my ears.

I've done a lot of scary shit in my life. But there is nothing more terrifying to me than people finding out I've got a weakness.

That my dark and twisted heart does actually beat.

And only for one person.

"What the actual fuck, Bro?" Alex barks a second after the lights come on around me, illuminating his bedroom at Dad's house.

He glares at me, his heart probably trying to beat out of his chest at finding me sitting on his bed in the dark.

I didn't know if he'd come back here, but seeing as it's closer to Damien's place than our flats, I took a punt that he might show his face—assuming he didn't stay the night with Calli, of course.

My stomach twists at the thought alone.

He pulls his piece from behind his back and places it on the side, making my brows pull together. Why the fuck did he need that for babysitting?

"Where have you been?" I ask, despite the fact that I know the answer.

"What the fuck is it to you? And why the fuck are you sitting in my bedroom in the dark like a creep?"

I shrug, as if this is fucking normal.

Truth is, I was waiting, waiting and drowning in the memories of the past that being in this house drags up.

There was a very good reason I was the first to move into our new building the second my flat was habitable.

I needed out of this place. I needed to no longer be the person I was when I lived under this roof, shackled by the opinions of those who tried to keep me down, to tell me I wasn't good enough.

"Because I am a creep," I say simply.

"Right. Well, if you don't mind, I kinda wanna go to bed," he mutters, swinging his door closed and pulling his hoodie off.

Ignoring my existence as if I'm going to disappear into thin air, he walks into our Jack and Jill bathroom to take a piss.

"So where have you been?" I ask again.

He hesitates, and I start to think that he's not going to tell me. But after a few more seconds, he sighs before flushing the toilet and shouts, "At the boss's, babysitting with Calli. Why?" he asks, emerging again, kicking off his jeans and throwing himself onto his bed behind me.

"Just wondered. I hear the others were having a private party in Hades."

He glares at me. "How is it that you're mostly absent from our lives but know exactly what everyone is doing?"

"It's a talent you obviously didn't get, much like your ability to shoot a gun."

"Fuck you. I'm a good shot and you know it."

"What was with the gun if you were just babysitting the minions?"

He shrugs. "It was in my car. Figured I should bring it in." There's something in his eyes as he says those words which makes me frown.

"You're lying."

"So fucking what if I am? You're off the clock,

remember? Daddy wants you to play teacher's pet for a few weeks."

"Yeah, I got that fucking memo."

"Taking it well, I see," he quips, getting himself comfortable and pulling the sheets up to his chin. Lucky motherfucker will no doubt fall straight to sleep the second I stop talking to him and be out of it for a solid eight hours. He's always been the same. And once he's out, that's it. There's no fucking waking him until he's good and ready.

"What the hell do you think?"

"Just accept Theo's help, man. There's no shame in that. He wants to do it."

"I don't want his fucking charity."

"He's your friend. He wants you to pass. He wants you happy."

"I'll think about it if you tell me why you needed a gun for babysitting."

"You're being kept out of the loop for a fucking reason, man. Dad wants you to focus, not worry about Italian shit."

A warning growl rumbles deep in my throat as I stare down at his sleepy eyes.

He rolls them in exasperation. "Dad's worried the Italians are about to strike. We're just on high alert."

"He thinks they could go after one of us?" After Calli, is what I really want to ask, but I swallow those words down.

"Nothing is confirmed. They want the businesses, but seeing as we made the first move by killing their men, Dad isn't ruling it out. We're just being cautious. Protecting those around us."

"If that's the case, I need fucking back in," I growl. "You need to talk to Dad."

"No," he barks, determination that I don't hear all that often, deepening his voice. "What you need is to pass these exams so you can reclaim your life. Let me help, let Theo help, hell, let Isla help if you want. But you have to do this."

"And what if I can't?"

"You already know the consequences. And if that is the case, then you could have no more part in this war."

"Fuck," I bark, scrubbing my hand down my face.

"You can do this, D. I've got faith in you. Just stop being so fucking hard-headed and accept that your friends are here for you. Even if you're not always here for us," he adds just to drive the knife in a little.

"When the fuck have I not had your back, A?"

The shoulder he's not laying on lifts.

"I'm going to sleep. Go study, seeing as you probably won't get any."

"Why exactly are you still coming back here when you've got your own flat? Dad's house is nice, but shit, man."

"I like it," he mutters sleepily. "The view is often pretty good."

"Jesus Christ," I mutter, pushing to my feet and walking through the bathroom to my old room.

I hate the weak and pathetic little boy this room

represents, and no sooner have I walked in do I walk straight back out again, quickly leaving the house.

I don't care how nice Dad's new housekeeper is to look at, she's not worth me hanging around—not that she'd be here gone midnight anyway. Or at least, I hope she's not. Wouldn't be the first time I've stumbled into one long before her shift started, wearing just one of Dad's shirts, since Mum left a few years ago.

22

CALLI

The weekend has been long and dull. Probably the exact opposite of how the first weekend of the school holidays should be, but there we are.

Mum and Dad have been suspiciously present upstairs, which has meant I've spent even more time than usual locked down in my basement. I've studied until I can no longer focus, and I've spent hours playing around on my iPad, coming up with new designs. I've even looked into setting up an online store as Emmie suggested, but just the thought of turning this into something more than a hobby scares me shitless.

Emmie and Stella have delighted me with tales of their night in Hades with their guys, most of which conjured up images I never ever needed in my head. I'm still trying to get to grips with the fact that Toby has some major kinks he's kept hidden from us all, let alone them all indulging in the illicit things Hades has to offer.

Of course, I've never actually visited.

My knowledge of what's inside is purely from my own imagination, and a cheeky read of a certain trilogy last year when my curiosity became too much for me to ignore.

My final call with Stella ended with her telling me that I must be ready by midday today and that I needed to pack a bag for a couple of days away.

She's still refusing to tell me where we're going. Emmie too. And even my attempts to get the intel out of Alex on Friday night quickly fell flat when I discovered that he was as in the dark about the whole thing as I was.

My only relief all weekend was when my phone dinged on Saturday night and I found Ant's name staring back at me.

He might have told me Monday night that he wanted me, that he couldn't get me out of his head, but we both know that the most sensible thing to do is to put an end to whatever was between us before anyone else finds out. Daemon knowing is bad enough. But if my dad or Ant's uncle find out, then there's every chance one of us would end up six feet under. Maybe even both of us, if we're really unlucky.

At two minutes before midday, I throw my bag over my shoulder, hoping I've packed everything I might need for our mystery trip, and head upstairs.

Mum is lying on her chaise in front of the French

doors that look out over the garden, reading some interior design magazine, probably planning a makeover on a room that really doesn't need any work.

"I'm going away with Stella and Emmie for a few days."

"I know," she says without looking up from her magazine. "Have fun. Stay safe."

My brows pinch at her lack of care or effort.

"I'll see what I can do," I mutter, barely loud enough for her to hear me. "It's not like I was planning on being unsafe anytime soon."

I'm still rolling my eyes as I pull the front door open and find Stella pulling up in her matte black Porsche.

"You ready for a road trip?" she calls from her window as I jog down the stairs.

Am I ready for going anywhere with my girls and getting away from reality for a few days? Hell freaking yes, I am.

The second I throw my bag in the boot and hear more female voices from inside, my stomach knots.

"Hey," both Jodie and Brianna say excitedly from inside.

"What's this, the jolly girls' outing?" I ask with a smirk, my pulse thundering when my eyes lock with Brianna's knowing ones.

"The boys are meeting us there. We just thought it would be fun to have a bit of girl time."

I swallow nervously, slipping into the back seat beside Bri.

"Yeah, sounds good. We're getting food though, right? I'm starving."

Stella and Emmie laugh. "Would it even be a road trip without food?"

"I guess not," I mutter as she spins the car around and heads back out to the road. "So are you going to fill me in on the details yet?"

"I wouldn't get your hopes up. We have no idea either," Jodie says with a laugh.

"It's good to see you, Jodie," I say sincerely, looking around her best friend. "How are you feeling?" She smiles brightly at me, but I don't miss the darkness of her suffering flicker through her eyes.

"I'm good. Really good, actually. I've moved in with Toby," she blurts, focusing on the good aspects of her life, as if hearing it is going to be a shock.

"We're all just surprised it took so long," Stella offers.

"She's not wrong," I agree. "When those boys want something, there isn't much to stop them from getting it."

"Is that right?" Bri asks, eyeing me closely.

"Yep, so you'd better watch your back with Nico," I warn before she gets a chance to turn this on me. Honestly, I don't think she would. I think she's loyal to the core. After all, it's been a week since she found me running from Daemon's flat like I had the devil snapping at my heels, and I have no reason to believe she's told anyone that she rescued me with her emergency knickers.

"Ah, but there's a difference there. He doesn't want me. He—"

"No, he just wants your pussy," Jodie finishes for her.

"Ew," I complain lightly. But in all honesty, I'm pretty numb to conversations that involve sex and my brother. They've almost become normal, which should probably be concerning, but this is Nico we're talking about. I swear the guy only possesses one brain, and it's not leaving his cock anytime soon.

"And my mouth. He reckons I was the best head he's ever had."

"Nico is a bullshitter, Bri. I wouldn't put too much weight on anything he tells you."

"I think she probably figured that out when he dropped his trousers and she realised he wasn't rocking the thirteen-inch beast he probably promised her," Emmie barks.

Laughter rips through the air and joy fills my heart. I've missed this so much. I was starting to feel like a prisoner in my own home. It's so good to be free and kicking back with my girls.

"You don't always need the size if he knows what to do with it," Bri announces happily.

"I don't know about that," Emmie states. "I've got both, and I couldn't be happier."

"Tell us more, girl. What's Theo got packing in his pants?" Bri asks, leaning forward between the front seats, sounding way too serious about this conversation.

"Uh-uh," Emmie tuts. "That's for me to know, love and abuse only."

"Spoilsport. I haven't got laid in..." She uses her fingers to count. "Three days."

"Three days, seriously?" Stella laughs. "If you want sympathy, you'd need to be dry for at least a week."

"A week?" Emmie blurts. "There's no way you've gone a dry week since you and Seb started hooking up."

"Did I say I had?" she scoffs, shaking her head as she pulls into the Burnt Coals for burgers. "I was just saying that as a suitable amount of time to complain about."

"Well, good thing you've got Nico's not-quite-thirteen-inches to keep you company for the next few days then," Emmie says loudly as Stella pulls up to the window, revealing an embarrassed-looking kid staring back at us.

"Give the guy your orders then, ladies, and let's get this show on the road."

***

Unsurprisingly, the conversation stalled once we all had bagfuls of junk food on our laps. And once we finished, thankfully the topic of conversation was no longer anything to do with my brother's body parts.

We talked about nonsense shit, sang along to the music Stella had pumping through the speakers, and just relaxed as we left real life behind. Although it was easy to see that Jodie struggled with that prospect more than the rest of us.

I sit forward when the GPS in the middle of Stella's dash shows that we're only two minutes out.

"You're aware that we're in the middle of nowhere, right?" I ask, getting a little concerned that this trip is going to involve tents and dirty toilet facilities. I don't want to be a princess or anything, but I'm kinda fond of being warm, dry, and having access to running water.

"Trust me, Cal. Have I steered you wrong yet?"

"Pretty sure my brother and parents would suggest you have," I mutter lightly.

"Well yeah, I threw the doors open on your ivory tower and started showing you the world."

"And things have never been the same since," I quip.

"Right. And you even live in the den of sin now."

"Please, don't call it that. Just stick with den."

Or Batcave.

Shit. I shake that thought from my head.

I tried banishing him from my thoughts after I watched him walk away from me on Friday night. But the insistent dick just keeps popping up. No pun intended.

"So are all the guys coming?" I ask, hoping that the question doesn't sound too loaded. Although the second it's out of my mouth, I feel Bri's intrigued stare as I lean forward and hold onto Stella's headrest to get a better look at where we're going.

"Well, not Daemon, obviously. Seb invited him.

Gave him the address in case he changes his mind. But he's being antisocial as usual."

"He's been even weirder recently," Emmie murmurs.

"He's having a hard time with school," I blurt, regretting it the second the comment leaves my lips.

"Oh?" Stella asks.

"Alex told me," I say in a rush.

"I heard you two had a babysitting date Friday night," Emmie says, glancing over her shoulder and wiggling her brows at me.

"It wasn't a date. He just came to keep me company. It was nice."

"Nice, sure," Jodie joins in. "That boy is so hot for you, Calli."

"I'm not interested in Alex. He's my friend. That's it," I sulk, crossing my arms over my chest and falling back into my seat.

"Have you told him that?" Stella asks.

"Of course I have. Over and over. He's like a dog with a bone."

"Oh, there's definitely a bo—"

"Don't say it," I growl, fighting a laugh as I interrupt Emmie.

"We're here," Stella sings as she turns off the main road and begins down a bumpy track.

"I swear to God, Doukas, if you're about to pull up to tents, we're going to be having serious words about our friendship. I don't think— holy shit," I gasp when she turns the corner and what I'm hoping is our accommodation appears through the trees.

"Oh wow, that's... cute," Jodie breathes, her nose damn near pressed against the window to get a better look.

"Looks like we beat the boys, too," Emmie says.

"Did you see the length of the shopping list we sent them off with? They'll be a while yet."

"I can't believe you put some of that stuff on there," Jodie laughs.

"What did you ask them for?" I lean forward, intrigued.

"Oh you know, the usual. Tampons. Vag wash."

"Jesus," I mutter, climbing from the car. "They're gonna love you lot for that."

"We'll make it up to them," Emmie says as I move forward.

"So what do you think? Better than camping, right?" Stella says, closing in behind me as I take in the tipis in the trees before us.

"This place is incredible."

"Officially, it's not open until the weekend. We're the guinea pigs."

"I'm not even going to ask how you found out about this."

"Just enjoy it, Cal. Come on, let's go explore."

We step through two of the tipis to find a huge decked courtyard, complete with hot tub, bonfire, barbecue and benches, logs, loungers, and hammocks to chill out in.

"The big one is the communal kitchen living area," Stella says, pointing it out. "And the others are all bedrooms." I spin around, looking at the little bridges that connect the five smaller huts to the main area. Fairy lights are strung up between them all, and I can only imagine how magical this place will be when the sun goes down later and the bonfire is crackling away.

"I really landed on my feet with you lot, huh?" Jodie mutters, her eyes wide in shock.

"There are six of these set up, scattered through the woods."

"I take back everything I said about reevaluating our friendship," I say with a laugh as Stella leads us to the main tipi to check it all out.

It was almost two hours later by the time the rumble of an engine carried over the crackling of the fire that the five of us had managed to start and keep going.

Stella and Emmie looked at me like I was crazy when I admitted that I'd never started a fire before. I have no idea why they were so surprised—they point out often enough just how smothered I've been by all the males in my life since the day I was born.

Their eyes all lit up, much like I'm sure ours did, as they walked toward us, taking in our lodgings for the next few days.

Unsurprisingly, Alex's eyes searched me out and he

quickly made a beeline toward me, squeezing his arse onto my lounger and wrapping his arm around my shoulders, much to Nico's annoyance.

But his reaction was the last thing I cared about in that moment as the five of them made themselves comfortable. All I could think about was the person who was missing. The one who'd once again been left behind. It didn't matter that he'd been invited and refused. My heart still ached for the boy who was always on the sidelines as we grew up, watching the guys all form bonds and experience things without him.

And as the night went on, that knot in my stomach and dull pain in my heart only got worse.

"You waiting for an important call or something?" Alex asks, dropping onto the bench beside me. The others are all sitting around the bonfire, drinking and roasting marshmallows as instructed by Stella.

In a rush, I push my phone into my hoodie pocket and plaster a fake smile on my face.

I'd sent the message to Daemon hours ago.

He's read it, too.

Those little blue ticks have taunted me ever since.

But he's not so much as sent me a fucking emoji back.

I silently fume as Alex gets comfortable beside me.

"N-no. I was just scrolling through Insta," I lie, hating that I've been reduced to this. Hating everything.

His stare burns into the side of my face, and my

shot nerves over this whole situation almost get the better of me.

"Alex, I've got something I need to—"

"NICO," Brianna squeals. Her chair crashes against the decking as she jumps to her feet, her bottle of beer going flying as she takes off, Nico chasing after her.

"He wants her," Alex mutters with amusement.

"What gave you that idea?" I quip, watching as Nico catches up to Brianna and throws her over his shoulder, effectively flashing us her thong-clad arse in the process.

"You barbarian. Put me down," she squeals, slamming her clenched fists down on his arse and kicking her legs frantically.

"I never thought I'd see the day," Alex mutters as the others all laugh, enjoying the company and our freedom.

"What day?" I ask absently.

I might be watching the scene play out in front of me, but inside, I'm still worrying about Daemon, still panicking over the fact I almost told Alex, and still waiting for a damn message.

"That Nico got himself pussy-whipped."

"Oh right, yeah. Same."

"You know, if those two hook up, you're gonna have to bunk in with me again. Seems to be becoming a bit of a tradition for us, huh?"

I swallow nervously, ripping my eyes from my brother, I look back at Alex.

"Uh…"

"Sorry, you were about to tell me something," he says, smiling at me encouragingly.

I shake my head, pushing to my feet and walking away.

"Calli?" he calls after me, but I don't stop. I can't.

"I just need the bathroom," I shoot over my shoulder as I head toward the tipi that Brianna and I claimed as ours long before the boys even got here.

The second I'm hidden from the others, I pull out my phone and bring it to life.

"Where are you?" I hiss, hating that I'm losing my mind over a boy who still insists on holding himself back.

I shouldn't care that he's not here. I shouldn't care that he's missing out. It's been this way for years, and it's never bothered me this much before.

So why now?

Why do I feel like we all left a massive part of us behind all of a sudden?

Because he's let you in. He's let you see more than all the others do, even if he doesn't want to admit it.

You've seen his pain, his loneliness, his demons.

23

DAEMON

I stare at my phone with my teeth clenched and my hand shaking with my grip.

Angel: Are you okay? You should come join us.

Confusion wars inside me. I've done the right thing since being sent away from Damien's house on Friday night. Or at least, I've let her think I have. Truth is, I've been watching her every night, feeding my obsession and soothing my worry over the fact that neither Alex nor Ant has visited her.

It allows me to be able to lie to myself that the words I growl to her every time I near her could be true. That she could be mine.

She sent this message hours ago. It was the final thing that shattered my restraint—if I have any, when it comes to Calli—and I got straight in my car and followed the dots of their trackers, all the while making myself invisible so if I decided to make my presence known, I could turn up as a ghost in the night and have none of them expecting it.

The second I open the car door, quiet laughter floats down, making my stomach knot and my chest ache.

Yes, I was invited. But like every invite I get, I never feel it's sincere. They ask because they feel it's their duty to try to include me instead of actually wanting me here.

With the sun long set, I'm able to stalk through the trees while having almost perfect vision of their... camp, I guess.

Seb had explained the place to me, shown me pictures even in his attempt to convince me to come with them. But while it might have looked impressive online, it's nothing compared to reality.

There's nothing around here. Literally nothing. And the only thing that can be heard aside from them all enjoying themselves is the sound of a couple of owls somewhere behind me.

It's heaven.

I allow my mind to wander, imagining what it might be like to spend time with Calli alone somewhere like this. Somewhere we don't have to hide, sneak about and pretend this thing that I've craved between us doesn't exist.

A shriek of laughs startles me, and fear of being

caught spying on them all has me lifting myself up a tree so they don't accidentally walk into me.

Nico and Brianna burst through the trees only a few seconds later, both of them with wide, happy smiles on their faces before he backs her up against one of the tipis, pinning her against it. Leaning in, he whispers something in her ear which makes her body sag with need before he claims her lips in a kiss that makes my stomach tumble and my balls ache.

Fuck. I need my girl.

Ripping my eyes from them, I search her out. But while everyone else might be hanging out around the fire, I can't find her.

My heart jumps into my throat at the thought of her hiding, or even being sick in one of those tipis and no one being with her. Then she bursts out of one, her phone in her hand and a deep frown etched onto her face.

Her thumbs race over the screen as she furiously types something out, and I can't say I'm wholly surprised when my phone vibrates in my pocket.

I continue watching as Emmie calls her over.

But she doesn't go straight there. Instead, she detours into the biggest tipi, and when she emerges a few minutes later, it's with alcohol.

Dropping into the space beside Alex, she twists the top of her mixer drink and tips it to her lips.

He leans in to speak to her, but she barely even registers it as she focuses on drowning out reality.

I hate that she's doing that because of me. I fucking

hate that I have any effect on her, almost as much as I love it.

Once I'm confident that the light of my phone won't catch anyone's eye, I pull it free and read what she sent me.

Angel: You're a coward, Nikolas.

All the air rushes from my lungs as I stare at those words from the one person who can see me better than anyone else.

They cut deep, leaving me carved open and bleeding up in this stupid tree.

But still, I don't find it in me to do anything.

I sit there for the longest time as the moon moves across the sky, changing the shadows it casts across their camp as I just watch them all enjoy themselves.

Unsurprisingly, Nico and Brianna never rejoin the group. Instead, they slipped into one of the tipis a while ago.

The other couples around the bonfire get closer until, about the time I completely lose feeling in my arse from sitting up here, they start calling it a night.

Jodie and Toby disappear first, quickly followed by Emmie and Theo.

Seb and Stella finish their drinks with Calli and Alex, all of them laughing and enjoying themselves before Seb finally stands, throws Stella over his shoulder and marches her toward a tipi.

My chest constricts as Alex reaches out to tuck a

lock of hair behind Calli's ear. She's drunk. The last time she got up, she could barely walk in a straight line —and that was a while ago.

Grabbing her hand, he pulls her to her feet and wraps his arm around her shoulder, keeping her tucked into his body.

My temperature and frustration soar as he supports her in the way I'm desperate to.

They come to a stop at the tipi, and Calli looks up at him like he's the most important person in her world as he hesitates.

She says something to him, something I can't make out, before she retakes his hand and tugs him inside the tipi with her as my heart plummets out of my chest.

"No," I breathe, my grip tightening on the branch beneath me until my nails dig into the bark.

Squeezing my eyes closed, all I see is the two of them inside that tipi.

His lips brushing hers, his fingers dragging her shirt up, exposing her to him.

Their limbs are tangled, her back arching and her nails scratching down his back.

"Fuck," I bark, loud enough to send a bird flapping out of the trees in fright as I jump down.

My heart is in my throat as I make my way toward their camp and drop down in front of their glowing bonfire.

Reaching out, I grab a marshmallow and throw it into my mouth, letting the sweetness coat my tongue, all the while wishing it were something else I were tasting.

Finding a half-empty bottle of vodka that Stella and Emmie were making drinks with, I tip the neck to my lips and swallow down a couple of shots. Anything to get those images out of my head.

A loud female scream floats around the camp from one of the tipis. The sound is like a fucking bat to my chest, even though I know instantly that it's not Calli. The tone is all wrong.

It gives me hope that maybe she's just fallen into bed and passed out, and my horny brother is just lying there, watching her sleep, wishing he was man enough to make the move we all know he's desperate to.

Something's holding him back, though. He's never really been hesitant with girls. So why is he with Calli? Is it because he really does like her and is trying to treat her as she deserves? Or on some level, does he already know? We've never really been the kind of twins who feel each other's pain and all that jazz, but we've definitely got a connection that I don't share with anyone else. Can he sense something that's holding him back?

Or did that all shatter to pieces the second she towed him into that tipi?

My heart races with the thought of him experiencing a side to Calli that only I know.

Swallowing another two shots, I abandon the bottle on the table as I make my way toward the tipi they disappeared inside.

My heart threatens to beat right out of my chest as I peer around the door and look through the window.

It's dark inside, apart from the faint glow of soft fairy lights that are strung up around the ceiling, and my breath catches in my throat when I find both of them asleep.

The relief that floods me when I find that Alex doesn't even have his arm around her is something I've never experienced before.

Lifting my hand, I comb my fingers through my hair, fighting with myself to do the right thing. To walk away and let her sleep. To go back home, knowing that my brother doesn't have his hands all over her.

But when my feet move, it's not in the direction of my car.

And when my hand drops, it's not to my side but to the door handle that will let me inside their little haven.

The sound of their heavy breathing barely overpowers the roaring of my blood past my ears as I close the space between the door and the bed, my eyes locked on the lump under the sheets that belongs to my girl.

As I get closer, her sweet, floral scent fills my nose and makes my mouth water.

Friday night in Damien's bathroom seems like a lifetime ago. Or at least, my cock thinks it was.

"My angel," I whisper, brushing my scarred knuckles down her soft cheek and feeling that spark that always shoots around my body when we touch as strongly as ever.

Needing more, I pull the covers back, revealing her body to me.

She's wearing her standard vest, but instead of just a pair of tiny knickers that I'm sure she selects purely to tease me during my late-night visits, her legs are clad in a pair of cotton floral trousers.

My teeth grind as I think about the possibility of Alex helping her change. She looked pretty wasted from a distance. But maybe it was more my mind playing tricks on me, forcing me to see what I didn't want to. Punishing me for the way I treat her, the way I can't embrace what I really feel for her, who I really am.

Trailing my finger lower, I trace it down her neck, over her collarbone and down to the lace trim of her vest.

My body aches for her, my cock hard and desperate to sink inside her once more, and none of that gets any better when she lets out a wanton moan as my finger glides over her nipple. It instantly hardens for me, and I pinch it through the fabric.

Her moan grows louder and she rolls onto her back.

It's dangerous, I know it is, but I'm powerless but to reach out and do the same to the other, delighting in the noise that hits my ears as her back arches on the bed.

One glance at Alex and I find that he's still out cold, his snores slowly getting louder, I hope enough to drown out Calli's whimpers as I tug the fabric lower and wrap my lips around her.

"Mmm," she moans. "More."

And I do. I circle her peak, suck it deep into my mouth and sink my teeth into her just as I know she likes until she's panting and her fingers have found their home in my hair.

But to my amusement, she still seems to be asleep.

It makes me wonder just how often she has dreams that are quite this vivid for her not to immediately know something is up.

"Daemon," she moans, and my heart damn near stops, hearing my name falling from her lips as a plea.

My eyes dart up, expecting to find her watching me, but hers are still closed.

Moving to the bottom of the bed, I wrap my fingers around her waistband and tug her trousers and knickers down her legs.

Throwing them to the floor, I crawl between her thighs and force them wider.

I run my nose through her, breathing her in before I circle her clit with my tongue.

A low moan rumbles in her throat once more, and I up the ante by grazing her with my teeth.

Her groan of pleasure gets louder before she jolts and a loud gasp rips past her lips.

I smile, my eyes finding her wide shocked ones as she stares down at me eating her out as if I haven't got a care in the world.

To be fair, while I'm down here, I really fucking don't.

"Daemon, what the hell are you—"

"Shh, Angel. Lie back."

I slide my hand up her stomach, putting some force behind it so she has no choice but to crash back to the bed.

But she fights me, holding her propped-up position and staring down at me as if this really is all a dream.

"B-but Alex is—"

"I'm aware, beautiful. Which is why you're going to need to be really quiet. Unless you have the intention of him joining, of course."

"W-what?" she gasps.

My chest swells at the horror written all over her face.

"I thought twins was every girl's fantasy," I tease while her mouth opens and closes like a goldfish.

Pushing two fingers inside her, I curl them, finding her G-spot and making her eyes shutter.

"D-Daemon," she moans, rocking her hips into me. "J-just you. P-please."

Fuck yes. Whatever you want, Angel.

She finally lets her arms give out as I swipe my tongue over her again, and I don't stop until I have no choice but to cover her mouth with my hand and bring her to ruin.

All the while, my brother sleeps peacefully beside her.

24

———

CALLI

I awake with a start and immediately push my hands under the covers to feel if I'm dressed.

Alex is curled around me like a freaking spider monkey, snoring deeply in my ear. The last thing I need is for him to wake up and realise his cock is pressed against my bare arse.

I breathe a sigh of relief when I find my trousers are exactly where they were when I passed out.

But that doesn't mean he wasn't here.

I know he was. I feel him.

Goosebumps prick my skin, and I force my eyes open to look for him. But I'm flooded with disappointment when I don't find him beside me, and when I push to sit up, I discover the rest of the tipi is empty, too.

"Go back to sleep, baby C," Alex groans, dragging me back down. "I like you, you're warm," he mutters sleepily, making me laugh. Although, it makes my heart hurt.

He has no idea that while he was sleeping peacefully, his brother was here...

My temperature soars as I lie there, my heart racing with the memory of waking to find his head between my thighs.

For the briefest second, my alcohol-fuelled brain thought it was Alex. But I quickly realised that, A, that's not his style, and B, there surely was only one person on this planet who could play me as if I'm his personal instrument like Daemon can.

"I need to pee," I say, desperately needing to get out of Alex's arms and attempt to get my head on straight.

He growls but releases me.

Reluctantly, I push to the edge of the bed and swing my legs over. My thighs pull, just a little reminder of what happened last night. But that's nothing to the shock that rocks through me when my eyes land on a small origami bat sitting on my bedside table.

Reaching out, I wrap my fingers around the perfectly folded black paper, hiding it from Alex.

My cheeks blaze with heat at the hazy memory and I still, squeezing my eyes closed as I try to force it out.

"Cal, is everything okay?" Alex asks. His concern tugs at my chest. I am the worst person, the worst friend in the world.

Glancing back over my shoulder, I meet his sleepy

eyes, my heart only pounding harder at the concern I see there.

His eyes narrow and his brow furrows as he studies me, as if my sins are written on my skin for him to read.

"Y-yeah," I stutter, my stomach turning over with a mix of last night's alcohol and fear.

I should just tell him the truth. If both of us can trust anyone, then it's Alex. He and Daemon literally shared a womb. They're more than trustworthy of each other's secrets.

But when my lips part, those aren't the words that fall out.

"I'm just a bit hungover."

"You know what you need?" he says, dragging himself so he's sitting against the headboard, the covers draped over his waist and putting his sculpted chest on full display for me to drink in.

"Do not say your cock for breakfast," I blurt, much to Alex's amusement if his barked laugh and wide smile is anything to go by.

"Well," he laughs, "now that you mention it..." He shifts his hands as if he's about to shove the covers lower, and I jump up like my arse is on fire. "I'm joking, Cal. I know it's not like that with us."

His words make me pause, and I can't help but find his eyes once more.

I swear I see something within them.

Does he know?

Did we wake him last night?

"Anyway, I was going to say that what you need is a

good fry-up, and luckily for you, I make the best one," he announces, shattering the tension that had fallen between us.

"Sounds perfect. I'd love to eat your sausage," I joke before rushing toward the bathroom to the sound of his laughter.

"Touché, baby C," he calls just before I close the door and fall back against it with my head spinning and my nerves shot.

Surely, if he knew, he'd say something... right?

No?

"Shit," I hiss.

I'm so fucking confused.

But one thing I do know is that I shouldn't have let last night happen. Even if Alex does know that nothing is going to change between us, it was still totally disrespectful, and I'm ashamed.

If he'd woken up and seen... I drop my head into my hands as shame burns through me.

That's not the girl I am. Or at least, it's not the girl Alex and the others know me to be.

But there's just something about Daemon. And when he touches me, every single shred of my dignity just goes flying out of the window.

Thankfully, Alex's self-proclaimed legendary fry-up did actually make me feel a little better about the whole situation as we all chilled out around the fire once more.

It might be the Easter holidays and the sun might be shining, but we haven't exactly got the heatwave Stella promised. It's not overly warm without the added heat from the fire.

My phone still burns a hole in my pocket, and I spend almost all day looking over my shoulder in case he appears like the ghost he is. But as the hours pass, I really start to believe that he did just drive all this way last night to eat me out and has happily gone home alone again.

The concept is bizarre, but then I've never claimed to understand Daemon and the way he is. I just seem to have found myself along for the ride.

"What's the plan for tonight, then?" Jodie asks from the hammock she and Toby commandeered a few hours ago when she had a call with Jesse to get an update on Sara's progress—or lack thereof.

Nico and Brianna are once again sitting as far away from each other as possible. Last night's truce—the reason behind the fact that I was sharing a bed with Alex and not my actual roommate—seems to be well and truly over. I guess they both got what they needed and we're now back to service as usual.

"Barbecue and hot tub sound like a plan to me,"

Seb says, eyeing Stella up as if she's already wearing nothing but her bikini.

"I'm not getting in that water if you have plans to be fucking in it," I mutter, looking between the three couples with a smirk.

"Maybe it should be girls only," Emmie suggests.

"So you guys in there practically naked and us out here?" Seb asks, his nose wrinkling like a kid who's just tasted something sour. "Yeah, that's not going to work," he says, speaking for all the guys.

"Sex addict," Stella mutters lightly.

"That's rich coming from you, Princess," he shoots straight back.

I rest back in my lounger, smiling to myself as they bicker like an old married couple.

It makes me weirdly content, seeing them. It's so normal. I like knowing their worlds are happy and normal while mine feels like it's spiralling out of control.

The conversation moves on from hot tub activities, and I sit there with my weak vodka and Coke and just listen to them all.

My heart drops as I realise that in only a few months, all our lives are going to change. University is going to start, and Stella and Emmie will still be at Knight's Ridge. Daemon may or may not pass his exams and have to face the consequences, whatever they may be. Nico is going to dive headfirst into Family business, following in our father's footsteps with the view of being Theo's second in the years to come when he finally takes over from Uncle Damien.

It all makes my head spin. And where will that leave me?

Sadness washes through me at the thought of my friends moving on with their lives without me. Yes, I might get uni, although it's not something I'd really choose for myself. What else am I going to have while they're all living in the same building—a building my father has already told me I won't be having a flat in— and still enjoying hanging out together while I'm stuck in my rut of a life, waiting for my mum and dad to marry me off?

I let out a heavy sigh, which catches both Stella and Emmie's attention, but before they get a chance to ask me what's wrong, their eyes lift to something behind me and they smile.

By the time Stella speaks, I know exactly what she's going to say.

I feel it. The crackling electricity that has been between us whenever we've been in the same room—or forest—since Halloween.

My temperature spikes, and I have to clench my fists to stop my hands from shaking quite so violently.

"Daemon," Stella sings happily. Hopping up, she rushes over and throws her arms around his shoulders.

I can't help but laugh when I look around the side of my lounger to find him frozen with his arms at his sides.

"Ignore Stella, she's already drunk," Seb explains.

"I am not," she argues. "I'm just happy you're here."

She releases Daemon, and I swear he breathes a sigh of relief as she takes a step back.

"Well," he says, rubbing the back of his neck almost nervously, "I-I'm not sure I've ever had a welcome quite like that before."

His stutter, although only small, makes my chest constrict. I bet no one else even caught it. It takes me right back to being inside his bedroom the weekend before last, when for just a short time, he let me see the real him. His insecurities, his fears, his true self. I just wish he'd trust me enough to do it again. Do it more.

"You guys don't mind me crashing, right?" he asks, and I hate that there's a part of him that truly expects someone to say yes and to send him away. "I brought pastries." He holds up a bag before marching forward to put it on the table.

"We invited you. Of course you're welcome," Stella says, shaking her head as if she can't even understand why he'd say it. But then, I guess she doesn't. All she's ever known is this aloof guy who's happy living on the sidelines and doing his own thing.

I think it might only be me and Alex who seem to know just how much bullshit that is.

Daemon craves this. Craves this normalcy of hanging out with friends and forgetting about all the seriousness of his life. He just refuses to accept he deserves it, or that his friends really want him here.

"Come and grab a beer, Bro," Alex says, holding out

a bottle for him and nodding to the seat beside him. "It's good for you to show your face," he says quieter, once Daemon is beside him.

My breath catches at the potential meaning behind those words.

Lifting my drink, I take a massive gulp in the hope the vodka will help banish my nerves and the knot in my stomach. Probably wishful thinking, but it's the only solution I have right now, so I'm going to have to stick with it.

It takes a good five minutes for Daemon to actually look at me, preferring to keep his eyes on his feet as he listens to everyone around us chatting or talking to Alex, but the second we connect, I feel it like a physical blow.

Danger flashes in his dark eyes as he holds mine. Wicked promises and a whole host of dirty things flicker through his mind so clearly that I can almost see them playing out.

A smirk curls at his lips as he reads my thoughts before his tongue sweeps across his bottom lip, making me burn up for him.

Ripping my eyes away from his, I down the rest of my drink before pushing from my lounger and heading inside to take a breath.

The second I step into the main tipi, my phone buzzes.

Daemon: I can still taste you...

I'm tapping out a reply before I've even thought it through.

Calli: Anyone would think you want to get caught.

Daemon: With my head between your thighs, any day of the week, Angel.

"Jesus," I mutter.

"What's wrong?" a deep voice booms from behind me, making me jump to the point of dropping my phone.

"N-nothing. I'm good," I say fakely as I quickly grab my phone, which has of course landed screen-side up, and I turn to Nico with a smile plastered on my face.

"You're being weird," he says, narrowing his eyes on me.

"Me?" I ask, sounding guilty as fuck. "No I'm not. I'm just... enjoying myself. Excuse me."

Dropping my phone into the safety of my pocket, I dart toward the toilet and lock myself in.

Calli: I think Alex is suspicious.

Daemon: He knows fuck all. Our dirty little secret is safe. *winky face emoji*

My teeth grind and fire begins to burn in my belly.

Calli: I never said I wanted to be your dirty little secret.

His response is almost instant, as if he'd already typed it before I even hit send.

Daemon: You love it though, don't you, Angel? You were dripping for me last night with Alex lying right there. The risk of getting caught makes you burn even hotter for me.

"Motherfucker," I hiss, putting my phone to sleep and lowering my arse to the toilet.

My head spins from the vodka despite my attempts to keep my drinks weak, and I can't help but wonder if the effects are more from Daemon's appearance than anything else.

Suddenly, I'm regretting my decision to message him yesterday. It seemed like a good idea at the time, but right now, I can't help but wonder if he's going to get both of us in a hell of a lot of trouble. Because if Nico and Theo suspect anything like I think Alex might, then...

Fuck. I don't even want to think about the consequences.

I spend entirely too long in the bathroom, and when I reemerge, I feel a little stronger—until I walk straight into the one person I'd just silently told myself I'd stay as far away from as possible.

I still the second he looks up across the kitchen with two bottles of beer in his hands.

A smirk appears on his lips, dimples popping in his cheeks that make him look even more delicious and deadly than normal. His eyes drop down my body, and he studies me as if I'm standing here naked. In fact, I almost have to look down to make sure I'm not, he's so lost in me.

"Where did you go?" I ask.

"For a drive," he says simply, as if he hasn't been gone for well over twelve hours. "I was going to go home, but then I reconsidered. Why would I want to be there when you're here, sleeping in the same bed as my brother?"

"I wasn't meant to be, but Nico and Brianna... yeah." The less we talk about that, the better.

"I bet Alex thought all his Christmases came at once, getting you back in bed again."

"Nothing happened with Alex, Daemon."

"I know," he says arrogantly. "I'm more than aware that it was my face you were coming all over last night."

Ignoring the way all the muscles below my waist clench in desire, I push forward, desperately needing a refill if I'm going to have to spend the rest of the night dealing with this.

"I meant what I said, Daemon. I don't want to be this sordid thing that you're ashamed to tell your friends about."

I startle when the bottles in his hands slam down on the counter and my back is pressed against the fridge I was about to reach into.

"I'm not ashamed of you, Angel. Never think I'm ashamed of you. Of this."

His knuckles brush along my jaw and a shiver races down my spine.

"Then why are we hiding?"

"Because I'm not the one for you, Angel. I'm stealing something I never should have taken, and I'm a selfish motherfucker who can't stop despite knowing that it's exactly what I should do."

"No," I say, shaking my head and placing my hand over his heart. It pounds violently beneath my palm. "That's rubbish. If you didn't deserve it, I wouldn't have given it to you."

His jaw tics as he refuses to believe those words.

"I took, Calli. You didn't willingly give anything, and I'll never forgive myself for the lapse in restraint that led us here."

His eyes bounce between mine as he silently begs me to believe him, to believe he's not worthy of the happiness I'm sure we could find if he would just let himself be... well... him.

"You can drop the *bad boy soldier, I'm not worthy of anything,* bullshit with me, you know. I see right through it anyway," I warn.

"I-I've n-no idea what you're t-talking about."

Self-hatred darkens his eyes as he loses his fight

with his composure and I attempt to rip his armour away from him.

Lifting my hand, I cup his jaw.

"Show me that boy, Nikolas. The one you're scared of."

Silence stretches out between us, but before either of us gets a chance to say any more, the door opens and Daemon jumps back as if I've just burned him.

Spinning on my heels, I rip the fridge open and look inside, hoping the chill is enough to cool my cheeks and calm my racing heart.

"Did you forget you came in here for beer? I'm fucking dying out there, man," Alex says, making my heart jump into my throat.

Was he hoping to catch us up to something?

Cursing myself for my out-of-control, possibly misplaced paranoia, I finally start looking for what I actually want from in here.

"You okay, baby C? You look like you're trying to climb in the fridge."

"Y-yeah, just looking for the Coke."

The warmth of his body covers my back as he reaches over my shoulder.

"It's right here. Jesus, how many have you had?"

Nowhere near enough.

"Thank you," I whisper.

"Take them out, Bro. I'm going for a slash."

"Yeah, sure," Daemon says, picking the bottles up and walking out the door.

"You sure you're good? Did he say something or..."

He studies me, and I swear he's begging me to open up. To confirm what he already knows.

But I don't. I can't.

Plastering on a smile, I look up at him.

"Everything is great. I'm just enjoying the freedom before I spend the rest of the holidays studying."

"Not sure I'm a fan of the seriousness that's looming for us."

"No, me neither. We've all got it under control though, right?" I ask a little hesitantly, not really believing my words.

"Hell, yeah. Of course we have. I think the others are going to get ready for the hot tub in a bit. You packed a bikini, right?"

"You look way more excited by that prospect than you should be," I mutter.

"The five of you, bikinis, and a hot tub... my idea of heaven, Cal."

"They're all taken," I point out.

"Right, so is Scarlet Witch, but that doesn't stop me looking."

"Scarlet Witch? She's not even a real person."

"And? You've seen all that red leather and shit she wears, right?" He gets this faraway look in his eyes, and I can't help but laugh.

Yeah, maybe I'm not his type after all.

"Fair enough. Just remember that I warned you when you're sent home tomorrow with a black eye."

"Another one?" he asks with a smirk.

25

DAEMON

I knew coming back was going to be torture. I knew I'd end up watching Calli from afar while continuing to pretend that I didn't really care about anything either she or Alex did.

Calli's message earlier warning me that she thought he knew about us has been at the forefront of my mind since she sent it. But while she might be worried, I've seen nothing to suggest she might be right.

His flirting is as strong as ever, causing my jealousy to rage like a wild beast inside me. Of course, it isn't helped by the fact that all of us have squeezed our arses into a hot tub that's definitely designed for fewer people.

Calli is happily sitting on Alex's lap, wiggling her arse against what I can only assume is his hard cock. I fucking well know mine would be aching if she were on my lap right now.

Nico has spent the past thirty minutes growling at

the pair of them, and I can't say that I'm not all too far behind him with that. But seeing as both have kept their hands above the water to pacify him, I can almost cope. Almost.

The others are all loving life as they drink, and Seb, Alex, Nico and Toby pass a joint around, occasionally letting their girls have a pull on it.

Their laughter and joy is infectious, and after a few more beers and with the warm, relaxing water, I almost find myself enjoying this little break. Even more so when Nico gets dragged into a heated discussion with Seb and Theo about football, and Calli shocks the shit out of me when she slips her hand beneath the surface and twists her fingers with mine.

My eyes find hers as a wave of desire so strong washes through me that I almost reach for her, drag her on my lap, and claim her lips in front of everyone.

What would be the worst that could happen?

Nico puts a bullet through your head.

But would that be so bad?

Calli deserves so much better than me. She's had her twisted little rendezvous with me now. She's lost her precious V-card to the devil. She should be looking elsewhere for her future anyway. He'd just be forcing her arm.

"Daemon? Daemon?"

I have no idea how many times Theo calls my name, but I finally drag myself out of my own head after Calli squeezes my hand so hard I have no choice but to focus, noting the way every single person is staring at me.

"Yeah?" I ask as if everything is fine.

"Where'd you go?" Theo laughs. His eyes are blown and glassy, so he probably won't even remember this exchange in an hour, let alone tomorrow.

"N-nowhere, I'm g-good." I curse myself for allowing my insecurities to shine through with everyone's eyes on me.

Calli's thumb brushes across my knuckles and I breathe a sigh of relief, forcing myself to relax.

"I just wanted to know if you wanted some," Theo says, offering me his blunt.

"Nah, I'm good with beer."

"I'm not sure I can stay in here any longer," Brianna says, stepping out of the water to cool down.

Nico's eyes immediately drop to her tits.

"You wanna go cool off, Siren?" he asks, clearly more interested in her this evening now that they're both wasted.

"With you?" she scoffs. "No thanks. I think I've got it covered."

She throws her leg over the side, Nico's eyes eating her up like she's just offered herself as his next meal. Which is far from the case. If you believe her words, of course.

She shoots him a look over her shoulder once she's out that says everything her mouth doesn't, and Nico quickly jumps over the edge, leaving a tsunami in his wake which causes a huge splash on the other side of the tub.

Brianna squeals, and he takes chase and drags her into the tipi he's meant to be sharing with Alex once again.

"Looks like I'm bunking with you again, baby C."

"You'd think that if Nico had such an issue with you hooking up with Alex, he wouldn't make it so easy for you to do so," Seb points out.

"He's too busy thinking with his dick to worry about where Alex is putting his right now," Emmie slurs. "What the hell?" she squeals in shock as Theo stands and throws her over his shoulder. "Get off me, you oaf," she cries.

"Excuse me. I need to go and teach my wife a lesson."

Theo's hand slams down on Emmie's half-exposed arse with a loud crack.

She wails in pain, but something tells me she loved it a hell of a lot more than she makes out. I'm even more convinced when she meets my eyes over his shoulder and winks at me conspiratorially.

The final two couples soon bid the three of us farewell before they go racing toward their rooms.

"And then there were three," Alex announces as Calli finally gets off his lap, releases my hand, and drifts to the other side of the tub. "Space at last." Alex's knee knocks against mine as he stretches out.

"Oh, I'm sorry. You should have said if you didn't

want me there. I could have sat on Daemon's lap instead. I'm sure he wouldn't have minded."

Alex's eyes meet mine, attempting to read my reaction before he glances back at Calli when he realises that my cold mask is fully in place.

"You're good, baby C. Your arse was just getting a bit bony."

Calli's brows shoot up.

"You're complaining to me about bone issues? Sitting on your lap wasn't all that comfortable either, I'll have you know."

"Something you need to confess, Bro?" I ask with a smirk.

Alex shrugs. He literally has no shame.

"Not my fault. I had a hot girl's arse grinding down on my D and her tits bouncing in my face. I bet that would crack even your ice-cold resolve, devil boy," he teases.

The two of us glare at each other, and for the first time, a little unease seeps into my veins at the possibility of Calli being right, of him knowing exactly what happened only feet from him last night.

"Drink," Calli says, passing over two fresh bottles of beer from the side table behind her.

Alex lifts his straight to his lips, downing the lot in one while Calli and I watch.

"You know," Alex says, making my pulse spike, "you don't have to hide from us." His eyes drop to where I'm still wearing a t-shirt while the others spent the last few hours wearing as little as possible.

I shrug, lowering my gaze to the water.

"I'm not hiding," I say, wishing like hell it came out a little stronger.

Calli's attention burns into me, but I refuse to look at her because I know she'll see the truth in my eyes, just like Alex will.

He knows exactly what I'm doing. He's experienced it many times over the years, but that doesn't mean I'm going to magically change anytime soon.

An uncomfortable tension falls over us while I wait for Alex to say something that will inevitably pull the rug from beneath both of us.

But to my surprise, it never comes.

"So, baby C. You ready for a night of double trouble?" he teases, when I start to think that drowning in this damn tub might be the easiest way out of the situation.

"Huh?" She looks between the two of us like a rabbit caught in headlights.

"Don't worry. We know what we're doing. We'll be gentle." The smirk on his face tells both of us that he's joking, but still, the comments hit a little too hard for my liking.

We might have gone there in the past. And if we were possibly about to spend the night with any other girl than Calli, then I wouldn't blink at the prospect of sharing her. But just the thought of watching him touch her makes me murderous—even toward him.

"I think I'll pass this time. Not enough vodka," she

says, waving the now-empty bottle at us and moving to the edge of the tub.

Every muscle in my body locks up as she stands, revealing her banging body to us in her royal blue bikini.

"I'm going to shower. You two play nice, yeah?"

I don't need to look to know that Alex watches her every move. And as much as I hate that his eyes are locked on her curves right now. I also understand it. She's captivating. Mesmerising. And she's got me totally under her spell.

Grabbing a towel, she wraps it around herself and looks back.

She smiles at Alex before her eyes shoot to mine.

Just for that brief moment, I stop breathing. The invitation for me to join her is more than obvious in her blue, sparkling eyes, but I can't. And she knows it. Which is why her shoulders drop as she turns her back on us once more and walks away.

"Thought she was gonna invite us to join her then. Beer?" Alex asks the second she's disappeared from our view, making my head spin. He stands out of the water and reaches to the table beside the tub, knocking the lids off two bottles.

"Thanks," I mutter, taking one from him.

"So," he says, after swallowing a mouthful.

My heart pounds as I wait for him to call me out on what happened last night. For him to rip me a new one for going anywhere near our princess and forbid me from doing it ever again.

But then he throws me for a loop once again.

"How's it feel being normal for a change?"

"Uh..." His eyes twinkle with amusement. "Yeah. It's great. I should be banned from working more often," I mutter, frustration clawing at my insides.

"I know you hate it. But it'll be worth it in the end."

I stare at him, irritated by his constant positive outlook on life.

"I'm gonna fail those exams, A. Nothing about this situation is going to get better anytime soon."

"Only you can control that, Bro. You wanna pass, you've got the power to make it happen. You've got us. All of us. Use us. Let us help."

My lips twitch, begging to turn into a snarl at his comments.

"You're a hard-headed, stubborn prick, you know that?" he hisses, changing tack. "You're more than capable of passing those exams. You're not fucking stupid. You just allow everyone to get inside your head. You allow Dad and Gram—"

"Don't," I growl. "Don't fucking go there."

"They were wrong, Daemon. You are not the person they thought you were. You've proved that a million times over with everything you've done in the past few years. Why can't you get past it with the school stuff?"

"Because none of it makes any fucking sense," I snap. "They might have been wrong about all the other stuff, but they're right about me being a dumb-arse who'll never make anything of myself."

"That's bullshit and you know it. Dad is freaking the fuck out at the prospect of losing you. He needs you, man."

"Then he shouldn't have told me I'm out unless I pass."

"He's just pushing you because, like me, he knows you can do it," Alex argues.

"No, he doesn't," I boom. "He thinks I'm a fuck-up, that I should be more like you."

Alex shakes his head. "You're fucking delusional, man. You seem to think that I've got it so good just because I can pass a few exams. Did you ever think that all the things you're good at are all the things I'm bad at, and that I get held to the same impossible standards for those?"

"You're not bad at anything, golden boy."

"Delusional," he mutters again. "You don't want help from us? Fine. I get that your pride is too important to show the guys your weaknesses. But what about Calli?"

"What about Calli?" I snap, my hands trembling beneath the surface of the water.

"She'll help you. She won't judge you." I shake my head, refusing his suggestion. "Why not? She's done it before, right?"

Lifting my eyes from the water bubbling around me, I find his, my breath catching in my throat.

"I'm not an idiot, Daemon. And I'm also not fucking blind." My heart pounds as I wait for what's going to come next, and all the air rushes from my lungs when I realise it's not what I'm expecting. "I remember what she did for you when we were kids. You need that magic now. Just ask her."

He drains his beer and heads toward the steps to get out of the tub.

"I want you to be happy, D. And that means you need to be working. So you need to pull up your big girl pants and get it fucking done, one way or another. Asking for help does not make you a failure. Refusing to accept it does."

And with that little nugget of advice, he takes off.

"The bed's big enough for three, if you wanna try to get some sleep," he calls before disappearing into the tipi.

"Fuck," I breathe, tipping my head back and staring up at the star-filled sky above me.

He's right, I know he is. But fuck. Asking for help from anyone, even Calli, is the hardest fucking thing. Admitting I'm failing goes against everything I've ever been taught. It shows weaknesses I've always been told to hide.

I sit there for another few minutes, but my need to be close to my angel finally gets me moving.

Her eyes find mine the second I slip into the room and I freeze, dripping hot tub water all over the floor.

She's standing in front of the mirror, brushing her hair.

My gaze drops, taking in a similar vest to the one she was wearing last night, and arguably the most sinful shorts I've ever seen.

"You're making a puddle," she says, her voice still a little slurred from the vodka.

When I make it back up to her eyes, I find one of her brows lifted in challenge.

"Is Alex in the shower?" I ask, glancing at my bag that he threw in here not long after I showed up earlier.

She just continues to stare at me. She doesn't need to answer my question—we can both hear the more-than-obvious running water coming from the bathroom.

"I'll just wait for him to—"

"Or you could strip off right there," she challenges, standing straighter as she fully turns to face me.

"C-Calli," I warn as she places the brush down and takes a step toward me.

Her eyes run down the length of my body, but they linger on my chest.

I know I'm not really hiding anything. Everyone here knows the scars I bear. But that doesn't mean I want them on show. Ever.

"So I was right, then?" she taunts, continuing to close the space between us. "You are a coward."

Faster than she was expecting, I reach out, my fingers gripping her jaw tightly and giving her little choice but to hold my stare.

"I-I-I—" I close my eyes and suck in a deep breath through my nose, getting a hold of myself. "I'm not a coward," I state, my voice hard, cold, leaving no room for argument. Or so I think.

"Then prove it. Show me who you really are, Batman," she teases.

The shower cuts off behind me, but I don't move. I can't. I'm locked in her stare while my heart thrashes in my chest.

A beat before the door opens, I manage to get a handle on myself, release her and take a massive step back.

"Sorry, was I interrupting something?" Alex asks with a smirk, walking out of the bathroom with nothing but a towel wrapped around his waist.

Jealousy slams into me with such force I actually stumble back a little.

Why can't you be more like your brother? He's funny, smart, sensible, reliable.

"D, you okay?" Alex asks when he notices my reaction.

"Put some fucking clothes on," I scoff, storming past him and shutting myself in the bathroom so I can freak out alone.

26

———

CALLI

"What happened?" Alex asks, studying me with a deep frown marring his brow.

"N-nothing," I say, forcing a lightness into my tone that I certainly don't feel.

"Did he hurt you?"

"What? Daemon? No, of course not," I lie. The truth is, him refusing to be himself hurts me more than almost anything else he could do.

Why can't he just open up? Embrace who he really is?

"Cal," Alex sighs, clearly reading more in my eyes than I want to show him.

"Honestly, everything is good. He was just being... well, Daemon." And I want Nikolas. I want the version of him he's let me have just the smallest glimpses of in the past week. The one he's scared to let out but is so fucking incredible when he does.

"You want me to talk to him?" Alex offers.

"What? No. Don't be silly."

Turning my back on him, I walk around to what was my side of the bed last night and slip under the covers, hoping like hell that he can't see the tears that are quickly filling my eyes.

"Daemon can be a dick, but he doesn't mean it. Not really. He built himself some impenetrable walls a long time ago, and I fear they might just be indestructible," Alex says quietly.

I blow out a shaky breath as the sound of his towel hitting the floor fills the space, followed by the rustling of fabric that I really hope is him pulling some clothes on.

"You want us to leave you alone and go sleep in a hammock or something?" he asks.

Swallowing down the emotion that's clogging my throat, I flip over to look at him.

A smile twitches at my lips when I find him standing in his boxers, holding a pair of sweats like he's really hoping he's not going to have to put them on and go and sleep out in the cold.

"Don't be stupid, get in here." I throw the covers back, and he instantly throws his trousers to the floor and dives in. His fingers find my sides and he tickles me until I have no choice but to let go of the sadness Daemon caused, and I squeal out his name through my laughter.

When he lets me go, my chest is heaving and I've got a wide smile on my face.

"You're a good friend, Alex. And a good brother."

He smiles at me, his eyes already drooping with tiredness.

"I do my best," he confesses. "You gonna make the devil sleep on the floor or what?" he asks, nodding his head toward the bathroom, proving he's more aware of his brother's movements than I am.

My breath catches when I find Daemon hiding in the shadows of the dark bathroom, watching us like a creep.

"I dunno," I say, loud enough for him to hear. "I guess it depends if he can play nice or not."

Alex snorts a laugh.

"He wouldn't know nice if it bit him on the arse, baby C."

"Fuck off, Bro," Daemon grunts, stalking into the room, dressed in grey sweats and a white t-shirt.

"Whatever. I'm done."

Both of us stare at Alex as he snuggles down and closes his eyes as if the tension in the room doesn't exist.

"So?" Daemon asks. "Am I banished to the floor, or is there enough room in there for three?"

My lips part to respond as he closes the space between us and successfully steals all the air from the room.

The scent of clean, sexy boy gets stronger, and despite my better judgement, my stomach clenches and my thighs rub together.

Sliding back, I hold the duvet up as an invitation.

For a second, I don't think he's going to accept. His eyes just stare at the space as a frown forms on his brow.

But then, he takes a step forward and lies down in front of me.

He keeps a little bit of space between us and rests his head on the other end of the pillow.

His eyes bounce between mine as if he's seeing me for the first time, and he sucks his bottom lip into his mouth, deep in thought.

"What is it?" I whisper, unable to stop myself.

He releases his lip and sucks in a breath, whatever he really wants to say dancing on his tongue.

"Please, Daemon. It's just me," I breathe, sliding my hand across the space between us and brushing my fingers against his.

He sucks in a shaky breath, and his eyes shoot over my shoulder at Alex.

"A, you awake, Bro?"

As if on cue, Alex lets out a more-than-authentic snore.

"Arsehole fucking sleeps like the dead. Pretty sure he got my share of that shit," Daemon mutters sadly.

"It's just me and you and some fairy lights," I say softly, my eyes urging him to talk, to open up, to... fuck, I don't know, do something.

"I don't sleep, Angel," he confesses.

"We don't have to. We can just... lie here."

"You want me to just lie in a bed with you?" he asks with a smirk that makes my stomach twist.

I shrug the shoulder I'm not lying on.

"I don't do this, Calli. I don't talk about feelings or open myself up. It's just too—"

"Terrifying?" I finish for him.

He remains silent for so long that I don't think he's going to agree, despite it being the truth.

"Don't you think that scares us all?" I ask.

He doesn't respond. Instead, he slides closer, until his nose brushes mine.

"Daemon," I whisper so quietly that I'm not even sure he'd have heard it.

"Shh, Angel," he breathes against my lips. "I know what I should and shouldn't be doing right now, and I just don't fucking care."

His kiss is so soft it makes that lump of emotion I'd swallowed not so long ago rise up once more.

I expect him to just throw caution to the wind and be as rough as he usually is. But there's something very different about the way he kisses me, touches me, and I utterly melt for him.

His hand moves, wrapping around my hip and dragging me closer as his tongue pushes past my lips, searching for mine.

I gasp when he pulls me so close that I have no choice but to feel just how much my kiss affects him.

"It's always been you, Angel," he whispers into my mouth as his hand grips my arse, pinning us as close as possible.

His kiss, his touch, only adds to the effects of the vodka that's coursing through my veins, so when he slips his hand beneath the waistband of my shorts and into my underwear, I don't stop him.

Hooking my leg over his hip, I shamelessly grind against him.

"You're not really an angel at all, are you?" he groans as he kisses across my jaw. "You're pure devil."

I gasp as his cock hits my clit just right.

"Love watching you come apart for me."

"W-we… we can't," I argue, seeing his intentions in the dark depths of his eyes.

"We can do whatever the fuck we want, Angel. Come play on the dark side with me."

Releasing my arse, he lifts my leg higher and tugs the fabric of my shorts and knickers aside, running his fingers through my wetness.

"Fuck," I gasp, pressing my face against the pillow to smother my voice.

"My dirty, dirty angel," he growls, sinking two fingers inside me.

I groan into the pillow as he starts shifting around.

Risking a look, I just catch sight of his bare cock before he repositions me as if I weigh nothing more than a feather and rubs his head against me, teasing my entrance with his fullness.

"Oh God," I whimper before biting down on my lip, wishing I could suck those words back in.

"Lips, Angel. I want all your moans and cries for more."

Unable to deny him, I tilt my chin up and let him

claim my mouth as he thrusts his hips forward, giving me everything my body needs.

He rocks into me, slowly, gently, and I feel every single one of his movements right in my soul.

He gives me exactly what I demanded of him. His soft side. His vulnerable side. I was just expecting to have it with words, not actions. Choked with emotion as our kiss continues, a tear slips free, soaking into the pillow beneath me.

He never picks up speed. He just kisses me passionately and loves me deeply. And I soak up every single ounce of it, terrified that it might just be a one-time deal from him, all the while praying it's not.

I wake up hot. No. Sweltering and pinned to the bed.

Just like the day before, my first thought is to panic and drop my hands down my body to make sure I'm dressed. Thankfully, I soon discover that panic is for nothing, because my pyjamas are fully intact.

What quickly becomes obvious, though, is the reason why I'm so freaking hot and pinned in place.

Daemon is passed out in front of me, still fully dressed and laying on top of the duvet. And that's not just the reason why I'm stuck. His arm is also slung over my waist.

I move slowly so as not to wake him. He told me

himself last night that he doesn't sleep, so it's the last thing I want to do right now.

My legs don't move as I twist around, and I realise that they're twisted up with someone else's.

Jesus Christ. What am I doing in bed with these two?

Twisting farther, I gasp when my eyes land on a pair of amused silver ones.

"Morning, baby C. You sleep well?" Alex whispers.

"I-I... uh... y-yeah. How long have you been awake?"

"A while. I didn't want to wake you. Either of you. He doesn't get to rest often, so..." He trails off.

"He told me," I confess quietly.

Alex nods, like he's not surprised to hear that.

"You're good for him, Cal. He's different when he's around you."

"I'm not sure about that," I whisper, thinking of all the moments we've shared.

Daemon shifts in his sleep, his arms tightening around me, pulling me closer, and we both fall quiet in fear of waking him.

Alex's eyes drop to where Daemon is holding me, but I figure that doesn't really mean anything. I've woken up in Alex's arms more than once now, and there's certainly not anything going on there.

Once he's confident Daemon isn't going to wake up, Alex continues.

"He needs our help."

"I know," I agree, looking back at the man in question.

"He's got to pass his exams or he'll—" Alex cuts himself off.

"Or he'll what?" I breathe.

"I don't know, and it terrifies me."

I nod, my heart in shreds for the complicated man sleeping before me.

"I know he probably doesn't deserve it, but... will you stay with him? Just until he wakes. I have no idea when he last got a full night's sleep without any medication."

"Sure."

Untangling his legs from mine, Alex slips out of bed and disappears into the bathroom.

My heart races as I lie there in silence, listening to Daemon's steady breathing. Does Alex know? Or is he just worried about his brother and sensing that I might be on his side?

After only a few minutes, Alex emerges, pulls on some clothes and disappears out of the tipi, leaving us alone.

I don't move, too scared to wake him when I know just how desperately he needs his rest.

I'm unable to take my eyes off him as he continues to sleep. He looks so peaceful, so... free.

My fingers itch to touch him, but I resist and just continue to lie beside him.

His eyelids flutter with whatever he's dreaming about, and his lips move every few seconds.

I can't help but smile to myself, feeling grateful and more than a little bit overwhelmed that the boy who hides from everyone, the boy who claims never to be able to sleep, is lying right here beside me, completely relaxed.

I have no idea how much time passes as I remain motionless and lost in my own thoughts. But others are awake. I hear voices as I assume they find Alex starting the fire or whatever it is he left us to do out there.

My stomach knots, knowing that they're all going to know we're in here together. Although I doubt they'll second guess it. Brianna might get some ideas, but I'm pretty sure the others all think I'm banging Alex anyway.

My cheeks flame at the thought that Stella and Emmie's minds will go straight into the gutter about me sharing a bed with twins.

I smirk.

That would be a great way to tell them I lost my V-card. Two at once. Talk about diving into adulthood with a bang.

"You're so pretty when you smile."

My entire body startles with his words and I gasp, my eyes finding his.

"And so sexy when you blush like that. What are you thinking about, Angel?"

"You're awake," I breathe.

His lips curl up into a smile at my obvious statement.

"I mean... how did you sleep?"

"Like I haven't done in... forever. It was you." His words make my pulse pick up speed, and my heart soars. But I refuse to believe them.

"Or maybe it was Alex. Being close was like being a baby."

An amused laugh falls from his lips.

"You can think that if you want," he mutters around a yawn. "What time is it?"

"No idea. But I think everyone else is up, and we probably need to head off soon. Pretty sure I heard Stella say we needed to be out of here by midday."

"You think it's that late?" he asks, his wide eyes going to the door where the morning spring sun pours in.

A low growl rumbles in his throat when I lean over him to grab my phone.

"Best morning ever," he mutters with his face pressed right into my breasts.

Tugging the fabric down when I fail to reach what I need, he sucks my nipple into his mouth.

"Daemon." It was meant to be a warning, but it comes out more like a needy plea. "Anyone can see us right now."

My fingers wrap around my phone, and I roll away from him reluctantly. Just that one touch and my skin is tingling with desire.

"It's just gone ten," I tell him.

"Fuck."

"You were tired."

"It doesn't usually make a difference. Did you get

the dose right this time?" he asks, and it takes me a few seconds to grasp what he's saying.

"What? No. I didn't. I—"

"Shh, Angel. I'm joking. I know you didn't. I feel... fresh. It's... weird."

I smile, feeling all kinds of happy for him.

A shout comes from outside, and it's the reminder I really don't need that we need to move.

I wish we could stay locked in this little bubble for longer. That I could keep this gentle, fun Daemon to myself, maybe even get to work on unlocking a little more of what he's hiding. But now isn't the time.

"We need to get moving," I tell him reluctantly.

I attempt to slip out from his arms, but I don't get very far because his fingers slip into my hair and I'm dragged forward until my nose almost brushes his.

There are a million things he wants to say to me, I can almost read them in his eyes. But he fights every single damn one of them.

"It's just me," I breathe. "You can say anything."

"I-I—" he stutters, making my heart clench.

"Come shower with me? I'm not ready to lose..."

He blinks, and my words trail off, fear cutting through my chest like knives.

The second his eyes find mine once more, I know the moment is over. His mask is back in place.

"You're right. We should get ready. They'll be waiting for us."

He releases me and rolls away, sitting on the side of the bed with his shoulders slumped in defeat.

"Hide from them if you have to, Daemon. But not from me, please. I'm begging you."

Silence follows, and it wrecks me.

Pushing to sit up, I stare at his back, watching the controlled movements of his breathing.

"You have no idea what you're asking for," he says ominously before getting to his feet.

"I think I do," I argue, frustration making my words sharper than I intended. "I've seen your worst, and I'm still here, Daemon. I'm still asking."

He stops at the door, his fingers wrapped around the handle, ready to escape.

"Then maybe you need to really think about that. Because any sane person wouldn't be."

"Daemon, I—" But it's too late. He's already gone, and whatever side of him I experienced last night has vanished with him.

27

DAEMON

The others were still packing their shit up when I grabbed my bag from the tipi I'd shared with Calli and Alex and took off toward my car.

Unfortunately, the move wasn't as smooth as I was hoping for, because before I can get swallowed up by the shadows of the trees, a voice carries over to me.

"Bro, wait up."

I pause, aware that he'll just chase me if I try to keep going.

"You leaving already?" he asks once he's in front of me.

I look down at the bag in my hand, wondering if that wasn't obvious enough.

"I need to get back," I say coldly.

"Stay for food, then I'll come back with you, if you want. Keep you company."

"If by that you mean so that you can nag me about school and shit, then nah, you're all good."

"What if I just wanna hang out with my brother? Talk and shit."

"I need to get back," I repeat like an imbecile. "I've got work to do," I add, hoping that the promise of me studying will get him off my case.

"D, don't do this," he begs.

"Do what?" I ask, his pleading with me to be normal getting my back up.

"Walk away like you're not wanted here. That's bullshit, and you know it."

"That's not what this is. I just need—"

"To get back. Yeah, I got that fucking memo." He kicks a stone by his foot and it flies off into the forest before colliding with a tree.

"Have you at least said goodbye to Calli?" he asks as if he's aware of just how deep that will cut.

"What's that got to do with anything?" I bark, getting more and more suspicious that Calli might just be right.

It'll be my own fault if he knows. I was careless. Foolish. Pussy-whipped, addicted, fucking blindsided. Whatever you want to call it. But when she's close... goddamn it.

"You two just looked kinda cosy this morning, that's all."

"Oh yeah? Like I'm sure you two didn't yesterday morning when I wasn't here. Careful, Bro. You're looking all green over there."

His teeth clench and his jaw tics at my words.

"Fuck you, man. I still woke with my cock nestled nicely against her fine ass."

The thought alone sends a rush of fury through my veins, and my fists curl at my sides.

"I hoped you enjoyed jerking off in the shower to that memory," I scoff before spinning on my heels and marching through the trees.

"You're a pussy, Daemon. And a fucking coward." That word hits me right in the chest. I fight to suck in the air I need as I consider the possibility of him and Calli discussing it. "And I'm not surprised Dad doesn't want you on his team right now. You're a fucking liability."

The need to turn around and flatten him burns through me. It takes all the willpower I possess to just keep walking as his taunts repeat over and over in my mind.

The worst part is that they're true.

Alex knows it. I know it.

Hell, even Calli fucking knows it.

So why the fuck is she still trying with me?

I think of her offer to shower with her, to strip bare and finally give her all of me, and a violent shiver rips down my spine.

I really am a coward.

———

I head for home, but when I come to a junction that I should turn right on to get back into the city, I find myself turning left.

It's a dangerous move, one I know I'll probably regret, but while I'm feeling so... vulnerable, it's the only place I can go. Home isn't a good idea right now, and Calli is still back with the others, so it's my only option.

I just have to hope she's in.

I don't remember any of the journey after making the decision to come here, and I have to do a double take when I pull up onto the driveway and kill the engine.

I throw the car door open without any hesitation. I've made my choice now, and despite the fact that I'm questioning it, I know I can't back down. She's probably already seen me, after all.

I discover I'm right not two seconds later when the front door opens.

"Daemon," Mum sings happily, her smile bright and wide despite the obvious exhaustion etched into every inch of her face.

She opens her arms for me and I act on autopilot, walking straight into them as if I'm a kid again.

"You want coffee?" she asks as soon as she's closed the door behind us.

"I'll make it. You look wiped."

"Thanks, Son," she mutters lightly. "I'm on nights, but I ended up staying late. Or early, I guess."

"Shit, you want me to go so you can—"

"No," she interrupts. "I'll take that coffee, though. I'm just going to change."

It's only as she says it that I notice her blue scrubs under her jacket.

I want to argue again, but she's gone before I get a chance.

I'm just sitting at the breakfast bar with two steaming mugs of coffee when she reappears, her face clear of makeup and her pyjamas on, ready for bed.

"I won't stay long," I promise.

"You're welcome here as long as you like, you know that." I smile softly at her, not realising until this moment just how much I've missed her.

The last time I was here was with Alex, the night of the Wolves' riot, so that Mum could patch up his hurty and stop him crying like a little bitch.

"So... how's it going?" she asks, her brows pinching in concern.

"You already know, I assume?"

"Of course. Is there anything I can do to help?" she offers despite the fact that she already knows I won't accept it.

I shake my head.

"If you need to get away for a bit, clear your head, focus, then you know you can always make use of Gran's place. It's just sitting there empty. And I'm sure there are plenty of jobs you could find yourself when you need a break."

"Thanks," I mutter. "I'll think about it." Although

really, just the thought of being that far away from Calli, even if she hates me right now, makes me feel all kinds of uncomfortable.

She might not need me, or even want me really, but I can't say that the feeling is mutual. She's always been my solace, even long before I allowed her to see just a tiny hint of how important she is to me.

"It's there if you need it. Alex said you were all away in some tipis or something. Did you have fun?" she asks, steering the conversation to something a little lighter. But that doesn't mean I expect her to drop the topic of my upcoming exams altogether.

She might understand me better than Dad does, and she might even have been on my side when I told them both I didn't want to formally further my education, but that doesn't mean her opinion holds any weight.

Just like mine.

I spend almost an hour with Mum, talking about anything I can come up with that doesn't involve school, work or Calli. But she makes it easy. She always does. She's just got this calming way about her that always soothes something inside of me.

When she and Dad split, I desperately wanted to follow her here. But I knew that if I did, I would be saying goodbye to the future I'd always wanted, the man I wanted to prove I could be, so I was forced to watch her pack up her things and leave.

It was one of the hardest fucking things I've ever

done. My only saving grace, I guess, was that my grandfather was already six feet under. If he were still around, then I doubt I would have been able to stick it. Being Dad's chew toy was one thing. But my grandfather's? No fucking thank you. The day his heart gave up was one of my best days. Almost all of my childhood nightmares were because of him. Because he didn't think I could ever possibly be good enough, being the 'runt' of the litter.

By the time I finally pull toward the underground garage of our building, I'm feeling a little more stable. Although, that all changes when my eyes lock on a figure loitering in the shadows.

My eyes narrow, my speed reducing as I try to make out who it is, and if they're a threat.

With my heart beating wildly in my chest, I blindly reach into my glove box for my gun.

Spinning the wheel, I pull into the closest space, my eyes locked on the hiding person as my adrenaline pumps.

Killing the engine, I push the door open and climb out, more than ready to teach this motherfucker a lesson.

My teeth grind as I close in on him, the grip on my gun tightening. But my reaction is nothing compared to the explosion of fury that rocks through me when he finally steps into the light and I get a look at who it is.

Lifting my gun, I press it against his forehead and force him back into the shadows of the alcove.

"What the fuck are you doing here?" I snarl, glaring pure hate into his dark eyes, my finger on the trigger and more than willing to pull the fucking thing.

28

CALLI

The drive home is much calmer than the one here. Mostly because everyone is hungover.

"My pussy needs a holiday from this holiday," Brianna moans after waking up from the nap she was having on my shoulder as we drive into the city.

"Not surprised," Jodie mutters. "You were going like, all freaking night. I'm surprised you can walk."

I roll my eyes at them, but I can't find it within me to even complain.

While Nico's been focused on getting inside Brianna, he hasn't been paying attention to what I'm up to, and I can only see that as a good thing.

"So how was your night with the twins, baby C?" Emmie asks, catching my eyes in the mirror.

"Exactly like I said it was earlier."

"Ugh," she complains. "Make it up then."

"I know that Nico would skin them with his bare

hands if they spit-roasted you, but can you imagine how hot that would be?" Stella muses.

"Seb know you fantasise about twins?" Jodie asks teasingly.

"I'm just thinking up hot ways for Cal to lose the V. There can't be many people out there who can say they gave it to twins."

"And I'm not going to be one of them. Sorry to disappoint, but there were no group activities in our tipi last night."

"I think I prefer Emmie's suggestion. Just pretend. How do you think that would have gone? Who'd have won the battle of the V-card and got in there first?"

"Daemon," everyone says at the same time before they start laughing.

"Jesus," I mutter.

"Alex would be livid, though," Emmie continues. "He's been dreaming about Cal's pussy for months."

"He has not," I huff.

The teasing continues as we get closer to home, and thankfully, less than ten minutes later, Stella is pulling into my driveway.

"So what's the plan for the rest of the week then?" she asks, putting the car in park and looking between us all.

"Studying," I say without missing a beat. "Don't be surprised if you don't see me again until school starts."

"Cal, come on. You can't lock yourself away for over two weeks," Emmie complains.

"I'm not failing my exams," I state.

"You won't. You're gonna smash it."

"I get it," Jodie says, leaning around Bri, who's half asleep between us again. "If you need any help, just shout, okay?"

"Thank you," I breathe, glad that she understands. "I'll text you later, yeah?" I push the door open and swing my legs out.

"Yeah. Just don't forget to have some fun, Cal. We're only young once."

"I'll see what I can do," I promise before grabbing my stuff and heading inside.

Mum and Dad are both here, or at least I assume so, seeing as their cars are, but I don't see them as I make my way down to the basement.

The familiarity and contentment of home hits me as I dump my bag by the kitchen counter and pull the fridge open to grab a can of lemonade, but I groan when all I find are bottles of water.

Fucking diet.

Walking over to my sofa, I flop down, staring out at the trees, searching for Daemon's preferred hiding space. But like every other time I've scanned the garden, I don't find it.

He could be out there right now, watching me, and I'd have no idea.

Pulling my phone from my pocket, I stare down at my lack of notifications.

"What are you playing at, devil boy?" I whisper.

Part of me wants to keep pushing him, to keep trying to discover that sweet, caring boy that I know is hiding. But there's also a huge part of me that tells me to remember the brutal, dangerous, obsessive side of him and to run the hell away.

But I can't.

Whether I like it or not, he's a part of me now. He's managed to brand himself on my soul, and no matter how many times he shuts me out, I can't stop craving him.

I let out a heavy sigh and lower my phone.

I sit there for the longest time, sipping on my water and reliving the last few days, wondering where the hell we're meant to go from here.

When my phone does ping beside me with a message, I startle.

But when I look down, I find that it's the wrong twin.

Alex: Did you get home safe?

Calli: Yep, home and ready to embark on a two-week study session.

Alex: You really know how to live, huh? If you need a buddy, you know where I am. *winky emoji* *book emoji* *pen emoji*

Calli: I'll keep that in mind. But I need to focus...

Alex: What are you suggesting exactly?

Calli: That you'll find an excuse to take your top off and distract me with abs. *winky emoji*

Alex: You know you love it.

Calli: Hmm…

Alex: Message if you need me. x

A smile curls at my lips at his offer. He really is a good friend. I just wish he'd stop looking at me like he wants me when I have nothing to offer him.

Pushing from the sofa before I end up falling asleep, I unpack and search through my cupboards for something to eat.

"Fuck," I hiss, finding them bare of anything decent, thanks to Mum's new bloody diet regime.

Refusing to settle for dried fruit and freaking nuts to study with, I shove my feet into my Converse by the stairs and grab my jacket and bag, heading back upstairs.

I'm almost at the front door when Dad's booming voice echoes off the walls around me.

"Where are you going?"

His tone immediately gets my back up. I spend most of my time in this house alone, with him not giving a shit about what I'm doing. But then the second he's here, he seems to think he can suddenly control my every movement.

"Out. Problem?" I hiss.

"Out where?"

Sucking in a breath, I turn to face him.

"To the shop for some decent food so I can study."

"Order it in," he demands.

"Crisps and chocolate?" I ask, my brow wrinkling. "I'm just going to the corner shop, I'll be like, ten minutes."

"Callista," he growls. "Just order it in."

"No," I state, for once not standing down the second he starts to get all authoritative. "I'm sick of this," I hiss. "I'm sick of being treated differently from everyone else. I bet Stella and Emmie can walk out of their houses whenever they need a sugar hit."

"You're not Stella or Emmie," he shoots back.

"No, because you've kept me locked up in my room while they've been out training to defend themselves. It's bullshit, all of it."

I storm forward and rip the door open.

"Wait, I'll come with you."

"Don't bother. You don't care any other day."

"Just wait," he demands. But I'm done, so over all this overprotective bullshit, and the second he turns toward the hallway to grab his shoes, I bolt.

Deciding against heading toward our closest shop, knowing that he'll be following me, I race down an alleyway a little farther down the street and damn near run in the opposite direction.

In only a few minutes, I emerge a couple of streets over from our house, and with no sign of Dad chasing my tail, I slow my pace. The sun is still out, and I push my sleeves up as I start to overheat.

The illuminated shop sign emerges up ahead and I continue forward, mentally listing all the things I want for the next few days.

I pass a few people, but I don't pay them any attention as I turn into the shop and grab a basket.

By the time I get to the till, it's full to the brim with everything Mum would ban me from eating if she were here. But she's not, and quite frankly, I don't give a shit.

I pack it all into a bag, keeping one of the chocolate bars free to eat on the way home. I sense that I'm going to need the sugar hit to deal with the raging bull that will be my father when I get back.

I rip the packet open the second I step back out into the sun and reluctantly head home.

I probably handled that all wrong. But after dealing with Daemon and his hot and cold bullshit, and then the girls' teasing about him and Alex all the way home, and then finding all my snacks banished... my patience at the way my life is going right now has all but run out.

Turning down the alley to lead me back, I take another angry bite of my treat when I sense movement behind me.

My heart jumps into my throat at the prospect of

being followed, and a little voice screams in my head that this was a really stupid idea.

I twist around to see what, or who it is, all while praying that I'm just being paranoid. But I don't get the chance to see anything, because hands grab my upper arms, something covers my eyes, and my screams are cut off by a large, strong hand.

Fear turns my blood to ice and I freeze when I know I should be fighting.

And the last thing I think before everything goes dark is that this might not have been the best time to disobey my father.

Calli and Daemon's story continues in Dark Princess.

ABOUT THE AUTHOR

Tracy Lorraine is a *USA Today* and *Wall Street Journal* bestselling new adult and contemporary romance author. Tracy has recently turned thirty and lives in a cute Cotswold village in England with her husband, baby girl and lovable but slightly crazy dog. Having always been a bookaholic with her head stuck in her Kindle, Tracy decided to try her hand at a story idea she dreamt up and hasn't looked back since.

Be the first to find out about new releases and offers. Sign up to my newsletter here.

If you want to know what I'm up to and see teasers and snippets of what I'm working on, then you need to be in my Facebook group. Join Tracy's Angels here.

Keep up to date with Tracy's books at
www.tracylorraine.com

<u>Knight's Ridge Empire Series</u>

<u>Wicked Summer Knight</u>: Prequel (Stella & Seb)

<u>Wicked Knight</u> #1 (Stella & Seb)

<u>Wicked Princess</u> #2 (Stella & Seb)

<u>Wicked Empire</u> #3 (Stella & Seb)

<u>Deviant Knight</u> #4 (Emmie & Theo)

<u>Deviant Princess</u> #5 (Emmie & Theo

<u>Deviant Reign</u> #6 (Emmie & Theo)

<u>One Reckless Knight</u> (Jodie & Toby)

<u>Reckless Knight</u> #7 (Jodie & Toby)

<u>Reckless Princess</u> #8 (Jodie & Toby)

<u>Reckless Dynasty</u> #9 (Jodie & Toby)

<u>Dark Halloween Knight</u> (Calli & Batman)

<u>Dark Knight</u> #10 (Calli & Batman)

<u>Dark Princess</u> #11 (Calli & Batman)

Dark Legacy #12 (Calli & Batman)

<u>Corrupt Valentine Knight</u> (Nico & Siren)

<u>Ruined Series</u>

<u>Ruined Plans</u> #1

<u>Ruined by Lies</u> #2

HATE YOU SNEAK PEEK
PROLOGUE

Tabitha

I stare down at my gran's pale skin. Her cheeks are sunken and her eyes tired. She's been fighting this for too long now, and as much as I hate to even think it, it's time she found some peace.

I take her cool hand in mine and lift her knuckles to my lips.

"It's Tabitha," I whisper. I've no idea if she's awake, but I don't want to startle her.

Her eyes flicker open. After a second they must adjust to the light and she looks right at me. My chest tightens as if someone's wrapping an elastic band around it. I hate seeing my once so full of life gran like this. She was always so happy and full of cheer. She didn't deserve this end. But cancer doesn't care what kind of person you are, it hits whoever it fancies and ruins lives.

Pulling a chair closer, I drop onto it, not taking my eyes from her.

"How are you doing today?" I hate asking the question, because there really is only one answer. She's waiting, waiting for her time to come to put her out of her misery.

"I'm good. Christopher upped my morphine. I'm on top of the world."

She might be living her last days, but it doesn't stop her eyes sparkling a little as she mentions her male nurse. If I've heard the words 'if I were forty years younger' once while she's been here, then I've heard them a million times. She's joking, of course. My gran spent her life with my incredible grandpa until he had a stroke a few years ago. Thankfully, I guess, his end was much quicker and less painful than Gran's. It was awful at the time to have him healthy one moment and then gone in a matter of hours, but this right now is pure torture, and I'm not the one lying on the hospital bed with meds constantly being pumped into my body.

"Turn the frown upside down, Tabby Cat. I'm fine. I want to remember you smiling, not like your world's about to come crashing down."

"I know, I'm sorry. I just—" a sob breaks from my throat. "I don't know how I'm going to live without you." Dramatic? Yeah. But Gran has been my go-to person my whole life. When my parents get on my last nerve, which is often, she's the one who talks me down, makes me see things differently. She's also the only one who's encouraged me to live the life I want, not the one I'm constantly being pushed into.

That's the reason I'm the only one visiting her right now.

When my parents discovered that she was the one encouraging my 'reckless behaviour', as they called it, they cut contact. I can see the pain in her eyes about that every time she looks at me, but she's too stubborn to do anything about it, even now.

"You're going to be fine. You're stronger than you give yourself credit for. How many times have I told you, you just need to follow your heart. Follow your heart and just breathe. Spread your wings and fly, Tabby Cat."

Those were the last words she said to me.

Tabitha

The heavy bass rattles my bones. The incredible music does help to lift my spirits, but I find it increasingly hard to see the positives in my life while I'm hanging out with my friends these days. They've all got something exciting going on—incredible job prospects, marriage, exotic holidays on the horizon—and here I am, drowning in my one-person pity party. It's been two months since Gran left me, and I'm still wondering what the hell I'm meant to be doing with my life.

"Oh my god, they are so fucking awesome," Danni squeals in my ear as one song comes to an end. I didn't really have her down as a rock fan, but she was almost as excited as James when he announced that this was what we were doing for his birthday this year. Although I do wonder if it's the music or the frontman who's really captured her attention. She'd never admit it, but she's got a thing for bad boys.

I glance over at him with his arm wrapped around Shannon's shoulders and a smile twitches my lips. They're so cute. They've got the kind of relationship everyone craves. It seems so easy yet full of love and affection. Ripping my eyes from the couple, I focus back on the stage and try to block out that I'm about as far away from having that kind of connection with anyone as physically possible.

I sing along with the songs I've heard on the radio a million times and jump around with my friends, but I just can't quite totally get on board with tonight. Maybe I just need more alcohol.

"Where to next?" Shannon asks once we've left the arena and the ringing in our ears has begun to fade.

"Your choice," James says, looking down at her with utter devotion shining in his eyes. It wasn't a great surprise when Shannon sent a photo of her giant engagement ring to our group chat a couple of months ago. We all knew it was coming—Danni especially, seeing as it turned out that she helped choose the ring.

Shannon directs us all to a cocktail bar a few streets over and I make quick work of manoeuvring my way through the crowd to get to the bar, my need for a drink beginning to get the better of me. The others disappear off somewhere in the hope of finding a table

"Can we have two jugs of..." I quickly glance at the menu. "Margaritas please."

"Coming right up, sweetheart." The barman winks at me before his eyes drop to my chest. Hooking up on a night out isn't really my thing, but hell if it doesn't make me feel a little better about myself. He's cute too, and just the kind of guy who would give both my parents a heart attack if I were to bring him home. Both his forearms are covered in tattoos, he's got gauges in both his ears, and a lip ring. A smile tugs at the corner of my mouth as I imagine the looks on their faces.

My gran's words suddenly hit me.

Just breathe.

My hand lifts and my fingers run over the healing skin just below my bra. My smile widens.

I watch the barman prepare our cocktails, my eyes focused on the ink on his arms. I've always been obsessed by art, any kind of art, and that most definitely includes on skin.

I'm lost in my own head, so when he places the jugs in front of me, I startle, feeling ridiculous.

"T-Thank you," I mutter, but when I lift my eyes, I find him staring intently at me.

"You're welcome. I'm Christian, by the way."

"Oh, hi." A sly smile creeps onto my lips. "I'm Biff."

"Biff?" His brows draw together in a way I'm all too used to when I say my name.

"It's short for Tabitha."

"That's pretty. So... uh... how do you feel about—"

"Christian, a little help?" one of the other barmen shouts, pulling Christian's attention from me.

"Sorry, I'll hopefully see you again later?"

I nod at him, not wanting to give him any false hope. Like I said, he's cute, but after my last string of bad dates and even worse short-term boyfriends, I'm happy flying solo right now. I've got a top of the range vibrating friend in my bedside table; I don't need a man.

Picking up the tray in front of me, I turn and go in search of my friends. It takes forever, but eventually I find them tucked around a tiny table in the back corner of the bar.

"What the hell took so long? We thought you'd pulled and abandoned us."

"Yes and no," I say, ensuring every head turns my way.

"Tell us more," Danni, my best friend, demands.

"It was nothing. The barman was about to ask me out, but it got busy."

"Why the hell did you come back? Get over there. We all know you could do with a little... loosening up," James says with a wink.

"I'm good. He wasn't my type."

"Oh, of course. You only date posh boys."

"That is not true."

"Is it not?" Danni asks, chipping in once she's filled all the glasses.

"No..." I think back over the previous few guys they

met. "Wayne wasn't posh," I argue when I realise they're kind of right.

"No, he was just a wanker."

Blowing out a long breath, I try to come up with an argument, but quite honestly, it's true. My shoulders slump as I realise that I've been subconsciously dating guys my parents would approve of. It's like my need to follow their orders is so well ingrained by now that I don't even realise I'm doing it. Shame that their ideas about my life, what I should do, and whom I should date don't exactly line up with mine.

Glancing over my shoulder at the bar, I catch a glimpse of Christian's head. Maybe I should take him up on his almost offer. What's the worst that could happen?

Deciding some liquid courage is in order, I grab my margherita and swallow half down in one go.

I'm so fed up of attempting to live my parents' idea of a perfect life. I promised Gran I'd do things my way. I need to start living up to my promise.

By the time I'm tipsy enough to walk back to the bar and chat up Christian, he's nowhere to be seen. I'm kind of disappointed seeing as the others had convinced me to throw caution to the wind (something that I'm really bad at doing), but I think I'm mostly relieved to be able go home and lock myself inside my flat alone and not have to worry about anyone else.

With my arm linked through Danni's, we make our way out to the street, ready to make our journeys home, and Shannon jumps into an idling Uber while Danni waits for another to go in the opposite direction.

"You sure you don't want to be dropped off? I don't mind."

"No, I'm sure. I could do with the fresh air." It's not a lie—the alcohol from one too many cocktails is making my head a little fuzzy. I hate going to sleep with the room spinning. I'd much rather that feeling fade before lying down.

"Okay. Promise me you'll text me when you're home."

"I promise." I wrap my arms around my best friend and then wave her off in her own Uber.

Turning on my heels, I start the short walk home.

I've been a London girl all my life, and while some might be afraid to walk home after dark, I love it. I love seeing a different side to this city, the quiet side when most people are hiding in their flats, not flooding the streets on their daily commutes.

My mind is flicking back and forth between my promise to Gran and my missed opportunity tonight when a shop front that I walk past on almost a daily basis makes me stop.

It's a tattoo studio I've been inside of once in my life. I never really pay it much attention, but the new sign in the window catches my eye and I stop to look.

Admin help wanted. Enquire within.

Something stirs in my belly, and it's not just my need to do something to piss my parents off—although getting a job in a place like this is sure to do that. I'm pretty sure it's excitement.

Tattoos fascinate me, or more so, the artists.

I'm surprised to see the open sign still illuminated, so before I can change my mind, I push the door open. A little bell rings above it, and after a few seconds of standing in reception alone, a head pops out from around the door.

"Evening. What can I do you for?" The guy's smile is soft and kind despite his otherwise slightly harsh features and ink.

"Oh um…" I hesitate under his intense dark stare. I glance over my shoulder, the back of the piece of paper catching my eye and reminding me why I walked in here. "I just saw the job ad in the window. Is the position still open?"

His eyes drop from mine and take in what I'm wearing. Seeing as tonight's outing involved a rock concert, I'm dressed much like him in all black and looking a little edgy with my skinny black jeans, ripped AC/DC t-shirt and heavy black makeup. I must admit it's not a look I usually go for, but it was fitting for tonight.

He nods, apparently happy with what he sees.

"Experience?" he asks, making my stomach drop.

"Not really, but I'm studying for a Masters so I'm

not an idiot. I know my way around a computer, Excel, and I'm super organised."

"Right..." he trails off, like he's thinking about the best way to get rid of me.

"I'm a really quick learner. I'm punctual, methodical and really easy to get along with."

"It's okay, you had me sold at organised. I'm Dawson, although everyone around here calls me D."

"Nice to meet you." I stick my hand out for him to shake, and an amused smile plays at his lips. Stretching out an inked arm, he takes my hand and gives it a very firm shake that my dad would be impressed by—if he could look past the tattoos, that is. "I'm Tabitha, but everyone calls me Biff."

"Biff, I like it. When can you start?"

"Don't you want to interview me?"

"You sound like you could be perfect. When can you start?"

"Err... tomorrow?" I ask, totally taken aback. He doesn't know me from Adam.

"Yes!" He practically snaps my hand off. "Can you be here for two o'clock? I can show you around before clients start turning up. I'll apologise now for dropping you in the deep end, we've not had anyone for a few weeks and things are starting to get a little crazy."

"I can cope with crazy."

"Good to know. This place can be nuts." I smile at him, more grateful than he could know to have a distraction and a focus.

My Masters should be enough to keep my mind

busy, but since Gran went, I can't seem to lose myself in it like I could previously. Hopefully, sorting this place's admin out might be exactly what I need.

"Two o'clock tomorrow then," I say, turning to leave. "I'll bring ID. Do you need a reference? I've done some voluntary work recently, I'm sure they'll write something for me."

"Just turn up on time and do your job and you're golden."

I walk out with more of a spring in my step than I have in a long time. I'm determined to find something that's going to make me happy, not just my parents. I've lived in their shadow for long enough.

I look myself over before leaving my flat for my first shift at the tattoo studio. I'm dressed a little more like myself today in a pair of dark skinny jeans, a white blouse and a black blazer. It's simple and smart. I'm not sure if there's a dress code—D never specified what I should wear. With my hair straightened and hanging down my back and my makeup light, I feel like I can take on whatever crazy he throws at me.

With a final spritz of perfume, I grab my bag from the unit in the hall and pull open my door. My home is a top floor flat in an old London warehouse. They were converted a few years ago by my father's company, and I managed to get myself first dibs. They might drive me insane on the best of days, but at least I get this place rent-free. It almost makes up for their controlling and stuck-up ways... almost.

Ignoring the lift like I always do, I head for the stairs. My heels click against the polished concrete until I'm at the bottom and out to the busy city. I love London. I love that no matter what the time, there's always something going on or someone who's awake.

The spring afternoon is still a little fresh, making me regret not grabbing my coat, or even a scarf, before I left. I pull my blazer tighter around myself and make the short journey to the shop.

The door's locked when I get there, and the bright neon sign that clearly showed it was open last night is currently saying closed.

Unsure of what to do, I lift my hand to knock. Only a second later, the shop front is illuminated, and the sound of movement inside filters down to me, but when the door opens it's not the guy from last night.

"Oh... uh... hi. Is... uh... D here?"

The guy folds his arms over his chest and looks me up and down. He chuckles, although I've no idea what he finds so amusing.

"D," he shouts over his shoulder, "there's some posh bird here to see you."

My teeth grind that he's stereotyped me quite so quickly, but I refuse to allow him to see that his assumptions about me affect me in any way.

"Ah, good. I was worried you might change your mind."

"Not at all," I say, stepping past the judgemental arsehole and into the studio reception-cum-waiting room.

"That's Spike. Feel free to ignore him. He's not got laid in about a million years, it makes him a little cranky." I fight to contain a laugh, especially when I turn toward Spike to find his lips pursed and his eyes narrowed in frustration. All it does is confirm that D's words are correct.

"Is that fucking necessary? Posh doesn't need to know how inactive my cock is, especially not when she's only just walked through the fucking door. Unless..." He stalks towards me and I automatically back up. I can't deny that he's a good looking guy, but there's no way I'm going there.

"I don't think so."

"You sure? You look like you could do with a bit of rough." He winks, and I want the ground to swallow me up.

"Down, Spike. This is Tabitha, or Biff. She's our new admin, so I suggest you be nice to her if you want to stop organising your own appointments and shit. I don't need a sexual harassment case on my hands before she's even fucking started."

I can't help but laugh at the look on Spike's face. "Don't worry. I'm sure you'll find some desperate old spinster soon."

He looks me up and down again, something in his eyes changed. "Appearances aside, I think you're going to get on well here."

I smile at him. "Mine's a coffee. Milk, no sugar. I'm already sweet enough." His chin drops.

"I thought you were our new assistant. Why am I still making the coffee?"

"Know your place, Spike. Now do as the lady says. You know my order."

"Yeah, it comes with a side of fuck off!" He flips D off before disappearing through a door that I can only assume goes to a kitchen.

"I probably should have warned you that you've agreed to work around a bunch of arseholes."

"I know how to handle myself around horny men, don't worry."

After finishing my A levels, before I grew any kind of backbone where my parents were concerned, I agreed to work for my dad. I was his little office bitch and spent an horrendous year of my life being bossed around by men who thought that just because they had a cock hanging between their legs it made them better than me. I might have fucking hated that year, but it taught me a few things, not just about business but also how to deal with men who think they're something fucking special just because they're a tiny bit successful and make more money than me. I've no doubt that my time at Anderson Development Group gave me all the skills I'm going to need to handle these artists.

"So I see. So, this is your desk. When you're on shift you'll be the first person people see when they're inside, so it's important that you look good. But from what I've seen, I don't think we'll have an issue. I've sorted you out logins for the computer and the software we use. Most of it is pretty self-explanatory. I'm pretty IT illiterate and I've figured most of it out, put it that way."

D's showing me how they book clients in when someone else joins us. This time it's someone I recognise from my previous visit, although it's immediately obvious that he doesn't remember me like I do him. But then I guess he was the one delivering the pain, not receiving it.

"Biff, this is Titch. Titch, this is Biff, our new admin. Be nice."

"Nice? I'm always nice. Nice to meet you, Biff. You have any issues with this one, you come and see me. He might look tough, but I know all his secrets." Titch winks, a smile curling at his lips that shows he's a little more interested than he's making out, and quickly disappears towards his room.

It's not long until the first clients of the afternoon arrive, and I'm left alone to try to get to grips with everything.

Between clients, D pops his head out of his room to check I'm okay, and every hour I make a round of coffee for everyone. That sure seems to get me in their good books.

"I think I could get used to having you around," Spike says when I deliver probably his fourth coffee of the day. "Only thing that would make it better is if it were whisky."

"Not sure the person at the end of your needle

would agree." He chuckles and turns back to the design he was working on when I interrupted.

My first day flies by. D tells me to head home not long after nine o'clock. They've all got hours of tattooing to go yet, seeing as Saturday night is their busiest night of the week, but he insists I get a decent night's sleep.

Continue reading Tabitha and Zach's story
HATE YOU!